THE
NORDEN AFFAIR

JEFF FUNK

The Norden Affair
© 2019 by Jeff Funk

Published by Insight Publishing Group
contact@freshword.com
www.freshword.com
918-493-1718

ISBN: 978-1-932503-64-7
E-Book ISBN: 978-1-943361-52-6

Library of Congress Control Number: 2018953108

Printed in the United States of America.

DEDICATION

I dedicate this book to the great love of my life, partner, and wife, Jan. She has indulged and supported my hopes and dreams during this very interesting journey called life. She is my devoted cheerleader, even when the chips are down. She keeps me on track and often reminds me anything is possible with faith, hard work, and a little good fortune. Her faith in me and the life we have built together proves she is right about that.

CONTENTS

ACKNOWLEDGMENTS

I'd like to thank the team at Insight Publishing Group for encouraging me to write this book. And it was fun to work with my long-time friend, John Mason, from beginning to end.

PROLOGUE

Mindful of the secret trust about to be placed in me by my Commander in Chief, the President of the United States, by whose direction I have been chosen for bombardier training . . . and mindful of the fact that I am to become guardian of one of my country's most priceless military assets, the American bombsight . . . I do here, in the presence of Almighty God, swear by the Bombardier's Code of Honor to keep inviolate the secrecy of any and all confidential information revealed to me, and further to uphold the honor and integrity of the Army Air Forces, if need be, with my life itself (underline added).

—WWII bombardier's oath to protect
the Norden bombsight

SEPTEMBER 1943

The B-17 Flying Fortress glided through the beautiful September morning over western Germany. The clear blue skies were interrupted only by the scores of milky-white vapor trails resembling horizontal icicles, towed by the large plane and its accompanying bomber planes, all carrying their deadly cargo. The contrails, however harmless in their appearance, betrayed the young men who made up the ten-man bomber crews, signaling to the enemy below their exact location. All the Germans had to do was look up.

The lumbering airspeed of 155 mph was much too slow for Josh Rinehart. The nineteen-year-old bombardier peered out his forward windscreen at the scene below.

The ground was an interesting and inconsistent mix of green and brown squares gradually moving below them. To Josh it seemed like they were moving in slow motion. The formation of nearly five hundred bombers had already been airborne for several hours in their narrow aluminum tubes. In spite of their heavy clothing, Josh and the other men in his crew were freezing. The air temperature outside was thirty degrees below zero, and everyone inside the unpressurized, unheated bomber felt the chill down to the bone. Many of the crewmen stomped their feet, clapped their hands, and resorted to other rudimentary measures in an effort to keep warm. Josh found himself continually rubbing his heavily gloved hands together, to little warming effect.

Numbingly cold wind gushed into the large, side openings where men manning .50 caliber machine guns kept watch for enemy fighters, adding painful windchill to the already subzero temperature. Touching the powerful guns with their bare hands in this extreme cold would fuse them to the metal. The loud, vibrating airplane, whose sole design was to deliver four thousand eight hundred pounds of bombs, provided no creature comforts. The only protection they had from enemy German fire below was the thin aluminum skin, barely an eighth of an inch thick.

"Hey Josh," came a familiar voice over the intercom, "how much longer to the target? My ass is getting cold and sore up here."

Josh smiled and took another look at the detailed map and saw they were getting very close. It wouldn't be much longer now. He pressed the button on his microphone. "Should only be another twenty minutes or so, Benny." Then he added to the top turret gunner, "Close enough that you should keep an eye out for the Jerrys. Don't want to be surprised like last time."

"Roger that," replied Benny.

The pilot, Captain Boyce, quickly rebuked both crewmen. "Cut the chatter. Gun check."

Immediately the plane began to vibrate with the loud retort of the .50 caliber machine guns positioned throughout the bomber, thirteen in all. No sooner than the deafening thunder began, it stopped.

Josh was the youngest member of the crew, many times referred to as the baby on the airplane. He didn't mind though, and even enjoyed the special attention he received. He grew fonder of his fellow crew members with each mission. An unmistakable bond had developed as a result of sharing the danger and uncertainness of war together, one that only battle in wartime can create. They all depended on one another.

Even with all its hardships, Josh and his fellow crew members had developed a fondness for their airplane, *Lucky Lucy*. So named after the pilot's mother, it sported a rather elaborate painting on the nose of the fuselage. It was of a middle-aged woman in a flaming chariot, smoking a cigarette, with her bright red hair streaming behind her. Underneath in equally bright red and yellow letters read *Lucky Lucy*. It was the most popular fuselage painting on the base.

When Josh first saw the airplane and its signature rendition, he asked the pilot whether his mother would approve. The pilot just laughed and replied his irreverent mother would love it. Also painted on the fuselage were sixteen painted bomb silhouettes, one for each completed mission over enemy territory. Most bombers would not reach that number. Josh had seen too many of their own aircraft being shot out of the sky. All too frequently he had witnessed long flaming spirals to earth without so much as a single parachute opening. The first time he saw the terrifying spectacle he stared in disbelief, hoping and praying he would avoid such a fate. Miraculously, *Lucky Lucy* always returned her very fortunate crew to their American home base in England without so much as a scratch. Perhaps *Lucky Lucy* was lucky after all.

Josh thought the long flights to Germany were quite boring and monotonous; that is, until they were within reach of German fighters and flak. Then the adrenaline raced through his veins, sending his heart pounding to a pace that at times he thought would force it to explode in his chest. After each bombing run, when German fighters and flak had relentlessly attacked their planes over and over again, Josh discovered he was drenched in his own perspiration, in spite of the cold temperatures.

For now, at least, *Lucky Lucy* was still some distance from their target and the deadly gauntlet that lay ahead. He could allow himself to relax to the drone of the four engines.

Admitting to himself he was more than a little homesick, Josh removed the glove from his right hand and retrieved a small photo he always kept in his zippered breast pocket. There were four people in the photo. His mother, father, himself, and the young woman he could not stop thinking about. Even more so, now that he was a long way from home.

He remembered how proud his Army veteran father had been with his decision when he informed his parents he had enlisted in the Army Air Force. He told them he would do his part for his country, with no reluctance to do so. His father beamed, then excitedly shook his son's hand. He saw his mother force a tepid smile as she fought back tears, and he knew she was all too familiar with the dangers of war and the knowledge that he may not return. Josh had often seen his mother shake her head and cry when neighbors were informed their sons were not returning home. She knew if her own son was fortunate enough to come back unscathed, he would be forever changed, no longer the adorable and naive boy she had raised for the last nineteen years, but rather a man with his own life and memories that may haunt him forever.

It would be much tougher for Josh to tell the special young woman who lived three doors down from his parents' house. His longtime sweetheart, Rebecca, had begged Josh not to enlist. She had seen all the boys heading in droves to the local recruiting office as soon as they were old enough to do so. She and Josh had also seen many of them come back in coffins, or had noticed the dreaded gold star hanging in the window of a neighbor's home. She pleaded with

Josh to wait. And of course, he would do anything for her. She had said numerous times, "You don't need to go, Josh. There are so many already serving, they don't need you. Your family and I need you here." She was right, of course, but *every* family needed their sons and daughters.

For Josh it had been love at first sight. Rebecca's short blonde hair, piercing blue eyes, and innocent yet inviting smile trapped him from the moment they met. It wasn't long before they were making plans for the future, and war did not figure into the equation. After dating for two years, Josh and Rebecca began talking about marriage, but only after he could secure a good job, of course. Josh even knew the number of children he hoped to have—two boys and two girls. Rebecca had often told him how excited she was about plans of marriage and raising a family with him. He told her their dreams were going to come true.

Wartime, however, had a way of changing one's plans.

Unsure of how to break the news of his enlistment to Rebecca, Josh devised a plan. He would invite her to dinner for one of his mother's signature dishes: roast chicken and fresh green beans, with mashed potatoes and gravy. That way Josh's parents, who loved Rebecca nearly as much as he did, could provide support if needed. After dinner they would retreat to the backyard where Josh and his dad would enjoy a game of horseshoes, as they had done so many times before. The two women would cheer them on from the sidelines and throw out wild challenges, as though much was depending on the game. It was all in good fun, and Josh treasured those moments when they were all together. Rebecca had become part of the family. After the game he would tell her.

The time had come and the plan was going well, so far. Josh's mother outdid herself yet again, preparing a wonderful dinner. Rebecca admired Josh's mother and exclaimed, "Mrs. Rinehart, I swear you make the best roast chicken I've ever had." And she meant it. The four of them ate until they were ready to burst, recited entertaining family stories, and talked briefly about life getting back to normal after the war. Josh was unusually quiet, and he could see Rebecca noticed.

Later in the backyard, another horseshoe game ended with his father winning, again. The two men shook hands, patted each other on the back, and then joined the women in the lawn chairs. Josh was obviously showing signs of nervousness, dreading what was coming. Rebecca noticed the troubled look on his face. The moment had finally arrived when Josh needed to break the news to Rebecca. The four briefly gazed up into the sky on that warm June evening as it darkened and the stars began to come to life. Josh swallowed hard and took a deep breath. He looked over at his father who nodded his encouragement to get it over with. Putting it off any longer would only make it more difficult.

He reached for Rebecca's hand and gently squeezed it. "I have something to tell you." His voice was shaky, betraying his nervousness. She smiled, the same one that had captured his affections long ago. A proposal, perhaps? Josh saw her glance over to his parents, hoping they would reveal a hint of what was coming. In what little light remained from the star- and moonlit sky, he saw what Rebecca saw; strained looks of anguish and fearful anticipation, tears beginning to fall from his mother's face. Josh quickly looked back at Rebecca. He could tell she knew immediately what was coming but needed to hear it from him. He saw her smile vanish in a second.

After telling Rebecca of his enlistment, she burst into tears and began to run home, Josh chasing after her. His father called after him to stop, counseling Josh she needed time to digest the news. It would be better, his father said, to wait and see her the next day after she had calmed down and had time to let his news sink in. Josh bowed his head in agreement, feeling ashamed and angry for hurting

Rebecca. How could he hurt her so? It was the last thing he wanted to do. Would she ever forgive him? She just had to!

Unfortunately for Josh there was little time for mending fences. He was catching a train in two days for basic training. After that it was eighteen weeks of additional training at the Army Air Forces Bombardier School before he would return home for a short leave. Then, as most young men knew, it was overseas to fight the Germans. It was anyone's guess how long he would be gone then.

Josh knew once he stepped onto the train, it would be months, perhaps years, before he would see Rebecca again. He needed her to forgive him, even though he believed in his heart he was doing the right thing. He wanted to hear her say she would wait for him. He wanted her to agree their marriage and a family could wait a little bit longer, that they had their whole future in front of them. He wanted to say he was sorry. He wanted desperately to see that smile again. Then everything would be all right.

No less than ten times over the next two days he walked three doors down to Rebecca's house. He knocked on her front door, praying she would appear. Only Rebecca's parents answered. Josh pleaded with them to persuade her to come out and talk to him. Her mother, who saw the anguish on Josh's face, eventually could bear it no longer. She begged Rebecca to leave her room and see him. She refused. He even camped outside her bedroom window and pleaded there as well. All proved unsuccessful. He tried everything he could think of, but in the end, in spite of his best efforts Rebecca stayed in her room and would not see him. Josh realized now how badly he had hurt her, more deeply than he ever could have imagined. Rebecca's father, who finally had enough of Josh's persistence, told him his daughter's heart had been broken and that he should go home and give it some time. Unfortunately, Josh was out of time.

With a heavy heart Josh hugged his parents at the train station, and then stepped on board to an uncertain future. As the train prepared to leave the station, he peered out the window to scan the large gathering of mothers, fathers, and girlfriends waving, sending their last farewells to the many young men leaving home for a long and uncertain future. He searched desperately among the crowd, hoping to see Rebecca. Perhaps she would come at the last moment to see him off. But she didn't. It was then Josh felt regret as never before, and his eyes welled up with tears at the very real prospect he had lost Rebecca forever.

<hr />

Josh's thoughts of his last days at home were interrupted by the pilot's voice over the intercom.

"Josh, have you done your equipment check yet? We're only ten minutes from the target. I want a good drop today. Let's ruin those Krauts' day."

"Doing it right now, sir!" Josh quickly stuffed the photo back into his breast pocket and maneuvered over to the Norden bombsight at the nose of the airplane. He still marveled at this technological wonder; its many dials, sophisticated gyroscope, and lenses were the heart of this ingenious piece of military equipment. He thought it was beautiful. As he leaned over the black and silver bombsight, he began running through the many adjustments, referring to his manual for the proper settings regarding how fast the aircraft was moving, altitude, and wind speed. Only a complicated procedure of calculations would synchronize the bombsight to accurately hit the target.

Josh felt privileged to be the bombardier. Not everyone who requested entrance to Bombardier Training School was admitted; first, they were tested and interviewed. Even then, many washed out during the eighteen-week school for not being able to manage all the complexities of this advanced piece of military hardware. The very first day of school Josh and the rest of his class were required to take an oath protecting the secrets of the bombsight with their very lives, if necessary. It was a serious affair for them, and one his superiors took equally seriously. He noticed all the students looking around at each other, finally realizing the importance of this technological marvel to America and the war effort. It made Josh feel more important than he had ever felt in his life.

Josh, along with his instructors, soon realized he had a knack for quickly picking up the information, and soon he was performing at the top of his class. He truly enjoyed the mental challenges and became so proficient that several of the instructors gave him the option of staying at the school to teach others.

Josh seriously considered their offer, but in the end, he wanted to serve as so many of his friends were doing. Initially he struggled with the decision, realizing by staying behind in the States, Rebecca would be relieved and would perhaps begin talking to him again. But he gracefully declined the offer, much to their disappointment. Josh believed it his duty to take his skills to the Germans, with deadly consequences. Perhaps even his minor contributions would soon help end the war. The sooner the war ended, the sooner he could get back home . . . and to Rebecca.

Josh's thoughts were suddenly and violently interrupted with the tremendous jerk of the plane as it rose upward and then downward in less than a second, nearly throwing Josh off his seat. Flak! Then he saw the familiar and harmless-looking black puffs of smoke all around the plane as the flak desperately searched for a target . . . any target. Josh knew the flak came first, then the fighters. He feared and hated both of them, but at least the Flying Fortress crew had some defense against the fighters—they could shoot back! Flak could be there and gone in the blink of an eye, and there was no telling when and where it was going to strike. There was also no way to prepare for it. You either got hit or you didn't. It was the luck, or unluckiness, of the draw. Now the flak was everywhere, the sky filled with so many black pockmarks the previously beautiful blue sky was now an ominous gray and white that threatened life itself. To Josh, it was the look of death.

Over the intercom he could hear frantic chatter from other planes' crews who were also struggling with the flak. This made it more difficult to keep the tight formation ordered by their superiors to concentrate the destruction from the bombing. Josh never understood this, as he thought the tighter the group the easier the target they'd be for their enemies. But their commanders assured them this was necessary, both for better bombing results and for safety from enemy fighters.

Lucky Lucy was shaking up and down now, and Josh wondered how the aluminum structure could manage to stay together. Thank God it did. He continued looking for fighters and saw the bomber on his left, *Betty Bye-Bye,* take a bad hit on its right wing. Josh winced, as he had eaten breakfast with three of its crew members just a few, short hours ago. It began dropping rapidly from formation as oily black smoke and flames began streaming from its right two engines. They were finished. Josh knew their journey had ended, and if lucky they would all get free of the plane and end up in a POW camp to sit out the war. There were much worse fates than a POW camp. Josh's fear was going down in the plane while conscious and being unable to get out. It would be a long and terrifying drop, one he certainly did not want to make. Better to die quickly or bail out safely and be captured by the Germans.

Over the intercom he heard the pilot say, "Open bomb bay doors! Thirty seconds to target! Josh, be ready to go to autopilot in fifteen!"

"Yes sir!" Josh was completely focused now as he leaned over the Norden sight to make some final adjustments regarding speed and altitude. He could clearly see the tops of smaller buildings on the outskirts of town getting larger as they neared their target. Having studied photographs earlier, he knew what to look for. It really didn't matter though, as Josh would release the bombs when the lead bomber in their formation released theirs—another strategy implemented to concentrate the destruction below. And it was working. A lot of people were going to experience hell in a minute, but Josh didn't feel much sympathy for them. The Germans started the war, and Hitler had to be stopped . . . even if it meant some innocent people had to lose their lives in the cross fire. He tried not to think about it as he prepared to drop his load.

"OK, Josh! You have the plane!" The pilot flipped on the autopilot that was in sync with the bombsight to help level and steady the plane as much as possible to facilitate a more accurate drop. The plane was bouncing up and down with hundreds of flak explosions surrounding them and the rest of the formation. Josh wondered how any of the planes would survive this onslaught and make it back alive. He knew the pilot was watching the lead plane, waiting for its bombs to begin falling, and then he would tell him to release the bombs. He flipped up the protective switch on the release button, his finger just an inch away, his eyes never leaving the sight.

"Bombs away!" he heard the pilot yell. He immediately hit the button, and within a couple of seconds, the plane lifted dramatically as it released its heavy burden. Just seconds later Josh could feel the plane make a steady tight turn to the left, climbing in the process. He knew they were trying to gain altitude to hopefully move above the deadly flak. He allowed himself a big sigh of relief, as now they were on their way home. They were not out of the woods yet, but at least they were going in the right direction, with their mission accomplished! He again scanned the horizon for fighters even though the annoying flak continued. It appeared the deadly projectiles were endless in number and were acting on a personal vendetta to bring down their plane.

Finally the flak stopped. Josh took a quick look around and began counting as many Fortresses as he could see. By his count, at least five had gone down already. The bombers on his left and right had been hit and were no longer in the formation. He peered down through the forward Plexiglas shield and did see some parachutes floating gently to the earth below. Enemy territory. He had heard stories that some locals would kill the American flyers on sight in retaliation for stray bombs that would destroy their villages, fields, and yes, innocent loved ones. Still, Josh would prefer to take his chances on the ground than ride a flaming tomb to certain death.

Josh was breathing a little easier now. They had survived the flak and there was no sign of enemy fighters. The German FW-190s and ME-109s would normally attack them prior to their bombs reaching their target, in hopes of shooting as many Fortresses down as possible before they had the chance to drop their deadly cargo. Not today for some reason.

Just then a dark blur screamed in front of his window. The intercom went wild with chatter. "Bogies, six o'clock high!" Then he heard Benny the top turret gunner. "Damn! There's about a dozen of 'em coming right at us out of the sun at twelve o'clock!" Benny was right, and it was like being in a hornet's nest, a nest of very angry hornets looking for revenge. The enemy fighters were so small and so fast as they swept by, it would take a miracle for anyone to shoot one down. How would they shoot down a dozen and save themselves?

Josh held the front .50 caliber machine gun in his hands, frantically trying to get a line on one of the planes, but they were coming by too fast. After a few seconds he saw one of the fighters coming straight for *Bonnie Bye-Bye*. He began to get a line on it and got ready to fire. Just then he heard "thump, thump, thump" in rapid succession from behind him and then felt a hideous and powerful punch to his left arm. It nearly knocked the wind out of him. He felt only a slight pain, but no feeling in his left arm . . . and definitely no control. His arm was useless. He slumped forward to support himself, removed his right glove with his teeth, then reached over with his right arm to begin feeling around. He felt something warm and slippery on his flight jacket where the numbness was. Even before holding his hand in front of his face, he knew what it was going to be. His hand was bright red with blood, and there was a lot of it. He felt unusually calm and began thinking of what he could use for a tourniquet to stop the bleeding.

Josh reached down and unbuckled his belt. Pulling with all the remaining strength he had, he removed it. With his right arm and teeth, he managed to loop the belt around his left arm up near the armpit and then he pulled as hard as he could. There was no way to tell if he had the belt tight enough to stop the bleeding. It would not go any tighter, so he would just have to hope that it would do the trick.

The intercom was still a flurry of screams, instructions, and an overall blur of chatter. But as the noise began fading a bit, the wound began hurting. And it was increasing by the second. He knew he had to get some morphine in him soon, as the pain would shortly become unbearable. He did not want to pass out now in case they had to bail out. He got up and was reaching for the first aid box when he heard more thumps, which opened up tens of holes in the fuselage just feet from where he'd been sitting moments earlier. One of the 20mm cannon shells struck the Norden bombsight and pieces of it shattered in an explosion sending small fragments of metal and glass into Josh's face. The top-secret instrument he had sworn an oath to protect with his own life was no longer something that needed protecting now.

Feeling weak and nauseous, Josh decided to lie down to conserve his strength. From this new angle he could see out the small opening in the fuselage. The number two engine was on fire, and quite badly. He pressed his intercom button. "Sir, this is Josh. Is everything all right up there?" No answer. He tried again; perhaps the intercom had been knocked out with the last salvo of cannon shells. "Sir?" Again, no answer. At that moment Josh had a sickening feeling the plane was beginning to drop. Slowly at first, and then with increasing momentum. He then realized both the pilot and copilot had probably been killed with the enemy fighter's last pass. No one was in control of the plane! Josh's worst fear was happening right then, and there was nothing, absolutely nothing, he could do about it. *Lucky Lucy's* luck had run out.

Josh still had his parachute. Did he have enough time, and more importantly, strength, to make it to the escape hatch and bail out? Josh gave his best effort to get up and crawl over to the opening. The increased speed of the diving and doomed plane was making what was a difficult job in the best of situations nearly impossible. He began crawling, but light-headedness and pain in his arm impeded his progress. The pain was now practically unbearable, shooting knives up his arm every time he moved. He was losing focus and feeling faint. It was too late, and he knew it. The plane was now moving at a tremendous speed and had rolled over onto its side in a fatal race to meet the beautiful countryside below.

The plane began to scream in its final agony of defeat. Moments before the final mission permanently ended for Josh, his thoughts drifted back to a smile . . . Rebecca's.

CHAPTER 1

THE DISCOVERY

PRESENT DAY

Illuminated numbers on the alarm clock read 12:20 a.m. David Keller's cell phone began to vibrate. He was in a deep sleep when after the third vibration he managed to reluctantly grab his phone off the nightstand and squint at the number on the screen. It looked unfamiliar. Late-night calls usually meant bad news, and he wasn't in the mood for any. For a moment he considered hitting the decline key but thought better of it just in case it truly was important.

"Hello?" he answered in an annoyed tone, keeping his voice low to prevent awakening his wife beside him.

"Is this David Keller?" asked the male caller, in an emotionless tone.

This can't be good, David thought. "Yes, who's calling?"

"I'm sorry to disturb you so late. My name is Robert Vargo. I'm the administrator for Regency Senior Care. Your grandfather, Eric, is one of our residents."

David sighed. What could it be this time? Another false alarm? "Sure, I remember. What is it? Did something happen?" He wanted to end the call as soon as possible and get back to sleep.

"Well, yes. I regret to inform you your grandfather passed away earlier this evening. We, I should say he, left instructions to let you know right away."

I guess it's not a false alarm, after all. David sat up in bed. "What happened?"

"One of the nurses found him during her evening rounds. Seems he was watching television when his heart just gave out. He passed peacefully."

David paused, his mind now racing to the last time he had spoken to his grandfather, and the subsequent argument they'd had. That was nearly three years ago now. Suddenly he felt guilty for not reaching out to mend fences with the man who, for the most part, had taken the responsibility for raising him after his parents tragically died in a car accident when he was just ten.

"Mr. Keller?" prompted Vargo after several moments of silence.

"Ah, sorry. I'm still here. Not really sure what to say."

"Please, Mr. Keller, there's no need to apologize. I completely understand. Forgive me, but I need to ask you about the key."

"Key, what key?" What the hell was Vargo talking about?

Emily was beginning to stir. David's conversation with Vargo, despite his best efforts to be quiet, had managed to waken her. Resting on her elbow, she asked, "Who is it? Is something wrong?"

David placed the phone to his chest. He didn't want to alarm her about Grandpa's death tonight; it could wait until morning. "It's about Grandpa. I'll fill you in later. Try and get back to sleep. I'll be done in a minute, sorry."

"It's probably another false alarm about his heart, nothing to worry about," she said as she rolled back over and pulled the covers snugly over her shoulders.

David rose out of bed and walked into the master bathroom, carefully closing the creaky door behind him.

"Sorry about that. You were saying something about a key."

"Yes," continued Vargo. "Part of our procedure after a resident passes is to check their file right away for any special instructions." He paused to make sure David was following, which he was.

"Go on," David said.

"Well, there wasn't much in your grandfather's file except a small note that said we were to contact you immediately on his passing and to make sure you had the key."

David's mind was a complete blank regarding a key of any sort. "Mr. Vargo, I have no idea what he's talking about. Not only don't I have any of his keys, but I don't remember him ever talking about a specific key. There must be some mistake."

"Oh, there's no mistake," insisted Vargo. "The note is in his own handwriting, and he specifically mentions a key, and that you're the only one to have it."

David looked up at the dark ceiling. He was at a complete loss. He and Grandpa Eric had talked many times over the years, even as they were growing apart. A key never came up. He must have imagined it.

"Believe me, if there was a key that important to my grandfather, I would have remembered. Trust me, there's no key. I certainly don't have it. Any chance it could be there in his file?"

"I'm afraid not. We've looked in his room, too, and nothing's there either."

In spite of the eventful news, David was exhausted and began to yawn. He needed his sleep after a very stressful day—and now evening. "Listen, I'm sure we can figure out what this is all about, but I really can't do anything about it tonight."

Vargo reluctantly agreed. "But of course. I know it's late and I am truly sorry to bother you at this hour. I'm only trying to fulfill your grandfather's last instructions. Why don't you stop by tomorrow and we'll take it from there."

"Tomorrow? Does it have to be tomorrow? I'm really busy right now; can I come by in a day or so?"

"I wish I could accommodate you, Mr. Keller, but unfortunately we need to make some arrangements tomorrow, if at all possible. Call me in the morning and we'll find a time that's convenient for you."

David let out a deep breath, resigned to the fact he would need to change his already impossible schedule. "All right, I'll call you tomorrow morning."

"Thank you, and again, I'm sorry for your loss." And with that, the line went dead.

Weary, David slowly opened the creaky door and walked back to bed. Good luck getting back to sleep now, he thought. And what's with this key anyway? Fortunately for David, he was asleep in less than five minutes.

⁜

His morning routine was the same every day, and David took comfort in it. There was something about doing the same mindless activities morning after morning that allowed him to slowly come up to full speed before taking on the world. It was his time; no one else made any demands on him while he was still in the worn robe and shabby slippers he would never throw away. He didn't need an alarm to wake up. He rose around six every morning, as regularly as the sun rose. Emily would sometimes sleep much later, allowing him the rare privacy he relished more and more as he grew older.

He entered the kitchen with its cold tile floor, poured himself a glass of orange juice, and stirred in his daily tablespoon of Metamucil. Two Aleve, one aspirin, and one vitamin were also part of his early-morning regimen. He put on a pot of coffee. The familiar aroma reassured him and perked him up even before pouring his first cup.

While the coffee was still brewing, David unplugged his MacBook from the charger and sat down at the kitchen table. Quickly checking his emails, he made a mental note of which ones he would answer right away. Most could be put off until later. Nothing urgent, thank God. Logging into the *Wall Street Journal*, he began skimming the headlines until he found something interesting. He frowned, as stock futures were down again. His own stocks were highlighted on his custom home page. Those were not doing so well either.

The skimming was mindless; however, his thoughts were preoccupied with Grandpa Eric and any memory whatsoever of a key. It was hopeless; his memory was blank. Surely Vargo had made a mistake when he was going through the file. If the key was so important, Grandpa would have mentioned it or given it to him. If the key actually existed it was most likely to a safety deposit box, a locker, or something like that. Maybe he'd get lucky and find a stash of cash or something very valuable, and he could retire early. Wouldn't that be a treat? He chuckled to himself, thinking it may be nothing more than some old photos of Grandpa, or something else of little value. That made more sense—all this drama for nothing more than an old memory box. More perplexing, though, was the fact that it was missing from the file and no one else seemed to know anything about it. So where the heck could it be? Probably it wouldn't matter in the end anyway.

This really couldn't come at a worse time. Later this week was his big sales presentation. If only he could hit a home run with that, then his new consulting business would be well on its way financially. And no one had to tell him that he and his family desperately needed it to be, especially with Emily's medical bills and the college expenses rolling in for his daughter, Rachael. It hadn't been so bad when Emily was working. Pharm Ds made pretty good money, and she could set her own hours. It was always the plan to live on her income until the business took off, but as all families find out, cancer has a way of derailing plans. She continued to work until the chemo made her so sick she had no choice but to take an extended leave of absence. Overnight the weight on David's shoulders grew heavier. Until the money tree began to grow in the backyard, he would have to bet the farm on his fledging business. Savings were evaporating, the pressure was on.

Behind him he heard the familiar sound of shuffling slippers on the tile floor. Emily was moving slowly and she stopped behind David, placing her hand on his shoulder. "Morning, hon."

He reached behind and squeezed her hand. "Good morning. You're up early."

"Jonesy woke me up. We should start putting her in the basement at night. Were you able to doze back off after that phone call?" Jonesy was their six-year-old gray cat, a stray who pretty much invited herself to become part of their family after a bad storm one night. She seemed to fit in, so they kept her around as long as she wanted to stay. Her only bad habit was letting everyone know when she woke up. She'd jump up on the bed and paw at the covers until everyone else was awake too.

"Seemed to," he answered with a sigh.

"I don't know why you don't turn that thing off at night."

She walked over and grabbed her familiar "Lake Tahoe" cup, stained from years of heavy use, and poured herself some coffee. No cream or sugar, just black. One of the few comforts she could still enjoy. She set it on the table across from David and walked over to the refrigerator. She opened the door and removed a clear pitcher containing a greenish liquid, what she called her "health shake." Emily didn't see a juice glass in the cupboard, so she leaned over and opened the dishwasher door and found one on the rack. She poured the rather thick, awful-looking liquid into the glass and then set it on the table next to the coffee. Finally she opened another cupboard door and surveyed the medicine bottles, nearly a dozen in all, and took three of them down.

"Yeah, you're probably right," David said.

"Right about what?" She sat down at the table and began removing the tops from the medicine bottles. Why do they make these tops so difficult to get off, she wondered. David saw her struggling with the tops and reached over to take them off for her.

"These phones. Sometimes they're more trouble than they're worth."

"Well, I'm glad you agree," she said, nodding her head.

"Sorry it woke you. You seemed to get back to sleep . . . at least before I did."

"You know me," she smiled, "sleep and I are bosom buddies these days."

"How are you feeling this morning?" He looked up, and for the moment, gave her his full attention.

"About the same. This is the third day since the last treatment, so I should have a pretty good few days before I go back in." Emily then rolled her eyes, knowing what would follow. "Of course, then it starts all over again." As with many chemotherapy patients, the first couple days following the long day at the center receiving the potent drug were predictable with annoying regularity—exhaustion from the most minor of activities, nausea, and a general feeling of depression. Emily, who had always been quite outgoing and self-reliant, also became increasingly frustrated and angry as she secretly acknowledged her increasing dependence on David and the many other friends who were always offering to do things for her. Things she used to do on her own.

She truly hated the disease. As could be expected, she had a newfound respect for all who were either going through treatment now or had preceded her with their own personal battle for survival. She thought it cruel and evil. Cancer was nothing more than a thief that robs people of their productive lives and places unreasonable burdens on those they love. It had to be the most unfair, indiscriminate, and yes, degrading illness ever to exist. What made it even worse was the timing. Just as they needed her to be working more than ever with David's start-up business, she got broadsided with this health disaster.

"I'm really sorry," he offered. "Just wish there was something I could do to make it go away." David was still having a lot of difficulty adjusting to the emotion of seeing this once-vibrant, "can-do," beautiful woman who was the envy of her colleagues and friends, gradually and with eerie predictability, erode in all aspects of her previous self. It was truly sad. And he felt helpless. Many times he would run an errand just to cry privately in the car so she wouldn't see the complete effect it was having on him. For now he would be as strong as he could around her and do his grieving in private.

She reached across the table and squeezed his hand. She smiled that loving smile that had so many times reassured him in the past. "Hon, you don't have to be sorry about anything. You've been terrific, and quite the trouper to put up with this sickie and all the baggage that goes along with it. If anyone needs to be sorry, it's me."

"OK, so we're both sorry. We've had this discussion before. Shit happens. It's no one's fault, and more importantly, no one has to be sorry. It is what it is. We're dealing with this curveball the best we can." Now he squeezed back, giving her that reassuring grip he'd done so much of lately. "You're going to get better; it will just take a little more time than we'd hoped."

She hoped too, but that inner voice told her something different. "I don't know, it seems that things aren't really going all that well. My counts aren't getting any better and I just can't keep any weight on. I know they said this may happen, but sometimes you just know the situation isn't getting any better."

"Listen to me," he said, squeezing her hand a little tighter, "you're the strongest, toughest person I've ever known. I've always loved that about you. Don't you even dare think about giving up. As long as Rachael, our friends, and I aren't giving up, you can't either. You have to stay positive."

She smiled again. "I'll do my best."

"That's my girl," he said with a smile. "Anything I can do for you today?"

"Don't think so." She picked up all the pills at once and downed them in one gulp with the nasty green stuff. After a slight pause to allow the pills a chance to make their winding trip down into her stomach, she finished off the rest of the concoction. She grimaced just a little bit, revealing the stuff was perhaps just as awful as David imagined. Immediately after it was gone, she picked up her coffee and blew on the top of it, as was her habit to test its temperature, and took a sip. Had to get that taste out of her mouth as soon as possible!

"Speaking of Rachael," David said as he turned his attention back to the computer screen, "an email from her said she may come home this weekend. Sounds like her exam is on Thursday, then no classes on Friday, so she can have a long weekend."

"That'll be nice," said Emily. Both of them were extremely proud of their daughter now. It hadn't always been so—there were some early struggles with drugs and alcohol. After a small fortune spent on counseling, however, Rachael had managed to turn her life around with some good friends and *very* supportive parents. Now she was studying architecture at Ball State and maintaining a 3.6 GPA, a very pleasant surprise to everyone, especially Rachael. She had a newfound level of self-confidence that up until recently was nonexistent. She was actually growing up and, if you asked David, becoming her mother in many ways. A good thing, in his opinion.

"She wants to cook. Something Italian."

"Really?" asked Emily.

"I know. Who would have thought a couple of years ago that—"

"Let's don't go there," Emily interrupted in her soft, pleasant manner. "Those were tough times and they're behind us now. I'd rather not revisit those days. Let's just be happy things are going well now."

David looked up from the screen, realizing she was right. "Sure."

He decided to put down the screen to enjoy these moments with Emily; he may not always have them. They chitchatted for a while, and then out of the blue, Emily remembered the call.

"You were going to tell me about the call last night. Something about Grandpa."

David nodded. How in the world could he forget about that? "Do you remember a guy by the name of Vargo who works at the home where Grandpa lives?"

"No, not really."

"He's the one who called last night. Grandpa passed away—"

"What? Why didn't you say so last night?"

"I didn't want to bother you with it last night. I thought it could wait until this morning."

"That's kind of odd, don't you think? Calling in the middle of the night when you're not even that close."

"Well, that's the weird part. Vargo told me they always check their files when someone dies. Grandpa left a note saying I was supposed to be notified immediately. Then he said there's this key of Grandpa's . . . and only I was to get it. No clue as to where it is or what it's to."

"That is strange. Do you know where the key is?"

"That's just it. I don't know anything about a key. Do you remember me ever talking about one?"

Emily paused just for a second before answering. "No. The only thing I remember is you were quite upset about something that happened during your last trip over there. And that's been . . . years now, I think."

"Yeah, almost three years."

"Any idea what it could be to?"

"Nope." David shrugged his shoulders.

"What are you going to do?"

David leaned back in his chair in resignation to the fact that he would probably be the one to handle all the funeral arrangements, and perhaps the expenses as well. Just one more financial obligation they didn't have the money for.

"Vargo asked me to call him this morning to go over the details. At the very least I'll have to go in and sign some papers. I don't think he had any assets, or at least not very many. I just hope he has enough to take care of any final expenses. I'm not even sure if he wanted a funeral. Vargo said he had no visitors, so who's to say if anyone would come even if we had one. With any luck we can do with a simple cremation and a small memorial service. I just don't know yet."

Emily was taking all of this in, while trying to remember the old man she'd met only a few times. "Do you have to take care of it this week?"

"Yeah, I think so. It doesn't look like there's anyone else, so I'm the one."

She reached over and squeezed his hand. "I'm sorry, hon. I really never knew him. I think the last time I saw him was five or six years ago when we made a quick stop on our way back from Indy."

"I think you're right."

"The one thing I do remember though," Emily recalled, "is he was quite happy to see you. A lot less interested in me. It seemed to me he wanted to tell you something, but as long as I was there he kept whatever it was to himself."

"I didn't pick up on that. Are you sure?"

"Yes, I'm sure. Haven't you ever had the feeling you weren't wanted somewhere . . . kind of a sixth sense? Well, I definitely had it that day. It kind of gave me the creeps."

"Oh, come on. Now you're imagining things. He was very nice to you. I actually think he was ogling you a little bit."

"Very funny," she said with an ornery grin, "but he was not ogling me. I think he liked me well enough. My gut was telling me to leave you two alone for a while, but I didn't because we were in a hurry to get back."

"If you say so."

"I know you have a full week, but you may want to call this Vargo and get things rolling now. Otherwise, I know you'll just worry about it until you do."

David did not like this fact about himself. He was a constant worrier. He would even admit, at times he rose the worry bar to an Olympic level. Funny thing, nearly everything he worried about never came to pass. It drove both him and Emily a little crazy at times.

"Yeah, I suppose you're right. I'll call him in a little bit."

Emily rose from her chair. "I think I'm gonna head back to bed for a while. I know it sounds boringly familiar, but I'm very tired and just need to lie down."

"No problem. Want me to walk you upstairs?"

"Nah, I got it. Just call Vargo so we can get this behind us. There's too much other stuff going on right now."

"You got it."

As she headed out of the kitchen, she glanced back over her shoulder to say, "Who knows, maybe you'll get lucky and find out this key's to a box with a winning lottery ticket in it."

"Fat chance."

David waited until he heard her reach the top of the stairs, then he went back to the Mac and began responding to his emails. Emily was right. Better to meet with Vargo now about Grandpa and get the ball rolling. Then he could focus his energies on the presentation. After all, how long could it take? Grandpa was a widower for more than twenty years and pretty much a recluse his entire life.

Twenty minutes later he picked up the phone and dialed Vargo's number.

⎯◈⎯

David pulled up to Regency Senior Care around 11:15 that morning. After speaking with Vargo earlier, it was clear he wanted to wrap up Grandpa's affairs just as much as David did. In fact, Vargo made the comment that since calling David the night before, two other residents had passed away. Busy night. So the sooner they could get together on Grandpa's business, the more it would help Vargo and Regency's already-busy schedule. It didn't seem to matter all that much what David wanted.

He had checked on Emily before heading out, and thanks to the drugs, she was out like a light. With any luck he would be back before she woke up and not even miss him.

The Regency was just as he remembered it; aging and now in some need of cosmetic attention, but still retaining the look of a reputable establishment. That's reassuring, he thought. David found a parking place not far from the entrance and took his small, leather flap briefcase with him in the event Vargo gave him a stack of paperwork. He walked up to the front nurses' station and waited patiently while the lone nurse talked on the phone. She politely acknowledged him and raised her forefinger, indicating she would soon finish the call. David smiled and nodded, signaling no need to rush on his account. He turned and surveyed the lobby, remembering his last visit. Could it really have been three years ago? Now that he was standing there it seemed more like a few months than a few years.

There were several patients in wheelchairs, some with IVs, and one particularly frail-looking man with a walker who appeared as though he should be in a wheelchair himself. He stared at David and waved nonchalantly, and David smiled and waved back. Then the frail man continued to shuffle out of the lobby and down the hall. God, David thought, I hope I die a quick and merciful death before this is my fate.

He heard the nurse conclude her conversation and hang up. "May I help you?"

"Yes. My name is David Keller. Mr. Vargo called me last night about my grandfather, Eric Keller. He passed away. Vargo asked me to come in and see about finalizing his affairs." He hated the way that came out. Too formal and unfeeling. But, he really didn't know his grandfather all that well, so why try to feign true sorrow when he just wasn't feeling any?

"Sure, I remember Eric. A very nice man." You could tell the nurse had spent some time with Eric and even had a fondness for him. "Sorry for your loss. I didn't realize he'd passed away. I just came on at 10:00 and haven't seen the deceased list yet. You must be the grandson?"

"Well, yes . . . that's right. How did you know?"

She chuckled. "You're the only one he ever talked about. He would always tell anyone who listened that you were coming to visit. But . . . I don't think I've seen you in a while. You must have come during my off-shift, as I would remember you."

David sheepishly allowed his eyes to look down. "It's been awhile since I've been here." Then he thought of a convenient "un-truth" veiled in his truthful situation as to why he hadn't visited. "My wife's very ill which has kept me busy."

The nurse wanted to believe him, but it was obvious to David she wasn't convinced. "Oh, I'm sorry to hear that. I hope it's nothing too serious."

"Actually, it is." He didn't want to get into the details. "Is he available? I believe he's expecting me."

"Let me check." She picked up the phone and punched in some numbers. After a few seconds she spoke into the phone. "Hey Mel, it's Fran. Yeah, I heard. Is he in? OK, I'll send him down." She replaced the receiver and pointed down one of the four hallways. "He's down that hall all the way at the end in room 100. You can't miss it, there's a big Purdue basketball poster on the door. He's *quite* the fan."

"Got it. Thanks for your help."

"Don't mention it. Oh, sorry about Eric. Hope your wife gets better too."

"Thanks," said David. He started down the hallway and casually peered into some of the rooms, naturally curious about their occupants. Most of the rooms were empty. In others the elderly were sleeping or watching TV with the volume turned up loudly enough to drown out any chance of conversation with anyone else in the room.

There it was—wow, that was one big Purdue basketball poster! David was an Indiana University grad, but he had some very good friends and colleagues who had attended Purdue. The only animosity between them was during the basketball games; mostly of course, during the famous, or more appropriately labeled, *infamous*, "Bucket" game, which signaled the end of the IU-Purdue football season. Neither football program had enjoyed much success lately, and both alums drowned their alma mater sorrows in many a beer following the annual Bucket game. Most of the time both sides were relieved the season and its frustrations were over. Maybe next year.

David knocked lightly on the open door and smiled at the very attractive young woman sitting just outside what he thought had to be Vargo's office. She was about thirty, had on way too much makeup, and sported a tight knit top. She was snapping her gum, which instantly annoyed David. She slightly turned her head toward him while continuing to keep her eyes on the screen and tap away at her keyboard.

"Are you Mr. Keller?"

"Yes."

"I already told him you were on your way down. You can go in, he's expecting you." She never raised her eyes to meet his.

"OK, thanks."

David walked by her desk and couldn't help but notice the strong aroma of perfume. He didn't recognize it, but thought it was probably a cheap brand and then immediately and silently chided himself for assuming so.

As soon as he entered the office, Vargo stopped typing on his computer, rose and smiled at David. He extended his hand, which David shook.

"Mr. Keller, it's a pleasure to see you again. Is it all right if I call you David?"

"Of course."

"Good, please call me Robert." They both sat down. Vargo turned and pulled one of the manila folders from a stack of about twenty on his credenza. David could see "**KELLER**" written across the top in bold letters.

Vargo continued, "I really appreciate you getting down here so quickly. We normally wouldn't be in such a rush, but like I told you on the phone, two more residents passed away this morning, and well, it's been a little hectic. Our policy mandates we get the family involved right away in finalizing arrangements for the deceased resident."

David couldn't help but think how Vargo was all business. No bedside manner whatsoever. He was about as cold as they come, with not even a hint of condolence. Sure wouldn't want to put him out or jeopardize his sacred policy or schedule! David was already anxious to wrap this up and get out of there.

"I understand," David lied. He didn't understand. At all. Did Vargo treat everyone with this attitude and air of detachment? If so, he was in the wrong profession.

"This is your grandfather's file, and as you can see, there's not much in here other than our normal records." He handed it over to David.

David took the file and quickly leafed through it, not exactly sure what he was supposed to do with the dozen or so sheets of medical evaluations, detailed diet schedules, and a myriad of other nurses' reports. It was pretty much gobbledygook to him. Then he saw the note, the one Vargo had told him about. It was nothing more than a large yellow Post-it note with a handwritten message on it.

Call my grandson David IMMEDIATELY after I die!
Make sure he gets the key.
NO ONE ELSE!

Then at the bottom was a phone number he didn't recognize. Nothing more. No instructions. No mention of where to find the key. And no mention whatsoever of what the key opened.

Vargo waited for a few seconds and then said, "So, you still don't know anything about this key?"

Confused, David looked up from the file and stared at Vargo. "No, I don't." Then he asked Vargo, "Are you absolutely sure you don't have it, or at least know anything about what it's to?"

"Yes, I'm absolutely sure."

"I even asked my wife about it," said David, "and she doesn't remember anything about a key either. Can you tell me anything about this phone number?"

Vargo again shook his head. "No, afraid not. We thought about calling it ourselves to see who answered, but as you can tell by the tone of his note, this was meant specifically for you, and only you. We really didn't feel at liberty to call it."

David looked at the number again, believing his brain would reveal the answer. Nothing. He would have to call the number and hope it revealed something.

"Well," he said to Vargo with a tone of disappointment, "I have no idea what this number's to. I'll call it later and hope it leads me to this key. Or at least to something. If not, I'm at a dead end and it will remain a mystery. Unless you have a better idea."

"Wish I did, but I don't. I'm sorry I don't have any more information for you."

David sighed, "It's not your problem. You did what you were supposed to do. He was an old man, so I wouldn't be surprised if he imagined this whole thing."

"You could be right. Just the same, I'd call the number and see where it leads. If indeed it turns out to be a dead end, then you've done everything you can and it's just that . . . a dead end."

David nodded in agreement. "OK, what else needs to be done?"

Vargo spent the next twenty minutes going through various forms, many requiring signatures. To David's pleasant surprise, Grandpa seemed to have a fairly respectable bank account that Regency was drawing off of every month for his care. That account would now need to be closed. A trip to the bank was in order. Another relief was Grandpa had already made arrangements to be cremated and then the ashes dispersed off the Atlantic coastline near a town that David was unfamiliar with. Another unexpected peculiarity.

✦

When they were finished, David glanced at his watch. All told, everything with Vargo took thirty minutes. Better than he expected. He exited the building, giving Fran at the front desk a smile and a wave as she spoke on the phone, knowing he wouldn't return. She waved back.

He started the engine to his Volvo and sat there for a minute remembering Grandpa, realizing there was indeed some mystery about him. Had he committed some terrible crime? Or better yet, was he a closet millionaire who saved every cent he made, only to leave everything he had to David and his family? Doubtful. The odds were, there never was any key. Only an imagined one. David now wondered if he had made a mistake, not putting forth more effort to improve their relationship. Then, perhaps, many of these questions would already be answered. But, as he well knew, you cannot turn back the clock.

He reached for the folder while still sitting in the parking lot and opened the file to the yellow note, his eyes focusing on the phone number. His instincts told him the number was the last and only path to the key and its importance. At least important to Grandpa. Should he call it or not? It was probably nothing, and if someone did answer, it would surely be a wrong number. Or more likely lead to an "out of service" recording.

He turned on his iPhone and touched the numbers on the keypad. It began ringing, and after the third ring, a rough male voice answered with a cough and a clearing of his throat. David thought this was not a promising start.

After another cough, "Logan Law Firm. What can I do for ya?"

David immediately considered hanging up, believing no legitimate law firm would answer their phone in such an unprofessional manner. Now he wasn't sure what he should say. "Hi, my name is David Keller. I'm calling to see if anyone there has done any work or perhaps had other dealings with a man by the name of Eric Keller."

Another cough. "Maybe. Why do ya want to know?"

"I'm his grandson. He passed away last night. I have some of his papers here, and one of the documents has a phone number on it. *Your* phone number. I just wondered if you or anyone else there had done any work for him?" David knew it was a stretch to call the yellow Post-it note a "document," but what did it really matter?

"What did you say the name was?" It was obvious the name Eric Keller did not immediately ring a bell with this man.

"Keller. Eric Keller."

"Hmm . . . Keller. Can't say that I do. Are you sure he did some work with me?"

"No, not really. This document indicates you have a key I'm supposed to get." The note really didn't say that, but David thought it would sound more official.

"Wait a minute. I do remember an older man who was making a big fuss over a key and a box he left with me. It was about six months ago. He was quite a character, really full of some interesting stories. I thought they were pretty crazy. I thought his mind was starting to go and he was making this stuff up. Yeah, I remember him. Haven't heard from him since. Sorry to hear he died."

David's heart jumped! Finally, a clue. Logan at least knew something about the key. This was a good start. "Mr. Logan, this is very important. To be truthful, I'm not really sure what this key is to, and I don't know anything about a box. But the document he left behind is very explicit about the key, and that I should recover it as soon as possible after his death. Are you sure he left a box with you too?"

"Yep. The key is to the box, or at least that's what I think it's to."

"What kind of box?"

"Well," Logan said as he tried to recall the last time he had seen it, "it's an old wood box and not that big. Could fit in most desk drawers. It's kinda heavy and pretty beat up, as I recall. He was very protective of it, that's for sure. When I met him, he was holding it under his arm and at first wouldn't even let me look at it. After we talked for a while he said he wanted to leave it for his grandson, who I assume is you. He was absolutely sure you'd be coming for it one day."

David could not believe his luck. This was not going to be a dead end after all. "Mr. Logan—"

"Please," interrupted Logan, "call me Ralph. Everyone calls me Ralph."

"OK, Ralph. Do you still have it?"

"Yeah, I think so, unless he came and got it when I wasn't here. I told him if it was that important he should get a safety deposit box, but he was having no part of that. I don't think he cared much for banks. But yeah, I'm sure I still have it. I remember he pleaded with me to keep it here. I have an old vault downstairs that we keep some of our own important stuff in. Told him I could keep it in there, but he'd have to pay for it. Think he paid for a year's worth. I was pretty nice to him, only charged a couple hundred bucks or so. After all, that's not really what we do. Only for special clients."

"So do I understand you have both the key and the box?"

"Yep, I'm sure. The key opens the box."

David could barely contain his excitement. He was still quite skeptical anything of real value would be in the box, but his curiosity was almost more than he could contain. "That's great news. Grandpa really wasn't all that specific about where the key was . . . and the box. When can I come over and pick them up?"

"Well, pretty much anytime. When do you want to get them?

"I'm in Indy right now, where's your office?"

"I'm downtown just off Illinois."

David knew exactly where that was, and by good fortune, he was only thirty minutes away. "That's perfect. I'm just leaving the Regency home now and can be there in thirty minutes, if that works for you."

"I'll be here. Just wrapping up some paperwork on an estate case. I'll pull his file and get the box and key from the vault. I'll have it ready by the time you get here. Kinda curious what's in it."

"Me too. See you in half an hour." David confirmed his address. He pulled out of the parking lot driving just a little faster than he normally would have. His heart was beating fast in anticipation of learning what this key and box business was all about. He had the distinct feeling he was going to be surprised at whatever he discovered.

"Logan Law Firm" was imprinted in large, fading black letters on the etched glass of the tired-looking oak door. The door's varnish was peeling in numerous places and was really in need of some work. The etched glass had a nine-inch crack running directly below the word "Estates," and had probably been there for decades. Underneath the firm's name was Ralph's full name in smaller letters, and below that was "Personal Injury – Estates." Standing outside in the dimly lit hallway of this obviously undermaintained building, David knew this was not going to be a large office. Probably a one-man operation.

The enormous brass door handle was huge, badly tarnished, and at least a hundred years old, in David's estimation.

David took in his surroundings and quickly realized he wasn't working with one of Indianapolis's top attorneys. Maybe Logan was not a licensed attorney at all, just someone who failed the bar and was practicing law in spite of that minor detail. Absolutely no effort was being made to promote Logan's firm in a positive light. Calling this establishment a second-rate operation would be kind and generous—very generous. He began to wonder again what kind of man Grandpa was, and why all the mystery. At the same time, he was finding this exciting and a welcome break from his normal work routine and stress over Emily's health.

David wasn't sure at first if he should knock lightly on the door or just walk in. After a brief pause, he turned the doorknob and entered without knocking. The small lobby or waiting room, if you could call it that, was a disaster. It was unkempt, with magazines and newspapers strewn about. A white coffeemaker was sitting in the corner on a cheap end table, badly stained from years of use with no evidence of any cleaning whatsoever. Used coffee strainers overflowed the wastebasket next to the table. The chairs and sofa were of sixties vintage with torn and otherwise badly worn material in just about every location conceivable. He didn't think he could sit anywhere without taking the risk of catching some disease. And finally, there was a huge stain about the size of a basketball in the middle of a dark-beige area rug covering most of the wood floor.

"Hello?" David called out.

"I'm in here." From around the corner came the voice he recognized from the phone. "Are you Keller?"

"Yes."

"Come on in. Sorry about the mess."

"No problem," said David. He walked around the corner, not knowing what to expect of Logan or his office. He entered to see

Logan checking his computer. On the desk was an old box, just like the one he had described on the phone. The office was in about the same condition as the waiting room—a complete and disorganized mess. He wondered how anyone could get any work done or find anything of importance in this place.

Logan was a man of about fifty, short, about thirty pounds over-weight, with two days' beard growth; but, for the most part, he looked harmless. David also noticed no wedding ring. No shock there.

Logan looked up. "You weren't kidding about thirty minutes, you made great time. I've been to the Regency home many times myself and never made it that fast."

"The traffic was pretty light, and I hit all the lights." He was lying about that, but he didn't want Logan to know how anxious he was to take possession of the key and now the equally mysterious box. "Is that where you met Eric, at Regency?"

"As a matter of fact, it is," said Logan as he eyed David up and down, attempting to size him up in a few seconds. "I get out there every couple of months or so. I do a lot of estate work for some of the folks out there. I've also done a bunch of POAs, trustee assign-ments, that sort of thing. You may say I'm their lawyer on call." Logan motioned to David to sit down, which he did.

"I see." David was again wondering how trustworthy Logan was. One thing was certain; he would never be David's attorney.

"Yeah, I don't remember the exact circumstance, but as I recall, I was doing some estate work for one of the ladies out there." All of a sudden Logan began digressing, recalling an unusual episode. "I think she was getting up there in years and had never put anything down on paper. Well, her kids, and even her grandkids, began bending her ear about leaving a bunch of stuff to them and I think she just got fed up with all of them being so selfish and greedy. She used the word greedy quite a lot." This was much more than David wanted to know or cared about, but to avoid taking any chance of alienating Logan, he decided to be patient and hear him out.

"So she calls me one day and says she's had enough, and wants me to write a will for her. Seems *she* wants to decide who gets what, which is understandable." David was nodding in feigned agreement. "I get out there and after meeting her I think this little old lady doesn't have two nickels to rub together. Well, I go ahead and make out a pretty simple, straightforward will, and she's happy. All the time I'm still thinking she's as poor as a church mouse and all her relatives are going to be sorely disappointed after she goes. But she pays me and the check clears. Guess what? She dies a couple of months later, and come to find out, she's worth more than a million bucks."

"Really?" David asks in mock disbelief.

"Yeah, really. Who would have guessed she was a spinster who saved every dime she ever made? Had investments in stocks, gold, and even a couple of rental properties."

"I guess the relatives were happy after all," David concluded, still disbelieving the story. He was hoping this little tale was nearly over so they could proceed with *his* business. He could see the box sitting there on Logan's desk, begging to be opened. The key was sitting on the box.

"Not exactly," Logan smiled. "The family had pissed her off to the point where she left everything, and I mean everything, to the Methodist church down the street. Seems the church was on hard times, and she took pity on them. Let me tell you, that family was *not* happy. They sued to have the will thrown out and the old lady declared incompetent to make a will in the first place."

Now David was actually taking some interest in the story. Logan was pretty good at relating the tale, and it was obvious he was taking pleasure in reliving the events. "So what happened?"

Logan sighed. "Of course we had to go to court. At first I thought the church was going to sign over the assets to the family. They were as nice as they could be and understood why the family was upset. I don't think they felt right about getting *everything*. But, the family behaved like real jerks and began harassing the church trustees, calling them names, sending obscene emails, calling them at all hours of the night. Well, after a few weeks of that, the church took a vote and changed course . . . deciding the family was not worthy of this lady's assets. I believe their intent at that point was to distribute what they could to the poor and needy in the neighborhood, a much better use of the money.

So, we go to court a few weeks later and the judge hears the case. He listens to the church trustees and then to the family. I had a long list of people at Regency who testified to her mental soundness when she made out the will, and the judge ruled in favor of the church."

David was now very curious about how it all ended. "My God, what did the family do?"

"It was a real circus," said Logan, still amazed at the events. "Right there in court the family started swearing at the judge, and some were throwing papers and other stuff at the bench." Logan rolled his eyes, shaking his head. "I've been doing this a long time and I've never seen anything like that before. They had to call the bailiffs to get things back under control. Then they took all of them away in handcuffs. Each and every one of them deserved it. I think it's safe to say they had only themselves to blame. Worst and yet most entertaining case I've ever had."

"Wow, that's unbelievable."

Logan nodded. "The reason I bring all this up is I had just finished up my will business with this very lady when your grandfather, Eric, wandered over and stuck his head in the doorway. He asked if I was a lawyer and would I do a job for him. I said sure. So we walked over to his room and he began telling me this interesting story about how he wanted to get some things off his chest before he died. Something about the war. World War II, the *Great War,* as he called it."

"The war?" What the heck was Logan, and more importantly Grandpa, talking about?

"That's right, the war. Said he'd been carrying something around for most of his life and couldn't die with it on his conscience."

David leaned forward, nearly mesmerized with this new information. The mystery continued. "So what was it?"

"That's just it, he wouldn't tell me. He showed me a stack of papers bound with a huge rubber band, and then told me it was for his grandson's eyes only." Then Logan pointed at David. "*Your* eyes only."

David sat back in his chair and frantically searched his brain for any memory of what Logan was talking about. Nothing. "I have absolutely no idea what it could be. He never talked about the war . . . any war."

"Whatever it is, he wants to clear it up, *and* he only wants you to know about it. Or should I say be the first to know about it."

Then David's eyes looked over to the box. "I assume the papers are in the box?"

"That's right. At least I think they are. What else could be in there?"

David kept his eyes on the box, now fearing what the papers may contain. "Now I'm not sure I want to see them."

"Of course you do. *I* want to see it, and I'm not even family. It was all so secretive to him. After he held up the bound papers for me to see, he placed them in this very box, locked it, and then gave me the key. Made me swore on my mother's grave I would never open it or tell anyone else about it. That's when I told him it would be better off in a safety deposit box. You'd have thought I insulted his mother. Gave me a dirty look and cursed the banking system in general. Offered to pay me to keep them until you came one day to get the box . . . and the papers."

David tilted his head in complete bewilderment. "That *is* unusual." He wanted to conclude his business here and get home with the box. "Do you need me to sign something?"

"Yeah, afraid so. Also need to see some ID, just to be sure you are who you say you are. No offense."

"No, I understand. What else?" David reached for his wallet and pulled out his driver's license. Logan placed the license on his scanner-printer and made a copy for the file.

"At the same time he had me draw up some paperwork that makes you his PR so you can do whatever else needs to be done."

"PR?"

"Personal Representative. That way you can take the death certificate down to the bank and close out his accounts and anything else that needs attention. He has a one-page will that basically says everything goes to you." Logan pulled out a one-page document that he held up for David to see. "Last Will & Testament" was easily seen written across it in large letters. "Eric Keller" was clearly legible, signed near the bottom. "It was obvious you were the only one he thought much of. He talked about you quite a bit the day I was there. Pretty proud of you, that's for sure."

David felt like a heel, knowing he didn't deserve any praise or other form of adulation from his grandfather. If anything, he should be scolded for avoiding him and not making more of an effort to provide some company for the old man during his final days. He was not going to share these feelings with Logan though, that was for sure. Now he just wanted to get the key, the box, and get the heck out of there.

David smiled. "Mr. Logan, sorry, Ralph. I can't tell you how much I appreciate the work you did for Grandpa. That includes keeping the key and the box. I know you didn't have to do that."

Logan noticeably relaxed, as though he was relieved to be rid of the box and its contents. "Normally I wouldn't have kept them, but there was something about your grandfather's sincerity that compelled me to do it."

"Again, thanks. I'm grateful. Do I owe you money for your work?"

"You're welcome. I'll figure it out and send you a bill. Shouldn't be much." Logan paused, then asked the question he had wanted to ask since David walked through the door. "Would you like to open it here? You've got to be curious . . . I sure am."

"You're right about that," agreed David, "but I think I'll wait and do it at home. Running a little behind and really need to be moving along." He stood and grabbed the key, placing it in his pocket. Then, with some apprehension, he picked up the box from Logan's desk and placed it under his left arm. It was a little heavier than he had anticipated. He stuck out his right hand and offered it to Logan. Logan stood and took David's hand, shaking it firmly. David now thought he had misjudged Logan. Perhaps he was indeed a straight shooter who was just a little down on his luck.

"It was a pleasure meeting you," said Logan. Then he pointed toward the box. "I hope it's something you can use."

"Likewise. And me too." David turned to leave with the mystery items in hand, anxious to get home and see what it was all about. Logan couldn't resist a last sales pitch.

"Take one of my cards at the front desk on your way out. Who knows when you'll need a good lawyer."

"You got it."

During the drive home David couldn't keep himself from glancing at the box sitting on the front seat next to him. So many questions needed answering. And right now he had no answers, only more questions. What in the world could all this be about? The Great War? Carrying something around for years? And most important, who were you, Grandpa? He was about to open the box and find out.

He entered the kitchen from the garage and set the box and the key on the kitchen table. Then he stood there looking at the box, giving it the respect of a rare artifact—a very mysterious rare artifact. He desperately wanted to open it immediately, but Emily was still in bed and he wanted to check on her first.

He walked up the stairs and crept quietly into the bedroom. She was sleeping comfortably and had probably been doing so since he left earlier this morning. He stood at the foot of the bed and felt deep sadness for the love of his life, just as he had felt so many times before during the last few months. He felt a struggle between two emotions now, sadness and helplessness—the anger had mostly passed. He still loved her dearly in spite of some rocky terrain over the last twenty-three years. After working through Rachael's problems, now this devastating illness! Bad luck, for sure. As always, though, they would persevere the best they could. He checked to make sure the glass of water she always kept on the night table was full, then bent over and gently kissed her on the forehead before exiting the bedroom.

David stood at the top of the stairs and peered downward—down to where the box was, down to secrets exposed, down to perhaps unwanted revelations. As anxious as he had been an hour ago in Logan's office to tear open the box, now he had mixed feelings about diving into it and discovering Grandpa's words and what they exposed. Part of him believed he would be better off placing the unopened box in a closet, and leaving whatever secrets lay within it a secret. He was sure whatever the words revealed, it was not going to improve his life; perhaps only complicate it. And no one in the immediate Keller family needed more complications right now. Emily needed his full attention and Rachael his ongoing support as she continued to turn her life around. For the moment as he stood upstairs, he felt a sense of safety, for down in the kitchen was something, at least for now, a little frightening.

David slowly walked downstairs and into the kitchen. He stared at the box sitting on the table. It was about the size of his briefcase, only slightly taller. It was made of what he guessed was mahogany or perhaps walnut. It was intricately engraved and was inlaid with a lighter wood around the border. Although showing its age, it was still attractive, obviously made by a craftsman; this had been an expensive box many years ago when it was new. The keyhole was in the front and bore many scratches from the key being used to lock and then unlock the box. No name was on it, nor did he see any manufacturer's identification. In other words, to David it looked like any old box used to store documents, jewelry, or anything else of import to its owner.

He slowly walked around the table to the kitchen counter, never taking his eyes off of it. The coffeemaker was still on, so he poured himself a cup and sat down at the table directly in front of the box. Taking a deep breath, he picked up the key and gently inserted it into the keyhole. He didn't have to turn it far before he heard a small click and saw the lid pop slightly upward; not enough to peer inside it, however. David took both hands and timidly lifted the lid, revealing the contents.

He saw a stack of papers protected by a very old leather binding, all held together by a large rubber band, just as Logan had described. He gently removed them from the box, not sure how careful to be. He could see they were 8 ½ x 11 white, lined notebook papers, several hundred in all. David removed the rubber band, then opened the leather binder.

The papers were all handwritten in Grandpa's style; that much, he recognized. He laid the entire stack in front of the box, picked up the first sheet and his cup of coffee, and began to read. He had only read a few sentences, his cup of coffee still suspended in the air, when all his thoughts suddenly focused on the words in front of him.

"Oh my God!"

CHAPTER 2

THE SUBMARINE

His grandfather's words began...

During the Great War, I was a German soldier working in intelligence for the Fatherland. I came to America as a spy to steal the plans, and, hopefully, a copy of the most guarded piece of equipment used by the US Army Air Corps—the Norden bombsight.

It was November 1943 . . .

NOVEMBER 1943

Cruising at the abnormally slow speed of three knots, the German killer submarine U-313 was protected by a cushion of water separating it from the turbulent waters above, providing its crew with relative safety. At least for right then.

The waters off the North Atlantic coast of America could be treacherous during the month of November, and that year was no different. Seventy-five feet below the surface, however, the German submarine's occupants had no idea what awaited them once they reached the surface. Nor'easters were some of the most ferocious of all winter storms, known for their dangerously strong winds of legendary intensity that rivaled those of hurricanes. The residents, commercial shippers, and fishermen making their living there feared the low-pressure weather system moving in, knowing she would bully and intimidate all who entered her reach; she would grant quarter to neither man nor machine, and for all who lay in her grasp, peril awaited. They knew many would not escape the approaching storm and those who did would never forget the destruction and wrath it was about to wreak.

Even then, as the heart of the nor'easter was still hundreds of miles south of the New Jersey shoreline, the seas were becoming more violent by the hour as it approached. Mother Nature was angry, and just waiting for another unsuspecting victim. The sea was always unforgiving, and now even more so. Onshore residents were taking all precautions to protect not just their property but their very lives. Many planned to head inland after boarding up their homes and businesses. Why battle what could not be fought? Those who stayed behind hoped it would be less vicious than earlier storms. Still, they knew they were tempting fate.

The voyage from the German crew's home port in Bordeaux, France, had taken twenty-two days—much longer than normal to venture this far from home. This was all part of the plan, cruising at very low speeds to conserve as much of the submarine's power resources as possible. Avoiding detection was paramount, and surfacing only placed that priority in jeopardy. They still had to surface every forty-eight hours to recharge the batteries they used for submerged running, but it was always done under the protection of darkness. As soon as the batteries were charged, it was back into the dark abyss, seeking the invisibility, and thus safety, of the deep again. All contact with other ships, enemy or friendly, was prohibited on this trip.

Crews of the U-boats were considered the elite of the Kriegsmarine, the German navy, but even they—the members of U-boat 313—were becoming restless. This was different from what they were used to; never before had they been out to sea for so long without seeing any action. In spite of the inherent danger of battle, most crews looked forward to enemy confrontation and the excitement that followed, as it broke up the long, monotonous hours. On this voyage, many crew members were questioning in their minds, and amongst each other privately, what their mission actually was—why haven't we engaged the enemy, the Americans?

It had become common knowledge throughout the submarine that only two torpedoes had been loaded before departing, rather than the twenty-two normally used for hunting and killing enemy ships. Something was amiss, and Captain Gerhardt wasn't talking. This made the crew even more suspicious. Gerhardt had been selected by his superiors for his Atlantic Coast experience and ability to keep his mouth shut, and he was doing just that. He hadn't wanted to accept this mission, and he made his feelings known to his superior officer, but to no avail. His skills were needed, and to refuse would have been unthinkable. He was told only when and where to drop his "packages," and to keep quiet. The crew was not to be informed of his orders. No one could know: Do not draw attention, conserve your resources, and above all, deliver the packages exactly when and where ordered, no exceptions. Gerhardt reluctantly acknowledged his instructions, saluted, and would of course obey his orders to the letter. Not even his second in command was to be made aware of their task. Yes, this was very unorthodox indeed.

The 1WO, or First Watch Officer and second in command, was becoming increasingly annoyed with the situation as time passed. It was customary for the captain to share his orders with the 1WO—many in command would even say imperative. He did not appreciate being kept in the dark. And rightfully so, as he would be required to take over command should anything render the captain incapable of carrying out his duties. The 1WO, Hans Fahr, had approached Captain Gerhardt on at least three occasions about details of this most uncommon mission, citing that very reason. Gerhardt, true to his very explicit orders, relayed same to Fahr—he was under strict orders of secrecy and not at liberty to discuss details of the mission.

Finally, 1WO Fahr made a fourth and quite animated request for further information. All Gerhardt would say is they were on a secret mission coming from the highest authority in Berlin, and that all of them on board should be honored to have been selected for this important task. Fahr's request, or more like demands for more details, went unsatisfied.

There were four "packages" on board—four men in their early twenties and dressed in civilian clothes. They spent nearly all of their time on board in their compartments, which had previously been occupied by other officers. The officers weren't pleased, but Gerhardt had convinced them it was absolutely necessary for isolating the men and for secrecy. There was to be no communication or fraternization whatsoever between the four men and the rest of the crew, under any circumstance. This was not easy, as room on the submarine was very tight.

Conditions on board the U-boat, the four men all agreed, were extremely uncomfortable. Cold, damp, and wet in many places, even the air was unpleasant after only a week. Early on the "packages" had come to the realization that any man who willingly volunteered to serve on one of these cold steel contraptions had to be crazy. Two of the four men became seasick after a few days at sea, one quite violently. Most of the time the seasickness kept him in his assigned bunk in the small compartment. He took some inadequate medication to quell the sickness; it helped, but just enough to keep minimum quantities of food and water down. He spent a lot of time sleeping. The other three struggled with the tight quarters and made a conscious effort to combat claustrophobia. They did this mainly by playing cards, using hard, unused beans borrowed from the mess as chips.

Their only communication outside themselves was with the captain. Gerhardt kept them apprised of their location, assuring them they were on schedule and not to worry. But worry they did. The rendezvous was critical, with no margin for error. They had to be on time, at the correct location. Any deviation of either endangered the success of what they were about to do.

Gerhardt was doing his best to make their time in the uncomfortable surroundings less unbearable. He made sure they received their meals at regular intervals, provided ample blankets, and even furnished some reading material he had accumulated over numerous missions at sea. The four men were most appreciative and continuously expressed their gratitude, even though they were in a word, miserable.

Finally on the twenty-third day, Gerhardt knocked and then entered the cabin where he found the four men again playing cards. Their stone-faced expressions displayed boredom with the game. But to his relief, the fourth man who had days before been violently ill now had his color back and even offered up a smile for Gerhardt.

"Well, gentlemen," said Gerhardt, "we are just thirty minutes from our drop-off location. And we will be on time." He was proud he was going to fulfill his orders, not to mention relieved that this odd and unwelcome mission was soon going to be behind him and the rest of the crew.

The senior of the four men, and the assigned leader, addressed Gerhardt. "Thank you, Captain. I think I can say for all of us we are more than ready to get on our way and relieve you of your duty to deliver us." The other three nodded in agreement.

"Good," said Gerhardt. "Then please make your preparations. We'll be surfacing soon and won't want to be up for long. The quicker we get you on your way, the better it will be for all of us."

"Agreed," replied Otto Langer, the leader. "We'll gather our things. Will you have your men prepare the rafts?"

"Of course. Anything else?"

"No, we're traveling light. There will be others onshore who will provide us with what we need."

"Very well." Gerhardt turned to exit the compartment, then looked back before shutting the door. "I wish you good luck. I don't pretend to know what your mission is, but I realize it must be very important for Germany. So … thank you."

The four men nodded. Gerhardt closed the narrow door, and then the four men immediately rose and began assembling their things. There was not much to collect. Each had a small satchel and that was it. They removed a few items from each of their bags and put them into their pockets—American money, counterfeit IDs, and some fabricated family photos to support their cover. It only took a few minutes to accomplish this. When finished they all sat in a tight circle looking at each other, as their time had come.

Langer spoke in soft tones, but still with the authority he was charged with. "We all know our jobs. Once we get to shore, we will cut up the rafts and hide them the best we can. We'll split up and meet within twenty-four hours at the address provided earlier. Be sure you have the map. Avoid all contact with anyone if possible. And remember, speak only English and begin thinking like an American. That's one of the reasons you were selected for this mission." Langer looked each man in the eye, conveying reassurance all was going to be fine; they were going to succeed. He was nervous yet hoped it didn't show. It did not. He continued, "Remember your cover. If you get delayed for any reason, still get to the contact location as soon as possible. Some contingencies have been made, so the mission *will* proceed. Understood?" Again, all nodded. He concluded, "Any questions?"

There was silence as the men focused on their task at hand, knowing full well their chances of success, and even survival, were not that high. All had been chosen for their unique qualifications. They were fluent in English, had spent time in America prior to the war, and had scored off the charts for intellectual and problem-solving ability. If any group of young men had a chance of succeeding, it was these four.

"There are just two rafts. Lars, you go with me," said Langer. "Erik, you and Kurt go in the other." The latter two glanced at each other and nodded. "Remember, what we're doing is for the Fatherland and all of our families. It's up to us to do our part. It's our turn to do something very important. We will *not* fail." He realized he was telling them what they already knew; there was nothing to be gained by belaboring the point.

A few moments later Captain Gerhardt's voice came over the intercom in their compartment. "We're ready to surface, gentlemen. Please make your way to the bridge. We have the rafts ready."

Langer pushed the intercom button. "We're on our way." The four men stood and shook hands. Langer opened the door and began the cramped walk to the bridge, the other three close behind. As they approached the submarine's control center, they passed through the cramped corridor of dripping pipes, large valves, and more dials than one could count. A lot of noise came from all directions, and all on board could now feel the bow of the submarine gradually rising. The crew was turning valve handles, watching dials, yelling instructions and readings to one another. They were busy. Even so, they momentarily stopped what they were doing as the four men walked past, wondering to themselves who these men were and what their mission was. Perhaps after the four men departed a sense of normalcy would return to the cold gray submersible.

Although the four men were uneasy about their upcoming mission, a general feeling of relief about getting off the U-boat prevailed. When they reached the bridge Captain Gerhardt and 1WO Fahr were waiting for them by the conning tower. Next to them laying on the ground were two small black bundles and four wood paddles. Nothing else.

"These are your rafts," explained Gerhardt, pointing to the bundles. "My men will inflate them once we surface and are on the deck. Not before. We'll help you into the rafts and when you're clear of us we'll immediately begin our dive. My apologies for not giving you a warmer send-off, but my orders are to leave the area as soon as you're off. If we're spotted, well, it only places you and us in more danger."

"I understand," acknowledged Langer.

Just then the U-boat began to rock, and everyone began to steady themselves by grabbing something. "Periscope depth!" barked Gerhardt. He glanced at Langer and then the other three. "Feels like rough seas. For your sakes I hope not."

A few moments later the 2WO, or Second Watch Officer, yelled out, "Periscope depth, Captain!"

Gerhardt walked over and peered into the periscope after it reached its maximum height. The U-boat was rocking even more now, and Gerhardt wasn't pleased with what he saw, yet not surprised from the way the submarine was pitching and yawing. He slowly circled three hundred sixty degrees, his eyes never leaving the periscope. He had obviously seen rough seas on many occasions, but this was a monster. How was he going to maintain any stability in such raging waters? There would be little chance of getting his four passengers off the U-boat with any safety, perhaps even alive.

With his arms resting on the periscope controls, he lifted his head in disappointment and concern. "Gentlemen, we have a problem. It seems we have wandered into a terrible storm. Waves are fifteen to twenty feet and exceed our allowable surface limit for these conditions."

Langer stepped forward in disbelief. "What do you mean?"

"What I mean, Herr Langer, is it will be nearly impossible to get you into the rafts safely. We should wait out the storm and then surface when the conditions are more favorable."

Langer, along with the other three agents, knew full well they didn't have the luxury of rescheduling their drop-off. "Must I remind you, Captain, that my orders—*your* orders—are to deliver us at this location at this time. Not tomorrow or days from now. There is no contingency plan. I have no doubt our superiors will show little sympathy for us due to some inconvenient weather."

"Herr Langer," said Gerhardt, now standing directly in front of him, "I don't think *you* understand. The conditions above are not just 'inconvenient weather,' as you put it. To surface now is foolishness and an unacceptable risk."

"This is simply not acceptable," replied Langer in complete disbelief and an irritated tone. "We must surface!"

Gerhardt attempted the reasonable approach. "Please understand, gentlemen," he said, peering into all four men's eyes, "it would be difficult to maintain the stability to launch rafts off the deck in *ten*-foot seas. These are twenty. The deck will be wet and slick. We'll all be in a rush to get the rafts off, and you in them. Accidents happen when doing things quickly, even in the best of circumstances. How are you to get into the rafts on a heaving wet deck when you have no experience on a submarine, or on any ship for that matter?"

"We'll manage," said Langer in a calm yet determined voice. "Now please, Captain, surface so we can be on our way."

"You do realize you will be placing my own crew in danger as well?"

Langer was becoming frustrated. "I can't help that. All of us are constantly in danger, are we not?"

Gerhardt sighed, looking over at 1WO Fahr for support, then back at Langer. "Yes, we have all placed our lives at risk for the Fuhrer. But that doesn't mean we need to risk them needlessly or recklessly. And trust me gentlemen, surfacing now is both."

Langer was at a loss for words, not sure what he could say to change Gerhardt's mind. He looked at his companions, almost in despair. Erik decided he would take a turn with Gerhardt. He stepped forward and spoke with the calm voice of reason.

"Captain, we know this is very dangerous, for us and your crew. We agree it may even be reckless. But we have our orders, and you yours. All of our superiors have placed much confidence in our abilities to fulfill these orders, regardless of whatever situation we find ourselves in." Erik was now pointing at all who were present on the bridge, indicating the inclusion of the crew. "All of us were chosen because they knew we would be successful when others may not. We obviously cannot share our mission with you, but please know this is our only opportunity to accomplish the very important task we've been asked to do. If we miss our rendezvous time, all will be lost, and another chance to succeed may not come. We will have failed our country."

Gerhardt was listening and considering Erik's words. Erik continued, "I believe it's worth the risk. We may not make it, but we have to try. Our leaders will accept nothing less. So please, Captain, I beg you to surface and let us be on our way. Then you can be on yours."

There was silence as Gerhardt weighed his options. He was a veteran of years at sea and had witnessed many bad storms. He had also seen ships and submarines alike founder in such waters, and it was a terrifying sight. He had survived by taking calculated risks, not foolish ones. He was not one to tempt fate when it was plainly looking him in the face; he would retreat and live to fight another day. He was smart and incredibly brave, accepting difficult missions in the past that others would forgo. No one had more confidence in their crew and machine than Gerhardt. He knew their capabilities and their limitations. He pushed his men and U-313 to the former, careful not to exceed the latter.

Under normal circumstances, if there were such a thing during a time of war, the decision would be easy. He would not surface. No, he would head out to sea, to deeper waters and the safety therein. Then, when the conditions were more favorable to success, he would return to complete the mission. This was his pattern of operation. This controlled behavior had served him well and kept him and his crew alive.

This was a different situation, however. Erik made a valid and indisputable point. All of them were under very explicit orders; orders to be dropped off at this exact location at this exact time, no exceptions. There was always risk—did these orders take precedence over what had worked so effectively for him and his crew in the past? And what would Gerhardt's explanation be to his superiors if he took it upon himself to alter Berlin's instructions? There was only one thing he could do.

Captain Gerhardt turned and looked at 1WO Fahr with a look of resignation. "Turn into the wind, heading south one-eight-zero. Then prepare to surface. Have extra lines ready. Let's be quick about it."

1WO Fahr barked out the orders, "Turn heading one-eight-zero, prepare to surface! Bring extra lines! Hurry, this is going to be quick!" Immediately all on board jumped into action and immediately felt the submarine turn to starboard.

Gerhardt turned back and explored Erik's eyes, acknowledging his point with a slight nod. He liked him and now feared what his fate may be. Erik returned the nod, more said in the silence than words could have conveyed.

"Thank you," Langer said to the captain.

"You may not be thanking me in a minute," Gerhardt said, glaring at Langer. He felt the opposite for him as he did for Erik. "It's unlikely we'll be discovered now. No one in their right mind would dare attempt to navigate these waters."

It was exactly 2:05 a.m. when U-313 slowly turned starboard and headed into the wind, to at least what Gerhardt believed was the correct heading for the safest rise to the surface. If he was off more than a few degrees, a rogue or otherwise large wave could roll the submarine while on the surface, then all would be lost.

"Heading one-eight-zero!" yelled out the 2WO as the submarine arrived at the heading.

With grave concern for their safety, Captain Gerhardt looked once more at the four young men. They would battle the furious sea in nothing more than two small rubber rafts and four paddles. Their odds weren't good. He secretly gave them less than a 10 percent chance to make it ashore.

Gerhardt caught 1WO Fahr's eye. "Bring up four life vests."

Langer immediately protested. "What? Captain, we will not be needing the vests, we have the rafts. That will just be one more thing we have to hide on shore. We'll make it."

Gerhardt was nearly dumbstruck at Langer's naiveté. "Herr Langer, even if you're an expert swimmer, which I strongly doubt, I assure you your very lives may depend on those vests. I'm confident you can find a place to hide them with the rafts."

Erik, now feeling emboldened by the silent connection he had made with Gerhardt just moments earlier, spoke his mind. "We'll take them and thank you. Little good it will do any of us if we drown within sight of the American shore." All but Langer nodded in agreement.

Langer knew he was outnumbered, and even though he was the assigned leader, it was pointless to bring up a leadership issue at this point in time. They needed to get topside. "Very well."

All began to feel the nose rise and even more rocking and yawing within the confines of the submersible. Lars, who had been violently seasick just days before, began to feel queasy once again. A weakness began to come over him. Surfacing, and then getting off the "hellish boat" as he continually called it, could not come soon enough. He needed fresh air, and soon.

The vests were delivered within seconds, and all four put them on, including Langer.

Gerhardt gave some last-minute instructions. "Four of my men will get topside on the deck first. They will inflate the rafts and secure them with the lines. We'll follow up thirty seconds later. I realize time is of the essence, but I cannot emphasize strongly enough how careful you must be when climbing down the conning tower and walking on the decks. It's dark, which will make this all the more difficult. As I said before, it's going to be wet and easy to lose your footing. Stay in a crouched position to reduce the effect of the wind. My men will lower the rafts into the water and secure them with the lines until all of you are safely aboard. As soon as the men release your lines, get away from the submarine as quickly as you can. When you're a safe distance away, we'll make our departure."

"How far will we be from shore?" asked Langer.

"I estimate about one-half mile. I cannot take the risk of getting you closer, in these seas. We'll be launching the rafts on the starboard side, which may provide a small windbreak. You're upwind from the shore, so you'll get quite a bit of help from the wind pushing you to the beach."

"Understood. Any thought on how long it will take us to reach the beach?" asked Langer.

Gerhardt knew there was little chance of them reaching the beach alive. "Hard to say. The wind will be in your favor, but the waves will be treacherous. My advice is to paddle as fast as you can until you come ashore. Whatever you do, try to keep land in sight. I realize it's dark, but our charts indicate there's a lighthouse that should be visible, and be assured, it will be working tonight. That beacon of light will serve as your guide." He again looked at all four of the men, wanting to make certain they understood how difficult and dangerous this was going to be. Their eyes showed both confidence and trepidation.

"Perhaps we should wear rain parkas, as we only have these clothes," suggested Lars, who was beginning to turn pale with the onset of more intense nausea.

"I would agree if this were a typical rainstorm," answered Gerhardt. "But this is not typical. There is a very good chance you may be thrown into the sea. If that happens, your clothes will become heavy and burdensome. Any type of rain gear will only make it worse. Everything you're wearing will feel like lead weights. You're going to get wet and cold, that's all there is to it."

"Yes, you're quite right," asserted Langer. "Getting wet is the least of our problems. Once we arrive our contact will have dry clothes and whatever else we need."

The sea was really having her way with the submarine. It was being tossed about like a leaf in a pond on a windy day. Men on board were grabbing anything within reach to steady themselves. Everything loose or not otherwise secured was tossed about and ended up on the bridge deck. All the crew members realized this was trouble and wanted to dump their "packages" as quickly as possible and head for deeper waters. The four men Captain Gerhardt ordered to help with the rafts were also the deck gunners. They were the most experienced at handling themselves topside, and thus, were the most qualified to assist the four young men.

The deck gunners were ready, standing in the well beneath the hatch. When 1WO Fahr yelled "Clear," the first crewman scampered up the tower and opened the hatch. Water poured in, drenching him and the other three who were waiting to exit. All in close proximity could hear the howling wind blowing over the tower hatch. Langer and Lars looked at one another, now realizing Captain Gerhardt had not understated the situation above. The remaining three crewmen quickly climbed up and out of the hatch one by one, out of sight of Gerhardt and the four young men waiting immediately below. The crewmen topside triggered the compressed air capsules, inflating the rafts in mere seconds. Gerhardt knew it would take all their strength to restrain the inflated rafts from being grasped by the wind like large uncontrollable kites. His prior instructions for more lines would prove to be wise.

Captain Gerhardt placed his hand on the first rung of the ladder. "OK, let's go. Remember, be steady. Don't be in too big a hurry. If you fall off the deck into the sea, we may not be able to rescue you in these conditions."

Gerhardt led the four men up the ladder toward the hatch. The sound of the screaming wind became louder and louder as they climbed each step toward the opening and the angry storm. Lars, already weak from the onset of seasickness, was struggling with each step, his feet beginning to slip as he approached the opening where the rain was pouring down. The life vests the men wore made it more difficult to maneuver the ladder up to and then through the hatch. Once each man exited the badly rocking U-313, however, all were relieved the vests were strapped to their bodies—even Langer.

Each young man carefully exited the hatch in the near-hurricane-force wind, driving rain, and twenty-foot waves. Rain and wind pelted their faces, feeling like hundreds of bee stings on their exposed skin. Their clothes and vests provided little protection from the fierce elements. It took all their strength and concentration to keep from tumbling overboard into the hungry sea. Erik thought the waves looked like angry hands reaching for victims to consume. None of the four had ever experienced the sea as it was now. All were wondering how they would have any chance of getting into the rafts safely, let alone making it to shore.

Gerhardt motioned to the crewmen topside to lower the rafts into the sea. All instructions were given with hand motions, as the volume of the wind drowned out any chance of hearing verbal orders. The crewmen were crouched and holding on to the lines as hard as they could. Not only were they securing the rafts but keeping the men themselves from being blown into the sea, as they fastened the other ends of the lines to the tower rungs. Even on the downwind side of the submarine the wind and waves were intolerable. The rafts bobbed up and down fifteen and twenty feet at a time. How could anyone get into them without being washed away?

Gerhardt motioned to one of the crewmen to pull the first raft up tightly to the hull of U-313, which he and another crewman did with great effort. Then Gerhardt motioned to Langer to move his men into position. Langer patted Erik's shoulder and signaled for him and Kurt to maneuver themselves into the raft. With much trepidation, Erik moved forward first and firmly grabbed hold of one of the lines the crew members were using to secure the raft. They reached for Erik's arm to keep him from slipping on the deck and to help him down into the raft. Erik concentrated on the bobbing raft, believing it impossible to get inside without a great amount of luck.

Erik and the crewmen were timing the waves to make their move at the crest of the wave. At that point the raft would be closest to them. The raft was coming up quickly and Erik prepared to jump. A split second before his timed leap, he felt two crew members push him into the raft. It caught him off guard, but by some good fortune, he fell into the middle of it. Although somewhat startled, he quickly regained his composure and realized he was sitting in three inches of water. He doubted the raft was leaking and knew it had to be from the driving rain. He looked around and found the two paddles laying in the bottom of the raft under the water.

The raft was rising again with a large wave and Erik could see Kurt being held on each arm by the same two crew members who had "helped" him into the raft. Kurt looked terrified. The wave and raft would crest in another second or two, and then Kurt would be pushed as well. Erik positioned himself as far back in the raft as possible to give Kurt a larger landing area. A second before the wave crested, Kurt also was pushed before he was ready. Erik was prepared and leaned forward to break Kurt's fall. Kurt's momentum carried him just outside the main section of the raft, however, and he landed on the inflated tube side and literally bounced into the sea.

The crew members standing on the deck were still holding the two lines, staring at Kurt in disbelief as he missed the raft and was momentarily swallowed by the dark water. Kurt quickly surfaced and immediately began flailing about in the frigid waters, struggling to stay afloat and find the raft. The vest had probably saved Kurt's life. Erik reached over and grabbed his arm, holding fast. Kurt's eyes were alarmed with fear and pleading for Erik to quickly get him inside the inflatable. With Erik gripping his one arm, Kurt managed to grasp the raft handle and pull himself up and into the raft. The two looked at each other in relief and astonishment—they both were actually in the raft!

The two crew members untied and threw off the lines. Erik and Kurt managed to catch and place them in the bottom of the inflatable. They immediately began to float away from the submarine, carried by the persistence of the enormous waves and controlling winds. U-313 was quickly becoming nothing more than a dark shadow in the murkiness of the night and raging seas. Erik looked toward the submarine and could barely make out Captain Gerhardt as he motioned them off and pointed toward the shore. He indicated with his arms to begin paddling for their lives. Within seconds the waves now lifted the raft up and away much faster from their home of twenty-three days.

Just minutes before, Erik had been secure in the safety of the submarine, more than anxious to depart the confined quarters and boredom of their transport. Now, however, he was having second thoughts. He and Kurt were bobbing uncontrollably up and down in the turbulent and ferocious water, in the darkness, in an eight-foot raft. The wind was pushing them at its own discretion, and paddling in these conditions seemed a fruitless effort in futility. Wet, freezing, and in genuine fear for their very lives, they had no other option. Erik quickly searched again for the paddles. He handed one of them to Kurt who was shaking with cold from his plunge into the sea. Kurt took it and began his aggressive strokes. Erik took the other and began paddling on the opposite side. Together they strained to build some momentum toward the direction Gerhardt had pointed. Erik realized they could very well be heading out to the vast and endless Atlantic, and to their deaths.

Erik looked back briefly to see if Langer and Lars had made it into their own raft, but it was impossible to see since he and Kurt were already several hundred feet from the submarine. The insistent winds were pushing them away from U-313 at a rapid rate. Erik could only hope they had made it and were on their way a short distance behind them. It was at that point he realized he and Kurt were completely alone. There was no one to help them if they ran into more trouble!

Kurt screamed over the howling wind. "I see it!"

"See what?"

"The lighthouse! I see the lighthouse!" Kurt stopped paddling and pointed ahead and to the left.

Erik was straining to see it, but they were near the bottom of a twenty-foot wave and could only see the black water attempting to batter them to death. Then, as if by a miracle, the raft rose and floated over the wave's crest, and he saw the small beam of light. Thank God. "Keep paddling!"

A few hundred feet east of Erik and Kurt in the fight of their lives, Captain Gerhardt was ordering his crewmen back into the submarine. Langer and Lars had also miraculously made it into their raft and were quickly being blown away from the submersible. U-313 had accomplished its mission. There was nothing more they could do. Now Gerhardt's immediate mission was returning his crew to the safety of deeper waters beyond the reach of the dangerous storm.

Crouching on the heaving deck, all of them struggled to avoid being swept into the hungry sea. Gerhardt motioned them to the tower, and back into the safety of the submarine. He glanced around, waiting for his turn, and believed the powerful storm was actually increasing in intensity. Could that be possible? U-313 must escape the violent storm soon or it may not make it at all.

One by one the four crewmen fought their way up the ladder of the tower, their clothes flapping wildly in the powerful wind as the storm tore at everything that dared defy its power. Gerhardt was the last to climb the rungs. Before lowering himself through the hatch, he took one last look in the direction he expected the four young agents to be heading. God help them, they'd need that *and* a lot of luck. He shook his head in disbelief at their naive persistence, and in admiration for their bravery in obviously difficult and dangerous circumstances.

Captain Gerhardt closed and locked the watertight hatch. Stepping down inside the conning tower he saw 1WO Fahr standing on the bridge, wearing a look of grave concern on his face. Gerhardt stood for a moment, water dripping from his clothes, happy and relieved to be back inside the submarine. His eyes met those of 1WO Fahr. "Let's get the hell out of here."

"Prepare to dive!" yelled Fahr.

Gerhardt swore he could hear a collective sigh of relief coming from the bridge. The nose of U-313 began to dip.

The small rubber raft was taking on much more water now, a combination of the rain and crashing waves. The water was at least six inches deep and continuing to gain on them. Then Erik heard a voice of panic.

"We're sinking! We're not going to make it!"

"Yes we are! Just keep paddling! We're getting closer!"

Erik was doing his best not to lose sight of the only thing visible in the darkness, the small beam of light coming from the lighthouse. Each time the raft would drop into the bottom of a wave, it would disappear for a frightening few seconds, then reappear again as they reached the crest. His arms were beginning to ache from paddling so hard, but to stop would be fatal for both him and Kurt. The fear of drowning kept both of them using every ounce of strength they had on the paddles. The rain continued to pelt their faces, driven by the relentless wind. Up and down the large waves drove the raft like a roller coaster. The sea was doing its best to overturn them.

On the next crest Erik was sure the beam of light was growing larger. They were making progress. He turned to encourage Kurt, who looked exhausted. Just as he was looking back at Kurt, he saw an enormous wall of water preparing to crash on top of them. He needed to warn Kurt to brace himself.

"Kurt—!" was the only word he could yell out before the twenty-five-foot wall of cold water washed over them and upended the raft. Both men were thrown into the bitterly cold sea. Erik was tumbling underneath the surface, completely disoriented. Which way was up? He began thrashing his arms, hoping his vest had not yet become waterlogged and would still take him to the surface. He felt himself continue to roll over like a rag doll with the undertows of the controlling black water. Erik fought panic. Never before had he felt so helpless. Nothing in his training had prepared him for this. Who in their right mind could have expected this nightmare? It didn't matter now. Erik must get to the surface, and the only lifeline he knew of—the raft.

After what seemed like minutes, Erik's head inexplicably popped to the surface and out of the water. He gasped for breath, knowing full well a few more seconds under water would have been the end of him. The coldness of the sea stung so much it actually felt hot on his skin. He was beginning to feel numb in his feet and hands. Recognizing this as hypothermia, Erik correctly surmised if he didn't get out of the water soon he would die. He had perhaps a minute, maybe less. A part of him was ready to surrender and end the suffering; there were worse ways to die than by drowning. He had always been told after the first inhaling of water you just go to sleep, then peace.

The raft! It was just twenty feet from him, and by good luck, was right side up. The wind must have caught it and turned it over again. His life vest was managing to keep him afloat. If he could just persuade his muscles to function for one last burst, he was confident he could make it to the raft and climb over its edge. He began kicking wildly and swimming as he had never done before. Even though the life vest was keeping him afloat, it was impeding the movement of his arms. Only ten more feet now. He saw one of the lines floating just a few feet in front of him—more luck when he needed it! He grabbed the line and began pulling himself and the raft closer together.

He reached up and took hold of the handle on the raft. Would he have enough strength to pull himself up and over the inflated tube into the relative safety of the raft? He took a deep breath and used what remained of his energy to pull himself up. He fell into the middle of the raft, totally spent. To Erik's great surprise nearly all the water had been jettisoned when the raft rolled over! But he saw no paddles. He was at the mercy of the wind and waves.

He sat up and began scanning the moving sea for Kurt. Nothing. "Kurt!" He kept yelling his name but could hear nothing above the roar of the wind and the crashing waves. Even if he did see Kurt, there was no way to maneuver the raft over to him. It was up to Kurt now. Erik had no energy left. He could offer no help. It was each man for himself.

On the next crest he looked over and saw the welcome beam of light, much larger now. He thought it a cruel irony the waves that had overturned the raft and nearly drowned him were now pushing the inflatable to the shore. He kept looking for Kurt and yelling his name, but it was hopeless. Erik tried to convince himself Kurt still had a chance to make it to the beach if his life vest held out. Then he remembered the biting coldness, numbing sensation, and racing heartbeat that followed. A sadness suddenly came over him. Kurt was dead. He had to be.

Erik laid back in the raft and let the sea do her work. He occasionally looked up to make sure the beam of light was still within sight. It was, and still growing larger. He was exhausted and thought of sleeping in a warm bed—even the small quarters on U-313 now had the feeling of home and would be a welcome sanctuary. There was no sleeping on the bobbing raft, however. He was cold, nauseous from ingesting so much seawater, and still afraid for his life. Even if he made it to the beach, what would he find? Or better yet, *what* would find him?

Something hard hit the underside of the raft! There it was again. Each time the wave bottomed out, he felt it. He had the sensation that the raft was sliding on something. Erik lifted his head and saw the breakwater on the beach. He had made it! A large wave pushed him up on the beach far enough where he and the raft were actually out of the water now. Other waves continued to push him up the beach farther and farther until the raft was only buffeted by the strong wind. Erik didn't know whether to laugh or cry.

He couldn't move; his muscles spent, his emotions run dry. He was empty. The relief and excitement of making land was short lived, since all his documents had surely washed away. He had no map and no money, only wet clothes. He might be the only survivor. For nearly a year the mission they had all planned and trained for was over before it began! Mother Nature was the victor—she must be working for the Americans.

As he rested in the raft, Erik assessed his situation while the rain persisted on pelting him. He wasn't sure if this was the correct landing point. He was in enemy territory with no weapon, no provisions, and no intelligence. The rest of his team had probably drowned at sea. He could imagine no positive outcome. He estimated his odds of mission success at zero, and of surviving at all, near zero. It was hopeless. Erik passed out.

✦

Erik wasn't sure how much time had passed when voices interrupted his sleep. He lifted his head and saw two flashlights searching not more than fifty feet from his raft. Too weak to run, he was prepared to give up and rely on the mercy of the Americans. The POW camps in America had been reported to be humane, and for many Germans a safe refuge from the ravages of war. His fight was over. He laid back down in the raft, shaking uncontrollably from the chill. He would just wait for them to approach and hope they didn't shoot him on sight.

The voices were getting closer and Erik realized they had spotted the raft. He could see their flashlight beams focusing on him as they walked up to the inflatable and peered down at him. He barely opened his eyes and was relieved to see they weren't wearing uniforms. No guns were pointed at him.

A man wearing a black civilian raincoat spoke first, yelling above the wind. "Are you Langer?"

Erik couldn't believe what he'd heard. "What?"

"Langer! Are you Langer?"

"No," replied Erik. "I'm Kaufmann."

The man with the flashlight smiled. "I'm Becker, your contact. Didn't think any of you were going to make it. Welcome to America!"

CHAPTER 3

THE FARMHOUSE

Erik was dreaming. He was home in the small village of Remseck where he spent his childhood. He could hear his two younger brothers laughing outside the window, playing a game. His beloved mother was cooking and telling him lunch was nearly ready. She was explaining how it wasn't healthy to be in wet clothes. How did he get so wet? He should take them off before he gets sick and hang them on the line outside to dry. Then come back and sit by the stove to warm up. Take the chill off. He could smell the stew she was simmering, and the aroma was comforting and delicious. He sat by the stove but couldn't stop shaking.

Different, unfamiliar voices were now coming from outside the window. They weren't his brothers' voices. Who were they, and why were they there? He wanted them to stop, but the voices continued. He was exhausted and wanted to sleep. His mother was annoyed at their interruption, and so was Erik. He was now shaking more from the chill. Why couldn't he stop shaking?

Then Erik's dream was interrupted, and he began to awake. He looked up to see two strange men looking down at him. He didn't recognize either one. They were talking in soft, low tones to one another. He was disoriented. Where was he, and how did he get here? He was in a bed covered by a sheet and a heavy blanket. He was stripped of all clothing. But despite feeling chilled and awakening to unfamiliar surroundings, he felt safe and comfortable.

The larger of the two men smiled at him. Erik thought he had seen the smile once before. "I'm Becker, the one who found you on the beach. How are you feeling?"

Erik began to recall. The raft on the beach, the terrible ordeal leaving the submarine in the violent waters. The enormous wave, overturning, *and Kurt*! What had happened to Kurt?

"I think OK," answered Erik. "Where am I? How did I get here?"

"You're in my home. Jon and I found you on the beach last night and brought you here."

Erik tried to remember but could recall nothing that happened after being discovered on the beach. "I can't remember anything after you found me."

"I'm not surprised," said Becker, "you passed out in the raft. It was all Jon and I could do to get you into the car."

"Where's Kurt?" asked Erik. He feared the answer but remained hopeful.

"We're not sure. But it appears he didn't make it. We searched for an hour, but unfortunately there was no sign of him. I'm afraid he might have been lost at sea."

Erik turned away, realizing Becker was most likely correct. The water was so cold and the waves so large! Their life vests had offered little protection against the frigid and violent waters of the Atlantic during the storm. He himself had nearly drowned. Then had he not been found by the two men, he could have easily succumbed to hypothermia. He knew he'd been on death's doorstep.

"How long have I been sleeping?" Erik had lost all track of time.

"More than thirty hours. It was the night before last when we picked you up. We decided it best to let you sleep. You had us pretty worried at first, you were in bad shape." Becker's voice was soothing and reassuring. Erik began to relax more, knowing he was in safe hands, at least for the moment. "We carried you to the car and covered you with one of the blankets we brought to warm you up, then looked for the others."

Erik interrupted. "Wait a minute. Our instructions were to meet at the house. All of us had maps. Why did you come to the beach?"

Becker looked at the other man standing there, then answered Erik. "We know that was the plan. But it wasn't difficult to assume that with the bad storm, you might have ... let's say ... difficulty finding us. Jon was the one who suggested the documents you were carrying, including the map, would probably be ruined. If that were true, how could any of you be expected to find us? We couldn't have four agents just wandering around. If any of you were picked up by the patrols, all would be lost and the mission a complete failure."

Erik nodded, "I guess you're right. Thank you." He acknowledged Jon with a thankful look.

"He was indeed correct," added Becker. "After we removed your wet clothes, our apologies for having to do that, we found what remained of the map inside your pocket. It was no more than a shred of wet and indiscernible paper. It's safe to say none of you had any chance to use what remained of *any* of your documents."

Erik assumed as much, even when he was riding the raft to shore. He realized again, luck had been with him. "What about the others?"

Becker looked down, disappointed. "We found Langer and Lars about half an hour later. Both were unconscious, but safely in the raft. They were in bad shape as well, Lars worse than Langer. I sent Jon back here with you. There wasn't room for all of you in the car. He got you into bed upstairs here, then rushed back to help me get the others. I stayed behind and kept watch. You never know when a patrol will wander by. It was unlikely during the storm, but one can never be too careful."

"So they're here too?" inquired Erik.

"Langer is in the other room, still asleep. I'm sad to say Lars was dead by the time we got back here. I think he died on the beach. We have his body in the barn at the moment. We'll figure out what to do with it later. Right now we want to get you and Langer on your feet. The mission must go on."

"Go on? How can it possibly go on?"

"Don't concern yourself with that right now. What's important is that you and Langer rest and get your strength back."

Just then an older woman lightly knocked on the door and entered the bedroom carrying a cup and saucer. Becker took them from her and immediately dismissed the harmless-looking woman with a look she recognized as her cue to leave. Becker set them on the table next to the bed.

Erik glanced over to see a cupful of steaming coffee, then addressed the two men. "I don't understand. This was a mission for four men, not two."

"Yes, you're correct about that. But Jon and I have been talking, and we believe it's still possible to proceed."

Erik frowned. "How can you be so sure?"

"I'm not going to go through those details now. Once you and Langer are up and around, we'll talk about it. Just the same, we did send a message to Berlin updating them on the situation. We believe they'll want us to proceed, with some changes."

Erik was positive Berlin would call off the mission, as all their training was based on four agents. He could not accept the idea two men could carry out the plan. Too many changes would need to be made, greatly diminishing the odds of success.

"How soon will you hear back from them?" asked Erik.

"I should think soon, perhaps later today. Tomorrow at the latest. You and Langer can use this time to rest, and it will allow Jon and I time to dispose of Lars's body."

Erik really had no choice in his current condition. He was still exhausted and had no place to go. Becker was right about using the available time to recuperate. He didn't care for his casualness in stating how they were going to "dispose" of Lars's body. Cold, impersonal, and all business.

"Very well," agreed Erik. "I too am curious what Berlin will say." And then, so there would be no misunderstanding, Erik looked

Becker in the eye to be sure his next point would not be mistaken. "Langer is my senior officer, so I'll be taking my orders from him. No offense."

"Of course," said Becker. "I understand and agree. No offense taken."

Becker looked over at Jon, who still hadn't said a single word in Erik's presence. "Now I think it best for us to leave you alone so you can rest. Mary brought you the freshly brewed coffee, which should help get rid of the chills. I've instructed her to make some soup for both you and Langer, and it should be ready soon. It will help you get some of your strength back."

"Thank you. Soup sounds wonderful."

"Good. Perhaps later when you're feeling up to it, you will share your experience on the submarine with Jon and me."

"Sure," said Erik. Although he would prefer to forget it.

"Mary will let you know when the soup is ready. There are clothes for you in the closet. Some in the dresser too. I'll check on you later." Becker and Jon turned and left the room, closing the door behind them.

Erik nodded. Even after thirty hours he was still tired and sore in more places than he thought possible; his muscles ached in every conceivable location. He realized Langer was undoubtedly going through the same unpleasant experience in the next room. Hopefully in a few days they would be well enough to continue on. Berlin would decide in what direction that would be—there was no denying that fact.

Erik's body pleaded for more sleep, but first he wanted to get dressed and explore his surroundings. He struggled out of bed, his joints and muscles protesting with every movement. He opened the closet door and found several changes of clothes. There were three of everything: three shirts, three pants on hangers, three very nice suit jackets hanging next to the pants, and even three ties of different colors and patterns. Hanging on a peg was a navy bathrobe. He reached for that first and put it on. One pair of shoes was on the floor, and a brown belt was rolled up in one of the shoes.

He picked out the most casual-looking pants and a plain white shirt. He took the shoes and tossed them on the bed. In the top dresser drawer were underwear and socks. He picked out one pair of each and threw them on the bed as well. In the second drawer were all the toiletries anyone would ever need. He wanted a hot bath; that alone would be a good start to feeling better. He noticed a mirror hanging on the back of the door. He walked over and didn't like what he saw. His reflection startled him—he thought he looked ten years older!

He ventured into the upstairs hallway and heard voices coming from below, echoing off the stairway walls. He saw an open door and peered in. A bathroom never looked so good. He stepped inside and closed the door. Five minutes later he was soaking in a hot bath. He thought it odd that two days ago water nearly killed him and did end Kurt's life. Now the water was comforting and even therapeutic.

Following the bath Erik dressed and walked downstairs to the kitchen. To his pleasant surprise the clothes fit quite well. The aroma of soup was leading him like a horse to water. His stomach was growling, and soup sounded wonderful. Mary was still standing over the stove. Eric couldn't help but remember the dream he was having, and how eerily similar it was to the current moment. Mary heard his footfalls, turned, and greeted him with a motherly smile.

"Good timing," she said. "It's just finished. You must be famished."

"As a matter of fact, I am." He pulled out one of the chairs and sat down.

Mary was a plump woman about fifty with a pleasant smile. She removed the pan from the stove and filled Erik's bowl. He was hoping for something German, something that reminded him of home. It was potato soup and looked pretty good. His stomach was beginning to pang from hunger, so everything sounded good at the moment.

"Has Langer been down yet?" asked Erik.

"You mean Arthur?"

Erik remembered all of them were to slightly change their names to be more American sounding when they arrived. Otto simply would not do. He would go by Arthur. Erik would still use the same name, just begin writing it as "Eric," with a "c" rather than a "k." He had actually practiced writing it for hours back in Germany to become familiar with the new spelling, to the point where it became second nature. Even though this particular change was quite simple, it took some getting used to. After writing it one way for all of his life, it never felt quite right. Kaufmann was now Keller. A last-name change was easier.

"Yes, I mean Arthur." He would always remain Langer to Eric.

"No, I think he's still sleeping. Mr. Becker will be getting him around soon if he doesn't wake up on his own."

The soup was delicious, and Eric was enjoying it. Potato soup, one of his favorites. Did she know? He gave Mary a smile, conveying his pleasure with her cooking. She smiled back, appreciating the compliment. It occurred to him this was the first meal he had eaten on dry land in more than three weeks. Mary was the first woman he had seen in months. How in the world did he manage not to lose his mind in the cramped quarters of the submarine? He would never look at playing cards the same again. In fact, he thought, he may never play again, period.

The hot soup was pleasing to his palate. Eric was certain his body was absorbing its nourishment like a dry sponge. First a hot bath, and now a freshly cooked meal. His spirits began picking up, even in spite of losing two members of their team, Kurt and Lars.

During their preparations over the past year, the four had become rather close colleagues. And even more so living in such close proximity for the last three weeks. How could anyone keep from growing close under those conditions? Lars was always the weakest link, to Eric's mind. Extremely bright and creative, he always had some difficulty with the physical part of the training. Even so, their superior officers were always committed to Lars's participation on the team due to his American education in the Midwest. He had a thorough knowledge of the American way of life. He even traveled extensively in Indiana, where most of the mission was going to occur. Lars had insightful knowledge the rest of the team would greatly benefit from to remain invisible to the American authorities. Lars was a great loss, and Eric had little confidence he and Langer would be able to succeed without him.

Kurt was the muscle. He also had lived part of his life in America. His father was a very successful businessman in Stuttgart and had sent Kurt to an all-boys school in America for his education. In a rare moment, Kurt had once confided in Eric that his father was extremely strict, emotionally cold, and even cruel at times. Kurt always appeared angry and distrustful of everyone. Eric sensed Kurt had a bullying streak running through him. Although Eric was never one to back down from a challenge, he made sure he never crossed Kurt. The only part of the mission Kurt feared was the submarine voyage itself. He wasn't a good swimmer, and water was perhaps the only thing he was really afraid of. To then drown, thought Eric, was a harsh fate.

"This is excellent, Mary," he said.

"It reminds me of home." He finished the last spoonful, leaving barely enough for a mouse in the bottom of the bowl.

"Thank you. It was always one of my son's favorites. He was about your age."

Mary noticed the empty bowl. "Would you like some more?"

"I should save some for . . . Arthur." May as well try to get used to calling him that.

She brought the pan and ladle over and began filling his bowl. Eric didn't protest. "There's plenty, so please have some more. It'll do you good." Mary placed the pan back on the stove, turned off the burner, and covered it. "I imagine Arthur will be down soon. This should stay warm for some time."

Eric nodded. Sitting at the table, enjoying his second bowl of soup, he began noticing simple things like the tablecloth, silverware, and even the baby blue bowls. Quite an improvement over the surroundings on U-313.

"Where is your son now?" asked Eric, as he continued to eat.

Mary was silent for a few seconds. "He was killed in battle."

Eric was mortified he had brought up an obviously painful memory for this sweet woman who had just fed him. "Please forgive me, I didn't mean . . ."

"No, it's all right. He died doing what he always wanted to do." Mary walked over to the table and looked into Eric's eyes with only the look a mother who had lost her son could have. "My son's name was Frederick. He was just eighteen when he joined the army. He was so excited to wear the German uniform! And I must say he did look quite handsome in it."

"I'm sure he did," offered Eric.

"He wanted to be part of the Wehrmacht, on the fast- moving front lines where all the glory was. At least that's what he used to write to me. Yes, Frederick was a loyal soldier and couldn't wait to invade France. He hated the French, feelings passed on by his father who fought in the first war. So, he got his wish when Hitler crossed the border into France that May. Of course Frederick was thrilled to be part of it. All of us at home knew the French would put up a fight, as they despised Hitler and everything he stood for.

"Well fight they did, the French. They were no match for the German army. Just the same they did put up quite a resistance at first.

Frederick was killed in an ambush the first week of June 1940. June 15th to be precise."

"I'm terribly sorry."

"Thank you. One of his friends wrote me a letter about his death. Frederick ran over to help another soldier who had been shot and was badly wounded. He was attempting to drag him to safety beside some trees not far from where they were fighting. He nearly made it when a bullet ended his life ten feet from the protection of the trees."

"How sad. He was a hero," said Eric.

"Well, I think so. He gave his life for another."

"I agree. Did the other soldier survive?"

Mary smiled. "Yes, he's the one who wrote me the letter."

"My God," replied Eric. "Then he truly was a hero. You must be very proud of him."

"It doesn't really matter now. I'd much rather have Frederick than some medal." Mary turned and walked back to check the soup. "Any more?"

"No, I'm full. And thank you, not just for the soup, but for sharing the story about Frederick. I know it can't be easy talking about him."

She was stirring the soup one last time. "On the contrary. I actually feel better when talking about him. In a way, it almost makes me believe he's still alive when I mention his name. At least for a moment. And I'll take those moments."

"Yes, I think I understand."

Eric looked around and began wondering where Becker and Jon were. Disposing of Lars's body? Retrieving the instructions from Berlin, and thus, the mission and their futures? He had to admit he was anxious to know what Berlin's decision would be, perhaps even more than Becker was.

Mary stood by the kitchen table and addressed Eric. "Is there anything else I can do for you?"

"No. You've been very kind. That's exactly what my body needed."

"Good, and I'm glad." She began to turn.

"Mary?"

She turned back. "Yes?"

"If I'm not imposing, may I ask how you came to America and became acquainted with Becker?"

Mary thought for a moment, not sure how much she should divulge. "I'm not at liberty to say how I know Mr. Becker. As far as coming to America, my husband died shortly after Frederick's death. I've always believed it was from a broken heart. We had no money, so the farm was sold. Frederick's friend, the one he saved, was reassigned to German intelligence and learned of my . . . difficulties. He came to me and asked if I would be interested in doing a job for German intelligence. The pay was good, and I would be serving Frederick's memory with even greater honor. So I agreed. What did I have to lose? They sent me here with false papers through Switzerland, and then Canada. My only task is to run this house and report anything I believe unusual to a man I've never met . . . even to this day."

"I see," said Eric. "Have you been here long?"

Mary hesitated. "About a year, I guess."

"That's a long time, do you miss Germany?" Eric was careful in his tone, attempting to make his questions appear innocent. He wanted this to be nothing more than small talk, which was what it was. In time of war, however, everyone was on their guard. And he was in enemy territory.

"Sometimes. Just when I get homesick, I hear how difficult it is over there. The bombings have destroyed so much. I even hear in many places food is in short supply. Maybe it's better I'm here. At least I can get whatever food I need."

"Have you had time to make friends?"

"Not really. I see some of the same women at the market. Occasionally we'll exchange pleasantries. No meaningful conversations. It's mostly about the price of food, rationing, and that sort of thing. I don't dare go beyond that. I'll never forget what the intelligence department said before I left Germany. 'Mind your own business, and no one else's.' I've never forgotten those words."

"Yes, probably a good idea." Eric realized it was probably best not to ask any more questions. He better check on Langer and see how he was doing.

Just as he was ready to head upstairs, the outside kitchen door opened. Jon and Becker walked in, looking at them suspiciously.

"What's going on?" asked Becker, looking directly at Mary.

Eric answered before Mary could utter a word. "I just finished the soup and was telling her how much it reminded me of my mother's. She was explaining how she learned the recipe from her own mother. Then we agreed I had better look in on Langer."

Becker was skeptical, but he had nothing more to go on. He changed course. "Are you feeling better?"

"Very much. You're quite fortunate to have Mary to do your cooking. My only fear is I may put on some weight while I'm here."

"I doubt there will be time for that," said Becker. He was still studying Eric and Mary to determine if anything else had transpired.

"Oh?" questioned Eric. "Have you heard something from Berlin already?"

"No. But I expect to soon. Whatever they decide, it's doubtful they will want either you or Langer here for very long. It will raise too many questions from the neighbors. And if there's one thing we don't want, it's attention." Jon nodded at that comment. He had yet to utter even one word in Eric's presence.

"Yes, of course, you're right. I just assumed you were out making contact about our plans."

"I wish that were the case, but Jon and I had to do something with Lars's body."

"What did you do with it?" asked Eric. He was at a loss at what they could do in broad daylight.

Becker looked at Mary, who was again fussing over the soup. "Mary, will you please excuse us?"

Mary smiled, showing both respect and fear in her eyes. "Of course."

Mary put down the wooden spoon she was using and covered the soup pan. She walked right past Eric and gave him a look of "tread lightly, don't trust them." Eric recognized the signal and decided to take her advice. Becker waited a few seconds after she disappeared from sight, then motioned for Eric to have a seat at the table.

"Please have a seat. We should talk," said Becker.

Eric complied, then Becker took the seat directly across from him and motioned for Jon to leave. Jon opened the outside door and walked in the direction of the huge barn, which was visible through the door window.

"Eric," addressed Becker, "I would appreciate it if you would not speak to Mary unless Jon or I are present."

"I was only—"

"Please understand," interrupted Becker, "that she is here in a very limited capacity. She knows nothing of your role here, or mine either, for that matter. All she's been told is that all of us report to German intelligence. That's it. Anything she sees or hears here she is to keep to herself. Like for instance, Lars's body. It was most unnecessary she heard about that!"

"I understand."

Becker continued to lecture Eric. "Mary's *only* role is to keep house. Cook, clean, do laundry, and file a meaningless report once a month. She never ventures outside the house. The only exception is going to the market once a week. And even then, she's to go on a different day each time to avoid running into the same people.

Nothing more. Nothing. She's not to know anything about us. Period. When our job is done here, Mary will be dealt with based on her obedience to these rules. It's really very simple."

Eric was beginning to take offense at Becker's remarks. "What exactly do you mean, be 'dealt with'?" Now he was worried for Mary.

"You don't need to concern yourself about that. You and Langer should only be concerned about whatever plans Berlin has for you, whether it's continuing the mission you trained for or something else."

Eric did not like the sound of this. Not at all. They had planned for nearly a year for a specific mission. And now if Berlin changed that mission, how would they prepare here in America? The odds for success when they boarded U-313 in France were already long. They suddenly got longer. He began feeling trapped and doomed, and he didn't like it. Everything now seemed out of control.

"Do we have an understanding?" asked Becker, with a sinister smile.

Eric didn't care for being boxed in, but what choice did he have? "Of course. I'll do whatever I'm ordered to do."

"Good." Becker stood. "Now, let's go and see how your friend Langer is doing."

Langer was up and getting ready for a bath by the time they knocked on his bedroom door. He said he would be down for some soup after he cleaned up. Becker and Eric left him to his bath. Thirty minutes later they heard him walking down the stairs and entering the kitchen. Mary returned to the kitchen and filled his bowl with soup. She set it down in front of a grateful Langer.

"Thank you." He blew on the steaming soup.

Eric joined him in the kitchen. "It's good to see you."

"Likewise," said Langer. He took a spoonful and blew on it before slurping it down. It was obvious he loved it! "Are you as sore as I am?"

Eric smiled in acknowledgement. "Perhaps more so. I ache in places I didn't know were there."

"I know what you mean." Then Langer's expression turned more serious. "You heard about Lars?"

"Yes. Becker told me. Didn't seem to bother him all that much."

"Really?" Langer wasn't sure he believed that.

"Yes, really. Kurt didn't even make it to the beach. Our raft over-turned about halfway in and that's the last I saw of him. I almost didn't make it myself. We lost the paddles, so there wouldn't have been any way to get to him. I knew he was afraid of the water. I should have done more to keep him in the raft."

"Yeah, and how were you going to do that?"

"I don't know, but I should have done something."

"Listen," said Langer," stop it right now. I was out there too, and it's a miracle any of us made it. It was every man for himself once we stepped off that submarine. Gerhardt was right; we should have waited out the storm."

"Maybe. But we're here now."

"True. Not sure what we'd have done if they hadn't come out to look for us. Good thinking on their part, orders or not." Langer was practically gulping down the soup. Mary looked over and saw how fast Langer was consuming it. She brought the pan over and refilled the bowl without asking Langer's permission. Langer just nodded his thanks and kept eating.

Mary's eyes met Eric's. He was now greatly concerned for her safety, even though she was one of them. "Mary, would you please excuse us for a few minutes?"

Mary then realized Becker had instructed him to alienate her from all conversations between the men. She also knew Eric was protecting her.

"Of course. I need to be getting to the market. Is there anything either of you would like me to pick up?"

"I would love some fruit if you can find any this time of year. Oranges would be wonderful," said Langer.

"I'll see what I can do," replied Mary. "How about you, Eric?"

Eric thought for a moment. "Nothing special for me. Maybe some cheese, if they have any. I'll be happy with anything you bring back. Something tells me you can work wonders with just about anything."

"Thank you. I'll see about the cheese." Mary removed her apron and folded it up on the counter by the sink. She exited the kitchen, the two men listening to her footfalls as they echoed down the hallway on the wood floors.

Langer glanced curiously at Eric. "What was that all about?"

"Becker," answered Eric. "He ordered me not to speak to her or have any conversations in her presence, other than about cooking or other house-related matters. He was *very* clear about that."

"You don't say."

"I do say," said Eric. "Becker is very suspicious of everything. Even us."

"Well, we are in enemy territory. I'd be suspicious too. He's just being cautious."

Eric shook his head. "It's more than that. I don't think he trusts us. There's something about him that makes me uneasy."

"Like I said, I'm sure he's just being cautious. He's at great risk being here just like we are."

"I know. Maybe I'm being oversensitive. Just the same, I think we should be wary of him . . . and Jon. By the way, have you heard him say one word?"

"No. But I don't find that unusual. It's obvious Becker is in charge. He's probably just following orders."

"Well," said Eric resignedly, "perhaps you're right. I'm still tired from the long trip over here. Not to mention the harrowing raft incident."

"That goes for both of us." He finished the last spoonful of soup, then wiped his mouth with the napkin. "Any news from Berlin?"

"Not yet, but I think we'll know today. I'm not sure, but I think they were out earlier meeting someone to see if there was any news."

"It may take a little time. It can't be easy getting messages back and forth to Berlin from over here. You have to be extremely careful. We may be here for a while."

"Of course, you're right," agreed Eric. "They also did something with Lars's body. Not sure what, but Becker assured me not to worry about it. I thought sure they'd wait for nightfall."

"Hmm," agreed Langer. "Well, they know what they're doing. At least I hope so. For now we're their guests, so we'll have to follow along until we hear what Berlin's plans are."

Eric nodded, signifying his agreement. "Becker believes we can still proceed with our plans, even with half our team dead."

"I don't see how, but he may be privy to information we're not. In the end, we'll do whatever Berlin orders. I do know certain contingencies were made before we left France. What those are I do not know. Something tells me we'll know sooner rather than later. They can't keep us waiting here for very long. Too risky."

"Yes, I believe you're right."

Just then they heard a phone ring from another room. Becker's voice could be heard, but his words were indiscernible. Moments later Langer and Eric heard his footfalls approaching the kitchen. Becker entered and looked pleased to see Langer up and around.

"It's good to see you. The bath and soup did you well?"

"Yes. Thank you. I'm sore, but all in all, in one piece."

"Excellent!" said Becker.

"Eric and I are grateful you came to the beach to get us. I know that wasn't part of your orders, but we would have died otherwise."

Becker nodded. "Sometimes you have to expand your orders to insure success. Just the same, I'm very disappointed we weren't able to save Kurt and Lars."

"Yes, that was unfortunate," agreed Langer. "Eric said you're waiting for word from Berlin for new orders."

"That is true. In fact, that was my contact on the phone just now. Berlin has made their decision—and quite quickly for Berlin—if you know what I mean." Becker smiled, trying to share a common complaint amongst those who worked for German intelligence. "It shows how much they value this mission."

Langer smiled, Eric did not. "So," asked Langer, "does this mean you can share their orders with us?"

"Not yet. Information like that is not relayed over the telephone. I will meet him shortly. Then I can share the orders with you."

"Yes, that makes sense," agreed Langer. "I understand you had to . . . take care of Lars's body. I hope that didn't pose any difficulties."

Becker thought Langer might be fishing. He was going to reveal nothing. "Not at all. It's unfortunate for Lars, and I do feel bad for him and his family. That said, we must stay focused on the mission."

"True."

"I'm heading out for a couple of hours. We'll drop Mary at the market. Please, for your own safety and ours as well, stay inside as much as possible. If you must go out, stay close to the house. We are fairly remote out here on the farm, but it's always wise to remain cautious." Becker looked at both men to make sure they understood, which they did. "Agreed?"

"Of course," replied Langer.

"Now, I must be on my way. Is there anything else either I or Mary can do for you?"

"I would love some cigarettes," answered Eric.

"I'll second that," said Langer.

Becker motioned to the hallway. "There's a hutch in the entryway. In the top drawer are cigarettes and matches. The cigarettes are American, much better than ours. Help yourselves."

"Where's Jon?" Eric inquired.

"He's outside and will go with me. OK, gentlemen, I'm off. Be back in a little while."

Becker exited the kitchen through the outside door and walked to the barn where a maroon four-door sedan was parked. Jon was behind the wheel. Langer and Eric watched him get into the car and drive off. Then Langer looked over at Eric.

"He is the most cautious person I've ever met."

"You got that right," said Eric. "How about those cigarettes. I can use one."

Langer nodded in agreement. Both men rose from the kitchen table and walked into the hallway toward the hutch.

The farm, as Becker called it, was just that. A farm. The first thing Langer and Eric noticed, however, as they sat on the front covered porch was little, if any, farming was actually being done. The fields had nothing growing in them other than weeds and families of rodents. There was a fenced-in area next to the barn for chickens, pigs, or other livestock. Surveying the immediate area, they saw no animals at all that would give the impression this was a working farm. Not even a dog or cat could be seen roaming the grounds. The siding on the white farmhouse was badly fading. The paint was peeling, and one large piece of siding was sagging and ready to detach completely and fall to the ground. The front door creaked when opened, and the outer screen door had several large holes in the protective screen mesh. Anyone visiting the property would immediately think the farm was being neglected and was perhaps abandoned.

A hundred feet from the house was a very large, and equally neglected, white barn. It appeared as though it hadn't been used in years. Surrounding the crumbling foundation, grass and other weeds had grown to at least two feet high. The name "Mail Pouch" painted on the front of the barn in red and black letters was badly faded and barely discernable.

A narrow gravel lane led to the main road. Cars passing by on the main road could barely be seen. It was quiet, and that was why Becker chose it. Quiet and private.

It was good to be outside, even in the cool November air. Langer and Eric were enjoying their American cigarettes in two old rocking chairs that creaked as they rocked. It didn't take them long to find a couple of jackets hanging in the front closet. They needed them; even though the storm had passed, the weather remained windy.

"I think we have the place to ourselves," said Langer.

Eric glanced around yet again, wondering where they really were. "I believe you're right. I'm surprised Becker would trust us to be here by ourselves."

"Don't be too hard on him. He's just doing his job. And it's not an easy one. There's a lot at risk."

"I know. Someone needs to tell him we're on the same side. It won't be Jon though. I'm beginning to think he's a mute."

"Funny," replied Langer. He put out the butt of his finished cigarette on the arm of his rocking chair. Then he reached for another. "These really are good cigarettes."

Eric leaned back in his chair and fully inhaled the delicious smoke. "Yes, they are."

The two men who had been through so much together over the last year were actually relaxing. And enjoying it. It was something they hadn't done since being introduced last year following their selection by German intelligence.

Once selected, there was no time for life's luxuries or relaxation. Training was fast paced and intense. There was no time to waste; Germany was slipping in the war. The Americans were bombing their once beautiful cities every day, and the bombing was extremely accurate and destructive. It had to stop! The Luftwaffe wasn't able to stop the persistent American planes, there were too many of them. Where did they get so many bombers? If one was shot down, they would send two more.

The once proud and invincible German people were now feeling a very noticeable chink in their armor. They didn't like it, not one bit. There was no time for leisure activities when the Fatherland was crying out for help. And that's what the four young men had signed up for, to help. Planning, training, then more training. Then three weeks on U-313, and finally the treacherous raft incident. They deserved some relaxation. Neither one had any feelings of guilt for this very brief reprieve.

Finally Eric broke the restful silence. "What do you think Berlin will say?"

Langer blew out a long trail of blue smoke, which was immediately grabbed by the wind and whisked away. "I'm not sure. If I had to guess, I'd say they'll want us to do something on a smaller scale. They have too much invested in the plan to cancel it now, even with half our team gone. How about you?"

"At first I believed they would cancel the entire mission. I still believe that's the right decision. Perhaps get us back and begin planning for something else. But Becker was very sure they would proceed on some level with the original plan. Now that I've thought about it, I think he may be right. All I want to do right now is sit here and enjoy these American cigarettes."

Langer smiled, inhaling another large breath. Then he tilted his head back and blew out one more long stream of blue smoke. "Great idea."

Twenty minutes, and a dozen cigarettes later, they saw Becker's maroon vehicle turn into the lane and speed up to the farmhouse. Langer and Eric walked down the porch steps and over to where the car had stopped. Jon stayed behind the wheel. Becker got out, looking pale.

"What's the matter?" asked Langer. He and Eric exchanged a quick glance, realizing something was amiss.

"Good and bad news," answered Becker. "I received the information from Berlin. That's the good news. The bad news is, my contact informed me the local authorities found a body washed up on the beach this morning. It's Kurt's. A couple of kids discovered it."

"How do they know it's Kurt? It could be anyone. Surely others drowned in the storm," said Eric.

"Yes, that's true. But it was a man in his twenties wearing civilian clothes and a life vest. A life vest with German writing on it."

"Shit!" exclaimed Langer. No one had thought of that when Gerhardt ordered the life vests brought up for them. His intentions were good, but that small deviation in the plan may cost them dearly now.

"Exactly," agreed Becker. "That's why I returned so quickly. We need to review Berlin's orders and make arrangements to leave as soon as possible." Then he walked over to Jon who was behind the wheel. "Pick up Mary at the market. She should be finished by now. While you're there, see if you can pick up on anything about finding Kurt's body. I'm sure the townspeople will be talking. We may learn something useful." Jon just nodded. He took off, spinning the tires in the process, leaving Becker, Langer, and Eric standing there.

"Wait a minute," warned Langer. "Let's not be too hasty. We need to think this through. Just because they found Kurt's body doesn't mean they'll show up at our doorstep any minute."

Eric looked at Becker, agreeing with Langer. "He's right. I'm all for moving forward, but first we need to make sure we have all our facts. Let's at least be certain of Berlin's orders, then move out.

Becker protested. "Berlin's orders will not matter if we're all arrested and thrown into prison!"

"OK, OK," said Langer, attempting to calm Becker down. "Let's go inside and see what Berlin wants us to do. Then we can talk about how to proceed. Above all, let's stay calm and focused."

"I am calm," said Becker, annoyed. He stared at the two agents as though they had no idea of what had transpired in the last few hours. Then he turned and stormed into the farmhouse, leaving Langer and Eric standing there in disbelief.

✦

Langer and Eric found Becker sitting in a large stuffed chair by the living room's front window. Becker didn't acknowledge the two men. He was holding the orders in his hand while staring out the window, deep in thought. Without saying a word, the two agents walked in and took a seat on the sofa positioned directly across from Becker's chair, a coffee table separating them. They waited patiently for a moment, expecting Becker to speak. The two agents were anxious to learn Berlin's instructions.

Finally, Langer broke the uncomfortable silence. "Are those the orders?" He gestured toward the papers.

Becker nodded, then continued staring out the window.

Waiting a moment for Becker to respond, Langer prompted him when he wasn't forthcoming. "Well, are you going to tell us what they are?"

Becker finally turned to face the two young men, then took a deep breath. "It's as I expected. We are to proceed per the original plan . . . with some minor changes."

Langer and Eric looked at each other. They were in disbelief Berlin would want to continue the plan without two very important team members *and* make changes at this late date. Why not call off the entire plan, or at least postpone it until new team members could be brought up to speed?

"What minor changes?" asked Langer. "And what do you mean by *'we'*?"

"What I mean," answered Becker, "is Berlin has instructed Jon and me to accompany you to Indianapolis to provide whatever support we can, in any capacity that may be."

Eric could not believe his ears and immediately objected. "You're not serious!"

Becker tossed the orders on the table between them. "I am *quite* serious, gentlemen. And so is Berlin. Read them for yourselves." It was plain to see from the look on Becker's face that he was just as stunned as the two agents. Langer quickly snatched the papers off the table and began reading, handing each sheet to Eric as he finished. Langer was quiet, and so was Eric as they read Berlin's instructions. When finished, Eric placed the papers back on the table. Now Langer was the one looking off into the distance, deep in thought.

"This was going to be difficult enough *with* Kurt and Lars," said Eric. "Now it's nearly impossible." He looked at Becker, then added, "No offense."

Becker not only didn't take Eric's reaction as an insult, he didn't acknowledge the remark at all. At the moment he felt betrayed, attacked by something he could not retaliate against—Mother Nature. All of Becker's preplanning, preparations, and extreme efforts in exercising caution had been undone by a storm: the storm had taken the lives of Lars and Kurt, the storm had forced Becker and Jon to deviate from their orders at great risk and venture to the beach in order to rescue the survivors, and now the storm was striking again! The blow of Kurt's body being discovered wearing a German life vest could be disastrous for all of them. It would only be a matter of time before the American authorities were on them. Becker was discouraged and angry. He was keeping score: Mother Nature 3- Germany 0. What would come next?

Langer reached over and picked up one of the papers. "If I understand this correctly, not only has our mission changed, it's expanded. Furthermore, Berlin has placed you in charge as commanding officer, Mr. Becker."

"It would seem so," replied Becker. "Be assured, that was not at my request."

"Perhaps not. But as you are now the senior officer in command, we will be taking our orders from you. So, now that Berlin has placed you in charge, what do we do? What are *your* orders?"

Becker leaned forward in the comfortable chair, realizing he had the undivided attention of Eric and Langer. "May I suggest we make immediate preparations to depart for our ultimate destination, Indianapolis? It will take us several days to journey there. That will give us many opportunities to discuss Berlin's instructions in more detail. Waiting only exposes us to more danger, of that I have no doubt."

The two young men had to agree. They realized Becker was much more aware of the local conditions than they were; they had been here less than forty-eight hours, while Becker had been here off and on for more than a year. They had no choice but to trust his judgment on this present dilemma.

"All right. What needs to be done before leaving?" asked Langer.

Becker's mind was racing, attempting to formulate the most efficient plan for wrapping up the operation at the farm and escaping to Indianapolis free and clear of the authorities. They would need to clean the farmhouse of any and all remnants from their stay in the small New Jersey farming community. Especially those of Eric and Langer. That should be easy, however, as they had just arrived.

Becker looked at Langer, then Eric. "Gather everything upstairs in your rooms that we provided for you, both clothes and toiletries. You will be needing them for our travels. You'll find suitcases in the closets. Take whatever clothes and other items you can fit into one suitcase. Those that don't, we will burn outside by the barn. I don't think I need to remind you that only absolutely essential items must be taken with you."

"Understood," replied Langer. Eric was nodding in agreement. "There's not much there. It won't take long to do that. What else can we do to help you?"

"Please don't think I'm discounting your abilities or efforts, but most of what needs to be destroyed only I can do. Not even Jon will be able to help me with that. There are some red cans of petrol in the barn just inside the door. A funnel is there next to the cans. If one of you will get the cans out and ready to fill the tank in the car when Jon returns, that will be most helpful. Filling it now will allow us to get far away before refueling. And getting as far away as quickly as we can should be our first priority. If we are discovered, or worse, detained, well, then it won't go well for any of us."

Of that, no one sitting there could disagree.

———✦———

As Langer had predicted, it took him less than ten minutes to pack. He chose two changes of clothes and all the toiletries, then packed them neatly into the suitcase. He threw the rest of the clothes into the hallway. He opened every drawer in the bedroom. Other than the top two drawers that contained the underwear and the toiletries, all the others were empty. He even checked under the bed. Nothing but a few dust balls. He realized he and Eric were the farmhouse's first and only guests, at least while Becker was involved there.

Eric entered the bedroom and looked around. "Not much to pack. Guess we're traveling light."

"Guess so, probably best. Have everything out?"

"Yeah, not much here," said Eric. "I think we're the only ones who have been in these rooms."

"I think you're right," confirmed Langer. "I'll take the suitcases down to the car if you'll gather up these clothes and take them to the barn. I'm sure Becker will want to burn them after it gets dark. Don't want the neighbors to see the smoke and call the fire department."

Eric smiled. "You're right about that." He set his suitcase down and grabbed the small pile of clothes on the floor.

Langer walked down the stairs first, carrying the two suitcases, followed by Eric with the discarded clothes. They passed the living room where Becker had just hung up from a phone call.

"Just got off the phone with our Indianapolis contact. He was not expecting us for another week, but he understands our situation and agrees we should leave immediately. I told him to expect us in two or three days. We leave tonight."

Eric was still holding the clothes in his arms. "I assume you want these burned after dark?"

"Yes, of course. Thank you. Jon and Mary should be back from the market soon. I'm hopeful Jon will have a positive report on Kurt. And what I mean is that it's quiet in town, very quiet."

"I hope so too," said Langer.

"Is Mary coming with us?" asked Eric.

Becker paused. Eric sensed danger in what Becker might be thinking. Becker looked first at Langer, then at Eric. "Well, we do have a problem there."

"What do you mean, a problem?" Eric inquired.

"Surely you must know Mary can't come with us. First of all, there is only room for four of us in the car. Second, she knows too much about us. Even though she's not been privy to who we really are or our orders, she does know we all work for German intelligence. *That* is the problem. If she were to be captured and questioned, well . . ."

Eric threw the clothes on the sofa. "What exactly are you saying?"

Langer set down the suitcases and waited for Becker's reply.

"Gentlemen," explained Becker, "we are at war. And at the moment Germany is struggling a bit. More than a bit, if we are to be completely honest with one another. We cannot risk this mission for the life of a lonely widow who has pledged herself to Germany, and more importantly, to the success of our mission." Becker paused for a moment, allowing what he had just said to sink in. "It's unfortunate, I agree, but Mary must be eliminated. The risk is too great to let her try and make a run for it. She would be detained within twenty-four hours."

"You don't know that," protested Langer.

"And you don't know that she won't," countered Becker. "Do you want to risk your lives on a homemaker with no training in enemy territory?"

Eric gave Becker a steely gaze. "And just who is going to 'silence' Mary? You? Jon?"

Becker lowered his eyes and sighed. "Gentlemen, gentlemen. You did not know this, but your friend who washed up on the beach this morning had orders to end Mary's life upon our departure."

"I don't believe that!" declared Langer.

"Just because you don't believe it doesn't mean it's not true. Kurt was a trained assassin by the SS prior to joining German intelligence. Jon and I were to wrap things up here as soon as the four of you were on your way, and then be gone two days later. Mary was always going to be an unfortunate loss to the plan. She was chosen because both her son and husband are dead, and she has no other surviving relatives. They wanted someone with no family, no traces. Mary, I'm sorry to say, fit the bill. She has to die."

Eric and Langer stood there in shock, Eric more than Langer. The innocent and sweet woman who had suffered so much was going to suffer one more injustice. He wasn't sure he could tolerate it.

"We are not going to let you kill her," objected Eric.

"Mr. Keller. These are not my orders. These are Berlin's orders. Are you prepared to defy your superiors? Are you prepared to jeopardize all of our lives? Are you prepared to assume the risk of this mission and perhaps the fate of continued bombings in Germany for the life of one woman?"

Eric was at a loss for words. Becker was quite persuasive; he made valid points. In a court of law he would have his way with a jury and judge. But this was not a court of law. An innocent woman's life was going to end. And he did not want to be part of it.

"She's done nothing wrong. She's innocent."

"Oh, I see. And are not the lives of all our countrymen innocent? How about the harmless women and children who are indiscriminately slaughtered every day by American bombers? Are they not also innocent? So you tell me, Mr. Keller, what would you have us do? You be in charge. You make the decisions. You be responsible for the success or failure of this mission and all it implies. Then tell me you will place all of it at risk for one person's life."

"It's wrong, and you know it."

Becker had enough of the arguing. "She dies, and that's that. An order is an order, and I take no pleasure in it. I'm going up to pack my own things." Then Becker left the room and went upstairs. They could hear his bedroom door slam.

Outside Langer attempted to slide open the extremely large barn door. He could only get it to move a foot or so. Eric saw him struggling and dropped the clothes. They pushed together and managed to open the door a few feet. Langer stepped inside. The daylight from outside the doorway allowed him to see inside only ten feet from the entrance. True to Becker's word, there were three large red cans just inside the door on the ground. Langer set them outside.

"We can't let them kill Mary," pleaded Eric.

"I don't like it either, but Becker does have a point."

"Point or not, it's just wrong. I'm sure she could manage to stay hidden for a couple of weeks. By then it won't matter."

Langer skeptically looked at Eric before pulling the door shut. "Maybe, maybe not. Becker's in charge, it's his decision."

"I don't care if he's in charge or not. We need to stop him. This really isn't necessary."

"I know you like her. I like her. She's a very nice lady, and German! But we can't take the chance of her getting picked up by the Americans. If there were another option I'm sure Becker would at least consider it."

"I'm not so sure," said Eric.

Langer wanted to change the subject. "We have other things to worry about right now. Find a good place to burn the clothes, not too far from the barn out back. Pour a little gas on them before we fill the car. We'll light them right before we leave."

Eric picked up a can with one arm and the pile of clothes with the other. He walked behind the barn and looked for a suitable place to burn them. There were several bare patches of ground that he could use. The barn would serve as a windbreak. He threw them on the ground. There were some rocks piled up a few feet away. He grabbed a few and tossed them on the clothes to keep them in place. He removed the lid to the can and doused the clothes with petrol. Satisfied, he put the lid back on and walked around to the side of the barn where Langer was smoking a cigarette.

Just then they saw the maroon car pull into the long lane and park between the barn and the farmhouse. Mary got out first and waved to Eric and Langer. Jon remained behind the wheel, studying the two agents through the windshield. After a moment he exited the car and walked up to the porch and into the farmhouse without acknowledging either one of them. It gave Eric the creeps. He didn't trust him and made a mental note to always keep an eye on him. He then knew Jon would be the one ending Mary's life. And Eric thought he may actually enjoy the task.

"I got your cheese, Eric. And two oranges for you, Arthur," said Mary. "I'll set them on the counter."

Eric carried a can of petrol over to the car and looked into the shopping bag where the cheese was. "Thank you, Mary. That was very kind of you to do that."

"It was no problem. The oranges don't look all that fresh, but it's the best I could do."

Langer walked over, carrying the remaining two cans. "I'm sure they'll be fine. And Eric's right, that was very kind."

"I'm happy to do it." Then she looked up at the farmhouse. "You may want to head in. Jon seemed very agitated after he picked me up. I'm afraid something may be wrong. If so, I'm sure Mr. Becker will want to see you."

"Any idea what happened?" asked Langer.

"No. He didn't say a word the whole way back. Of course, he hardly ever says anything anyway."

"Why don't I find that surprising," smiled Eric.

Langer tapped Eric's shoulder. "Let's head in and see what's up."

"OK. I'll just help Mary with these bags."

"Don't be long." Langer left the two standing at the rear of the car by the trunk, which Mary then opened.

After Langer had walked up the steps to the farmhouse, Eric leaned over the open trunk and grabbed a bag of groceries. Mary was reaching for one too. Then Eric, trying desperately to avoid drawing attention to himself, said in a low tone, "Mary, listen to me *very* carefully . . ."

Becker, Jon, and Langer were standing in the kitchen when Eric and Mary walked in. Both were carrying grocery bags. Erik was talking to Mary nonchalantly.

"Well, my mother liked to use a little more cheese. But other than that, it's basically the same." Eric placed the two bags he was carrying on the kitchen table.

"Mr. Keller," said Becker, "if you're not too busy we'd like to see you in the living room." Then Becker turned and walked in that direction. Jon and Langer followed close behind.

"Of course," answered Eric. He gave Mary a quick glance, then also exited the kitchen.

The three men were all seated when Eric entered. He took a seat and then waited for Becker to initiate the conversation, which he did a moment later.

"Our problems continue," sighed Becker.

"How so?" asked Langer.

Becker looked first at Jon, then addressed the two agents. "The police have called in the OSS to help them identify Kurt's body and to find others who may have survived."

"The OSS?" asked Eric.

Becker gazed at him in disbelief, disappointed he wasn't more familiar with America's premier intelligence agency. The OSS, Office of Strategic Services, was dedicated to espionage and counterespionage activities during the war. The organization was enjoying some much-needed success of late, to the chagrin of the Germans. The OSS was America's answer to an otherwise ad hoc collection of independent intelligence services previously headed up by various departments of the executive branch of the American government: the departments of war, state, navy, and treasury.

As one might suspect, all were competent in their duties, but none were particularly effective in communicating with each other. Not only was there costly redundancy, critical information wasn't being passed from one department to another. Too frequently time-sensitive information was not being utilized where it was needed; instead it was being contained within the confines of just one department, costing American lives!

To become truly effective, the independent intelligence services had to be consolidated. President Roosevelt saw the problem and took action to correct it. In doing so, he began by choosing the right man for the job, the very competent Colonel "Wild Bill" Donovan. He was a highly decorated soldier from World War I, even receiving the Medal of Honor for his actions near Landres-et-Saint-Georges, France, in 1918. A man of action before and during wartime, he wasted no time in developing the now effective OSS. It was effective, but at times, ruthless.

"You *are* joking?" chided Becker.

Eric and Langer looked at each other, hoping the other one knew what Becker was talking about.

"Will you please enlighten us?" asked Langer. "We're familiar with America's army intelligence, but not with this OSS."

"I'll make this quick," lectured Becker. "The OSS is America's equivalent to our own German intelligence. The Americans have come a long way in the last couple of years in the intelligence department. They are better organized and are drawing on significantly more resources than we have. They are sharing their information with British intelligence as well, which unfortunately for us has been a thorn in our side. The fact that OSS is now involved has just made our job much more difficult."

"I see," said Langer.

"I hope you do. To underestimate them is a recipe for failure. We must double our efforts and exercise even more caution."

Both Langer and Eric believed that was impossible. "Anything else?" asked Langer.

"Yes. It appears both the police and OSS have begun going house to house looking for information on anyone who looks out of place, perhaps some new faces. In other words, they're searching for any strangers in or around town who weren't here prior to the storm. It's only a matter of time before they stop here. We're close to the water and remote for the most part, making this a perfect place for two foreign agents to hide out until the authorities relax their guard. They are looking for you, so we need to leave for Indianapolis as soon as it's dark."

"How would they know there was anyone other than Kurt?" asked Eric.

Becker looked at Jon before answering, as though he had failed to do his job. "Evidently there were two sets of identity papers found on the beach. One set was on Kurt's body. The other set was stuck in some bushes up from the beach. They belonged to Lars. I was assured the beach had been thoroughly cleaned, but I guess that was impossible during the storm. It doesn't matter now. The OSS has them, which means they are looking for at least one more person, dead or alive. So, we are now forced to act hastily."

"Agreed," said Langer. "What needs to be done until then?"

"For starters, I need to destroy everything else here that could possibly link any of us to German intelligence. That should not take very long. If you and Eric will fill the car with petrol, that will allow us to be prepared if we need to depart in a hurry."

"We've already placed the cans by the car. We'll do that right away. Anything after that?"

"I'm afraid not." Becker looked at his watch. "It's 4:47 right now, so it will be getting dark within an hour or so. Let's just hope it all remains quiet for the next ninety minutes. We'll leave at 7:00. Be ready."

Becker stood up to adjourn their little meeting when Mary rushed in. "Mr. Becker! A dark car just pulled up the lane!"

Becker shot the two agents a panicky look. "Trouble."

The sound of tires crunching on gravel could be heard from the living room. All four men stood, not exactly sure what to do. Becker glanced over at Jon and nodded, giving some sort of signal. Jon immediately headed toward the kitchen, Mary close behind. Becker yelled after her, "Just relax, Mary. It will be all right."

Then Becker instructed Langer and Eric. "Stay here and be quiet. If it goes that far, say both of you are visiting family from Ohio, nothing more. I'll do the talking."

The two nodded nervously. Becker walked to the kitchen where Mary was peering out the door window. Becker scolded her, "Mary, get away from the window. You want to draw attention to yourself?"

She stepped back from the door and looked at Becker, asking with her expression for instructions.

"Perhaps it would be better if you went upstairs until they leave," said Becker, trying to soothe her uneasiness. Then he added, "Remain calm, they just want to have a look around. Then they'll be on their way." Mary acknowledged his instructions with a quick nod, then headed toward the stairway.

Looking out the window from several feet away, Becker could see the entire area between the farmhouse and barn. Two men got out of the dark sedan and started looking around. They had parked just feet from Becker's car. He could see the two strangers exchange suspicious looks. One of the men was wearing a suit. He was obviously the senior of the two, and the one in charge. The other was an MP, military policeman. He was a very large, muscular man with both a sidearm and baton. He had a no-nonsense roughness about him. Becker believed him to be the more dangerous of the two, and the enforcer, if necessary.

The man wearing the suit was in his midforties. He was carefully studying the farm, sensing something was out of place. He walked over to Becker's car and noticed the suitcases and cans of petrol sitting nearby. He motioned to the MP to have a look around. Then the man in the suit walked up to the porch and knocked on the door with authority, startling everyone inside the kitchen.

Becker purposely waited a moment, then calmly opened the door. "Yes, may I help you?"

"My name is Ralph Conway. I work for the Department of Defense." He reached inside his suit pocket and flashed a wallet-sized ID at Becker. Becker didn't even look at it. He knew the man was from the OSS, not the Department of Defense. Becker played along.

"Well, Mr. Conway, what can I do for you?" The door was fully open to allow Conway to peer into the front of the farmhouse. Becker wanted him to have a look, implying he had nothing to hide. He stood in the doorway, however, preventing Conway from entering.

"I'm sorry to bother you, but we had a report there were some German sailors who had to abandon their ship during the recent storm. They found their way to the beach not more than two miles from here." Conway pointed in the direction of the beach. "We're just doing a precautionary search. We don't believe them dangerous. Just the same, they are Germans and we consider them the enemy. If found, they will be incarcerated."

Becker thought this a great story, fabricated to reduce the citizenry's fear. Very clever, and one he would have chosen as well if the roles were reversed: some harmless sailors washed up on the shore looking for nothing more than a chance to survive; still, you could never be too sure, and the DOD was just doing their job looking for the unfortunate few men.

They both knew full well what Conway was really looking for. Conway's eyes betrayed him, and each man was leery of the other. Becker continued to play along for a while longer.

"Oh my. What on earth would a German ship be doing off our coast?" asked Becker, attempting to show concern.

"We're not exactly sure," answered Conway. "Our guess is it was a German patrol ship doing nothing more than some reconnaissance and it got caught in the storm before it could escape to safer waters.

Wow, thought Becker, the OSS really had given this manufactured story some thought. He noticed the MP outside, snooping around the barn. Then he remembered Eric was to prepare their clothes for burning when it got dark. If the MP found the clothes, then alarm bells within both authorities would surely go off. That would be most unfortunate for everyone.

"How do you know they washed ashore?" asked Becker.

"One of the young sailors was found dead on the beach. He was wearing a German uniform. Then we found some other items that indicated there could have been others, exactly how many we're not sure." Conway was doing his best to peer inside and take account of the farmhouse. His antennae were sending off alert signals, but he was remaining calm, thinking of how to gain access to the house without raising unnecessary suspicion from Becker. Little did Conway know, it was too late. Becker was on guard long before Conway reached the front door.

"The poor man. That must have been terrible."

"Yes," replied Conway," I'm sure it was.

"We haven't seen any strangers lurking about, if that's what you're asking."

"So you're not alone here?" asked Conway.

"Ah, no," said Becker, realizing his slip-of-the-tongue—he should have said "I"! "We have some family in from Ohio. They're just visiting for the week. They planned to head back a couple of days ago, but I'm afraid the storm set things back a bit. I was getting ready to take them to the train station." Becker smiled, deciding he could be just as creative at making up stories as the OSS. He thought them believable. Over Conway's shoulder he could see the MP walking around the barn. It would only be another minute before he discovered the clothes. Becker's mind began racing, considering all his options to maneuver out of this latest obstacle.

"I'm sorry to hear that. Would you mind if I spoke to them? Perhaps they know something that could help us," asked Conway.

"Of course. Please come in." Becker backed away from the door, reluctantly allowing Conway to enter the foyer. He had no choice. The staircase was directly in front of Conway. He was looking up and surveying all he could from his vantage point. "They're in the living room. Follow me." Becker turned and walked toward the living room, Conway two steps behind.

As they entered the living room Langer, Eric, and Jon were sitting and reading magazines. All of them looked unalarmed and relaxed. Becker paused a moment as Conway entered the room.

"Excuse me, gentlemen," interrupted Becker. "This is Mr. Conway. He's with the Department of Defense. He would like to ask you a few questions regarding some mysterious German sailors who may be lurking about."

Conway was about to say something when Becker continued. "Jon, will you please check the coffee and bring some in for all of us?" Jon nodded and rose out of his chair.

"That's really not necessary," said Conway.

"Please, it's no trouble. And besides, we were just about to have some anyway. Do you mind?" Becker was as smooth as they come.

"Of course not," answered Conway.

As Jon walked past the two men, Becker gave Jon a quick look that he seemed to recognize. Langer and Eric remained seated and put down their reading material. Although appearing outwardly calm, on the inside they were anxious. Eric could have sworn everyone could hear his heart beating much faster and harder than normal. Each beat was nearly in his throat.

"I'm truly sorry to bother you," Conway proceeded. "I realize you're just visiting but I wonder if you've seen anything suspicious in the area. Perhaps even on this farm?"

Both Langer and Eric shook their heads. "No sir, but we haven't been here all that long," responded Langer.

Conway was measuring up the two young men, attempting to figure out who they actually were. He seriously doubted they were family. "I understand you're just visiting?"

"That's right," answered Eric.

"How long have you been here?"

Eric and Langer looked at each other. "I would say a week or so. Wouldn't you agree, Eric?"

Eric confirmed the answer with a nod. "Yes, that's about right." He looked at Conway. "We're heading to the train station in a little while."

Conway didn't respond at first. Then he said, "Are you sure it's today?"

"Yes," answered Eric.

"I don't see how that's possible, as there are no trains on Thursdays. You must be mistak—"

Just then Jon snuck up behind Conway and put his left hand over Conway's mouth. With the swift and expert movement of a trained killer, with his right hand he quickly stuck a six-inch knife in the side of Conway's neck and pulled the blade back toward him in a single powerful stroke. The result was immediately fatal, ripping a large and gaping slice through his windpipe. Blood was gushing out of Conway's neck and down Jon's right hand onto his sleeve. Becker rushed over to help Jon catch Conway's slumping body, just as he was collapsing. As they laid him on the floor Langer and Eric jumped to their feet.

"Damn!" yelled Langer.

"Shut up!" snapped Becker. He rushed to the window to see where the MP was. "Quickly, both of you come over here and help me drag the body to the basement. Come on, hurry!"

The two young men, still in shock over what had just happened, did as they were told. Each of them grabbed a leg while Becker and Jon gripped Conway's arms. They carried the body, its dripping blood marking a trail on the floor, to the basement door. Becker loosened his grip and reached for the doorknob. He opened it and the four men struggled to get Conway's body through the doorjamb. As soon as the torso was through the jamb, Becker motioned for Langer and Eric to move aside. Once they were out of the way, Becker and Jon pushed the body down the stairs. All four watched as it tumbled to the bottom in a crumpled and bloody heap.

"We're not finished yet," said Becker calmly, to no one in particular. "The MP will be here in a minute wondering where his boss is." A few seconds later there was a loud knock on the door. Everyone looked at each other.

Becker was checking all of their clothes. Eric had virtually no blood on him. "Eric, go let the MP in. Tell him we're all in the living room, and that Conway is having coffee and asking us some questions. Ask the MP to join us. Do it now!"

Eric double-checked his clothes, and to his amazement there were indeed only a couple of small spots of blood near the cuffs of his pants. He gave Langer a bewildered look and then began to rush to the door.

"Slowly!" yelled Becker. "We want him to believe everything's normal."

Eric took a deep breath, and with extreme effort, deliberately slowed his pace. He rounded the corner in the hallway and could see the MP standing at the door. He was peering inside, looking for Conway, or anyone, for that matter. Eric smiled and waved. He opened the door.

"You must be looking for Mr. Conway."

"Yes, I thought I saw him come in. Is he still inside?"

"He's in the living room asking some questions. We brought him some coffee. He knew you'd be here soon and asked that you come in."

The MP looked very skeptical and did a cautionary inspection of the immediate area before entering the foyer. Eric led the MP toward the living room, knowing the room was empty. What was he going to do when they got there? Two seconds later he received his answer. As he made a slight right turn toward the living room, Jon stepped out from behind the corner by the basement door, pointed a revolver directly at the MP, and pulled the trigger. The sound made everyone jump as it reverberated off the narrow hallway walls. The bullet hit the MP directly in the forehead, the impact jerking his head back. Blood and brains spattered on the door behind him in a fine mist. The MP fell to the floor, crashing against the hat rack, bringing it down upon him. Jon casually walked past Eric and up to the MP. A pool of blood was beginning to grow on the wood floor surrounding his head. He stood over him, and with no emotion whatsoever, shot once more into the MP's head.

Then, everything was quiet. Becker walked up to the MP's body. He placed his hand on Jon's shoulder. "Good work. Throw his body down the basement with Conway's."

Jon placed the pistol back in his suit jacket. He glanced at Eric, waiting for him to help with the body. Eric leaned down and grabbed hold of the MP's feet. Jon grasped the shoulders. With Eric walking backward, together they dragged the body to the basement door, leaving another trail of blood. Eric dropped the feet when he reached the basement doorway; he couldn't back up any farther. He stepped aside. Jon struggled to lift the large man's shoulders up high enough to force them over his feet. Then he shoved him, letting the momentum carry the MP down the stairs and onto Conway's corpse. Jon stared down at the two bodies for a moment, admiring his handiwork.

Becker walked over and closed the basement door. Then he began barking out orders. "OK, there's no time to waste. We no longer have the luxury of waiting until it gets dark. Jon, move their car to the barn so no one will see it from the road. Eric, you and Langer go ahead and put as much petrol in our car as possible. I only need ten minutes to get what I need. I'll destroy it later when we're on the road."

"How long before anyone discovers they're missing?" asked Langer.

"Your guess is as good as mine. A few hours at most. It's getting late and the authorities will be checking in with each other soon. With any luck they won't find the bodies until tomorrow. That will give us plenty of time to put some distance between us."

"Good," replied Langer.

"Just one thing," added Becker.

"What's that?"

"We haven't had much luck lately." Becker gave Langer a sorry grin and headed up the stairs to the bedroom to gather what he could.

Eric brushed past Jon and rushed to the maroon car. Jon, following close behind, opened the dark government sedan and found the keys still in the ignition. As Eric opened the cap to the first can of petrol, he saw Jon motion to the barn, and more specifically, the door. Eric nodded he understood and ran over to the door. With all his strength, he pushed it open wide enough for the car to pass through.

Jon started the engine and spun the tires. He drove the car into the barn, nearly knocking Eric over in the process. He got out of the car and helped Eric close the large heavy door, except for a small opening. Eric believed Jon to be much stronger than his small frame indicated. Jon then walked to the back of the barn, reappearing a few seconds later with the clothes. He walked up to Eric and threw them through the doorway. Then he pushed the door completely shut. Eric understood what he was doing; perhaps it was better not to leave any evidence outside. And now there would be no time to burn the clothes. Even if there were, smoke during the daylight would draw attention. The last thing they wanted now were curious neighbors checking on them to see if they needed help. Jon went back to the farmhouse. Eric lifted the first can and began pouring the fuel into the car.

Five minutes later Becker and Langer walked down the steps and approached the maroon sedan. Becker was holding an attaché case. He opened the trunk and placed it next to the suitcases. He looked around, trying to identify anything out of place that would draw unwanted attention to anyone who may venture onto the farm. Other than appearing abandoned, nothing cried out that there was trouble inside. More specifically, two dead Americans.

Becker took the driver's seat. Langer and Eric sat in back. After a full minute Langer and Eric looked at each other, speculating on what was delaying Jon. Finally he walked out on the porch and caught Becker's attention. He shrugged his shoulders. Eric knew immediately what the signal meant—Jon could not find Mary.

Becker turned around and looked Eric in the eye. "What did you say to Mary?"

"What are you talking about?" answered Eric.

"You know very well what I'm talking about. If you revealed what had to be done, and she now conveniently disappears, then you have placed all of us at even greater risk."

"Mr. Becker," replied Eric with animosity, "I have not been alone with Mary. And furthermore, I take my duties seriously. Langer here will tell you I follow orders. And you are in charge. So as much as I would have liked to warn her, I did what I was ordered. Period! So don't begin accusing me of something I didn't do."

Langer spoke up in defense of Eric. "He's absolutely correct about following orders. If he said he didn't warn her, then he didn't warn her."

"Would you like us to find her for you?" asked Eric mockingly. "She can't be that far and is probably in the house somewhere."

Becker remained silent for a moment, not believing either one for even a second. He was out of time and out of options. He motioned for Jon to join them in the car. Jon trotted to the car and took the passenger seat. Becker gave Jon a look of disgust, then started the car. As he pulled out of the lane Eric took one last look at the barn, and undoubtedly, into Mary's eyes as she watched them leave. Then he smiled.

CHAPTER 4

THE DESTINATION

The petrol Eric had poured into the tank carried them over two hundred miles—even Becker seemed pleased with that! The farmhouse was now far behind them. Stops were short and infrequent, only for more petrol, food, and very short nights in roadside motels. Becker and Jon shared a room, as did Langer and Eric. Through the walls at night the latter two agents could hear Becker talking but weren't able to make out any of his words. At times his angry muffled tone revealed Becker's displeasure with the recent series of setbacks. Both Eric and Langer knew Becker remained furious about the way events had transpired since that first night on the beach. Nothing thus far had gone according to plan, with one failure after another. And now two bodies lay at the bottom of the basement steps in the farmhouse!

During their long trip both Langer and Eric fully expected some conversations about the recent change in their orders from Berlin. Every time Langer brought it up, Becker would immediately snap, "Later!" He was in charge now, so the two young men kept to themselves, the conspicuous quiet making them uneasy. As expected, Jon never said a word, only making hand gestures and occasional nods to acknowledge Becker's instructions. Eric, more than Langer, was afraid of Jon. Eric had killed before in battle, and at first, it had bothered him immensely. Never had he witnessed someone killing at such close range with so much ease and so little conscience about taking a life. To Eric, it was murder. Pure and simple.

Bare winter trees greeted their maroon sedan as it finally approached Indianapolis from the east. The four men, bored after the seven-hundred-mile drive, were more than ready to arrive at their destination. Two days of continuous driving had worn on everyone's nerves. Langer and Eric privately commented to each other the long hours of boredom in the car reminded them of their extended stay on U-313. At least they wouldn't face the same treacherous raft ride once they arrived.

At the same time, many living in the Midwest were facing depression as beautiful October faded and the shorter, cooler days of November dawned. Only two months prior an ample supply of lush, green foliage had covered the countryside and daylight still extended into evening, the sun soon rising again in the morning to welcome early risers.

One month later the much-anticipated cornucopia of yellows, browns, and oranges had begun as leaves commenced their annual death announcement. Mother Nature had spread her enticing display for all to enjoy. The colorful leaves had hung from trees like signs forewarning in the most pleasant of ways what lay ahead in the near future. Winter was preparing to make her grand entrance.

When beautiful October exerted its last, yet stunningly handsome, grasp on the remnants of summer, November snuck in like a reaper stripping trees and other vegetation of its vibrant costume. Radiant blue skies became grayer with each passing day. Winds increased, forcing the remains of stubbornly clinging, dying leaves to the ground in final victory. Residents put away their outdoor furniture, short-sleeved shirts, and bicycles. From their attics, they brought down coats and snow shovels, and outside, they cut firewood. Winter was just around the corner, so they wisely prepared.

Neither Langer or Eric had ever been to Indianapolis. Before the war, however, Lars had attended Butler University on the north side of "Circle City," so named after its original design and thought of by residents as a proud reminder of the famous Indianapolis 500 automobile race held there each May. At Butler, Lars had studied chemistry and done well with the very difficult subject; he was preparing to work as a physician, following in his father's footsteps. Doing so was becoming a family tradition, as his older brother had chosen the same path. He had proclaimed on numerous occasions to the other young agents his admiration for America and the hardworking people who lived there. To a person, the university's faculty and his classmates had made him feel welcome and encouraged his success.

He embraced his time in Indianapolis and, on occasion, entertained the idea of staying and making it his home rather than returning to Germany. In the end, however, he realized his family would never allow it. Germany, the Fatherland, was home and would always remain so. When Germany's hostilities continued to increase, Lars was called home by his father. Tensions in America were building against Germany, and Lars's father was becoming nervous. All young German men were requested, even demanded, to join her fight for supremacy. Lars would have to do his duty. Even if he didn't support Hitler and his aggression, Germany was still his country and he would do whatever was required of him. In May 1939 following completion of his junior year, Lars bade his farewells to his friends and faculty. He boarded a train for New York where a ship waited to take him home. For several weeks afterward he was overcome with melancholy, fearing he would never see Butler or Indianapolis again.

Lars was to be their guide during this all-important mission in the Midwestern city. To Eric's mind, the loss of Lars alone should have been enough reason to call off their mission. But Berlin had spoken—the objective of sabotaging the manufacture of the Norden bombsight was considered too critical to abort. So the mission would go on, even without the valuable knowledge and guidance of Lars.

Becker pulled the sedan over to a small diner on the outskirts of town. He looked back over the seat at Eric and Langer. "Let's stop for a minute. I need to call and get final directions to the house. We're not going to eat here, just order coffee. I want to be on our way in ten minutes."

Langer looked at his watch; it read five minutes after seven. His stomach was growling and would soon need food. He and Eric exchanged looks, both telegraphing their exasperation with the two men in the front seat. They opened their doors and walked up to the diner's entrance with Jon and Becker following close behind.

They chose a booth in the back, far from any activity. No sooner had they sat down than a middle-aged woman chewing gum walked up and pointed to the menus stacked upright by the napkin holder against the window. "Would you gentlemen like a minute, or do ya know what ya want?" She made no effort to smile. She was probably near the end of her shift, Eric thought, and looked exhausted.

"We're just going to have coffee," answered Becker. "I need to use your phone. Where is it?"

The look of disappointment on the waitress's face was clear. No meaningful tip from this table. At least she wouldn't have to do much, and then she could go home in another twenty minutes. She tilted her head back over her shoulder. "It's on the wall by the bathroom."

"Thank you," said Becker. He slid out of the booth and walked toward the phone.

"Do you have any cream?" asked Eric with a smile, trying his best to be polite to the weary waitress.

"It's on the table, hon. So is the sugar, right there by the menus. I'll be back with your coffee." She turned and walked over to the counter, reaching for four large cups.

"I'll be back in a minute," said Eric. Jon looked at him. "Relax, I'm just using the bathroom." Langer let him out, then slid back into his place.

Five minutes later all of them were back in the sedan, their coffees barely touched. Jon took the wheel, at Becker's instructions. Eric and Langer dreaded getting back into the car. They felt trapped in the submarine, then the farmhouse, and now the sedan. Would they encounter the same fate at their next destination? Hopefully not.

As they neared the city, the houses began to group closer together than in the countryside. They were luxurious and large. Eric and Langer were taking in their surroundings as well as they could in the predark hour. Another thirty minutes, and little if anything would be visible.

"Nice neighborhood," commented Eric.

"Indeed," replied Becker. "Berlin believed we would attract less attention if we located ourselves in a more affluent section of the city. Who would suspect German agents to spend so lavishly to set up an outpost?"

"I suppose you're right," said Langer. He couldn't help but notice how much larger the houses were getting.

Finally the car slowed down, hesitated, and then pulled into a narrow lane between two entry-gate masonry posts. The black wrought iron gates were already open. Jon pulled the car forward beyond the reach of the gate, and then Becker held up his hand.

"Stop here," he said. Becker got out of the car and walked back to the gates. He looked up and down the dark, quiet street, and then slowly swung the two black gates shut behind the sedan. He moved the hinge latch downward, then walked back and sat down in the car. He motioned for Jon to continue up to the house.

The lane was nearly a hundred feet long. As they approached the house they saw a man holding a flashlight and standing by a detached garage. It was nearly dark now. He motioned for them to park in the garage. The sedan slowly pulled in. Its taillights dimmed and then extinguished. The man heard four car doors open and then shut. Becker was the first to exit the large garage door behind the sedan. He immediately walked up to the man who was holding the flashlight.

"Ah, Gerald," said Becker, reaching to shake his hand, "it's good to see you."

"And you as well." Gerald took Becker's hand and nearly shook it off from excitement. He was wearing a genuine smile of welcome and of relief that the four men had finally arrived. He quickly looked over at the other three men. "Welcome to Indianapolis, gentlemen. I'm Gerald, your host during your stay here. I'll do everything within my power to make you comfortable." He went to each man and shook his hand with just as much enthusiasm as he had Becker's.

"I could sure use something to eat," said Langer.

"Of course. I had June prepare dinner just in case you hadn't yet eaten. Please, grab your suitcases and let's go inside. It's cold out here."

"Excellent," said Becker. The four men retrieved their suitcases from the trunk and followed Gerald to the side entrance door.

From outside, it was difficult to see many details of the large home in the darkness. Only two small outdoor lights were on, one each over the front and side entrances. Several rooms inside the house had their lights on but their draperies closed, prohibiting any chance to see anything inside. The street in front of the house was quiet. Eric only saw one car pass by.

Gerald opened the side entrance door, which led into a small mudroom. Eric noticed several coats hanging on hooks on the wall, and two pairs of rubber boots on the floor beside a large rug. Gerald turned and addressed the men.

"Hang your jackets in here. I'll take you up to your rooms, then we'll eat."

The four men kicked off their shoes and hung their light jackets on the hooks. With suitcases in hand they followed Gerald into a very spacious and well-equipped kitchen, very professional and businesslike in its layout and appearance. All of its cabinetry was white with glass cabinet doors, displaying all of the beautiful tableware. At one end of the counter, hooks suspended from the ceiling were holding an assortment of steel and copper pots and pans. Eric doubted any fine restaurant was better equipped.

The aroma of beef and kraut was in the air, immediately producing hunger pangs in everyone's stomach. They were starved, and thankful to have a home-cooked meal. They were finally here! In the kitchen was a young woman leaning over the stove and stirring a large pot of kraut. Her back was to them as she kept working. Gerald stopped the men.

"Gentlemen, this is June." She turned around with a large wooden spoon in her hand. "She is our housekeeper and cook. And, I may add, quite a good cook. I've already put on several pounds." He patted his stomach. June smiled as she acknowledged the newcomers.

"Welcome," she said.

"Is dinner about ready?" asked Gerald.

"Yes, ready when you are," answered June.

Becker walked over to the stove and leaned over the pot. "Smells wonderful. I'm sure it's delicious."

June was about to say something when Gerald interrupted. "Of course it's delicious. You'll find out soon enough."

Eric's eyes met June's. "Thank you, June. It will be nice to have something that reminds us of home." June smiled. Eric thought her attractive and wondered for a moment what circumstances had brought her to this house. Then he remembered Mary, and hoped she was somewhere safe.

From the kitchen they entered the dining room through a swinging six-panel door. Again, another large, well-furnished room with a sizable mahogany table and enough chairs to serve ten people. The equally large hutch was well supplied with crystal, blue Willow plates, and more silver than Eric and Langer had ever seen. A very exquisite and ornate chandelier was hanging over the table by a heavy gold chain. Five places were already set at the table. Eric chuckled to himself thinking of their cabins in U-313. He and Langer exchanged a quick look of approval of their new home.

They proceeded through another arched doorway into the living room. The size and opulence of the room nearly took the men's breath away. Walnut, oak, and mahogany furnishings upholstered in fine satins filled the room. Beautifully framed paintings of every possible American genre hung on the walls. Dark-stained beams supported the raised ceiling. The polished oak floors sparkled, and the enormous area rug in the center looked Asian and expensive. A large grand piano sat in the corner, and even a tall, stained glass window at the far end bore some kind of family crest. Eric was in awe! Gerald took great satisfaction at the impact the house was having on the men.

"Quite impressive, isn't it?" asked Gerald.

Eric and Langer just nodded. Jon showed no emotion. Becker did answer, "It's magnificent. I find it hard to believe Berlin would approve of such extravagance."

Gerald smiled. "Yes, you would think so. But, they thought this would be the perfect disguise. And I must admit, I think their idea was brilliant. Not to mention, I receive the benefit of living here, even if for a short while."

"This home surely has a story?" inquired Becker.

"Indeed, it does. It was constructed in 1917 by an industrialist who was manufacturing pistons for the Liberty aircraft engine during the First World War. It made him a very wealthy man. He invested millions in the American stock market and was becoming wealthier every year, that is, until 1929 when he lost everything in the stock market. He lived in the house until 1932 when the housekeeper found him hanging in the garage. His house was going to be seized for unpaid taxes the following week. The rest of the family moved back east to Boston where his wife was originally from."

"Most unfortunate," said Becker.

"It was for *him*, but not for *us*. The home sat unoccupied with most of these furnishings until we purchased it a little over a year ago. These days no one really has any money for such extravagances. And who was going to purchase a house like this when America was involved in two wars? Both the bank and the city were most anxious to have a willing buyer, especially one with cash. The house was acquired for less than half of its original construction cost."

The men continued to gaze at the wonderful home, conjecturing what the walls would say if they could talk. Gerald walked over to the splendid staircase and placed his hand on the carved mahogany railing. "Let me show you to your rooms, then we can eat."

He led the way up the staircase, which ended in a landing with two sitting chairs. Gerald walked past them and stopped by the first room. It was large with one double bed against the opposite wall. He looked at Becker. "I thought you would like this room, as it's closest to the stairway."

Becker nodded approvingly. "Thank you. It will do quite nicely. And much nicer than the farmhouse." He smiled, trying to make a sarcastic, yet humorous comment. He walked in and dropped his suitcase.

"Dinner in ten minutes," reminded Gerald. Then he led the remaining three to the next door down the hallway, opening to a smaller, yet just as lovely bedroom, one containing a simple single bed with a writing desk. "Well, gentlemen?"

"I'll take it," said Langer. "I'll be down in ten minutes."

The next room across the hall was identical to Langer's. "This will do just fine," said Eric. It also had a single bed with a writing desk, as well as a large window facing the front of the house.

"Well, Mr. Kreuger," said Gerald, "it appears you will be staying in the bedroom at the end of the hall." The two men walked down to the last door.

Now Eric knew Jon's last name! Still, not a single word from the man. He was relieved he wouldn't be sharing a room with the killer.

Ten minutes later all the men were standing around the table, doing their best to make small talk. Gerald had opened one of the doors to the large hutch, exposing a well-stocked bar. June had placed a bucket full of ice on top of the hutch and several packs of Lucky Strike cigarettes on one of the hutch's shelves. Eric and Langer each took a pack and then made themselves a cocktail. Langer poured himself a scotch and soda, while Eric had vodka with some ice. Becker decided on a red wine and filled his glass nearly to the brim. Jon had nothing to drink but did light a cigarette. He was quiet and studied his surroundings. Eric could tell he disapproved of the lavishness, in spite of what Berlin thought.

After they seated themselves, June walked in and began to place the food on the table. The men appreciatively gazed at steaming plates of beef and bowls of kraut, a basket of warm biscuits covered with a checkered napkin, and last, a hot apple pie she set down at the far end of the table. Eric could not believe his eyes! When she finished filling the table with the eagerly anticipated food, June looked at Gerald.

"Will there be anything else?" she asked.

"No, my dear. Everything looks fantastic. Thank you so very much. You can clean up in the morning."

"Very well," said June. Before she turned to leave, she glanced at Eric, happy to see a young man for a change. Not many were around during wartime.

Eric studied her for a moment. June was a very attractive young woman in her early twenties. She had a petite build with blonde hair that hung just below her shoulders. She possessed naturally pretty features that needed no makeup. He remembered those large blue-gray eyes from meeting her earlier in the kitchen, eyes that conveyed both warmth and beauty. June showed no awareness of her attractiveness. Yes, she was beautiful in Eric's eyes, a good catch for some lucky man in the future.

Once June had left the dining room and the swinging door had closed behind her, Becker raised his wine glass. "Gentlemen, I'd like to propose a toast to Germany and the final success of this mission."

"I agree," replied Gerald. He and the others all raised their glasses in unison. Jon halfheartedly raised his water glass to join in on the toast.

"Tell me about June," said Becker. He reached for the beef while Gerald helped himself to the kraut. Eric took a biscuit and passed it to Langer.

"Well," started Gerald, "June has been here about four months. She's staying in the small room next to the kitchen. It was originally the servant's quarters, but it's actually quite comfortable." Gerald had everyone's attention while they enjoyed their meal. "Her parents are German born, but June was born here in Indianapolis. She was also raised and educated here, so she fits in naturally. June's a replacement for another housekeeper we brought over from Germany."

"Really?" asked Becker. "What happened there?"

"Gretel was her name. She was quite a bit older, and I was surprised Berlin selected her in the first place. Even though she was efficient at keeping house, she was sometimes ... shall we say ... indiscreet."

"How so?" persisted Becker.

"Perhaps 'careless' would be a better word. I would pick her up from the market and always see her talking to the other women. And here, sometimes I would notice her conversing with the postman, deliveryman, or others. She would always claim it was just small talk. *But,* in our business, small talk is not permitted or prudent amongst strangers. I had warned her on numerous occasions to be careful and to mind her own business. Even an innocent slip-of-the-tongue could spell disaster for our ongoing operations. I, of course, notified Berlin of the potential problem." He paused.

"And?" inquired Becker, wanting to know the conclusion.

Gerald took another sip of his cocktail. "At first they considered the idea of sending her home but then decided against that. After all, would she be bitter and perhaps talk more about her situation? We could not take the risk of her revealing our ambitions here, even if innocently. In the end they decided she would need to be . . . silenced. Here, in America."

Eric was again uncomfortable with the ease in which Berlin would order the death of one of its own loyal countrymen, but not at all surprised. Especially after learning how they wanted to deal with Mary back at the farmhouse. He decided to keep quiet and just listen.

"May I inquire as to how the situation was . . . resolved?" asked Becker.

Gerald looked at all the men around the table. "As I'm sure you can imagine, it's never a pleasant thing to end the life of one of our own countrymen, *especially* a woman. All of us desired a quick and painless method to solve the problem. Each night before Gretel retired to bed, she would have a glass of wine. Berlin sent me something to . . . shall we say . . . prevent her from waking up. It was painless. She fell asleep and never woke up."

"And what of her body?" Langer questioned.

"Does it really matter?" It was obvious Gerald wanted to change the subject.

"And you trust June?" asked the always-cautious Becker.

"Absolutely. She still has family back in Germany, and they hold high positions there working for Herr Goebbels. June's parents are still here and have been useful in providing important information back to Berlin. That, along with Herr Goebbels's endorsement, is good enough for me. She keeps her own counsel, runs the house with even more efficiency than Gretel, and," said Gerald with a smile, "she's much easier on the eyes."

"Very good." Becker seemed satisfied.

After a moment, while the men enjoyed their meal, Gerald put forward a question that had been on his mind since Becker's frantic call a few days earlier. He looked all the men in the eye but settled on Becker. "Tell me," said Gerald, "what happened at the farmhouse? My superiors are most concerned and agitated."

Becker took another sip of his wine before answering, formulating his answer. "Up to now, nothing has gone according to plan, forcing us to adapt very quickly to changing conditions."

"And those would be . . ." probed Gerald.

"Those would be the loss of two men off the submarine, the discovery of one dead agent on the beach wearing a German life vest, and the abrupt attention of the OSS."

"The OSS?" asked Gerald. He was alarmed with that bit of information.

"Yes. Shortly after I spoke to you on the phone, an OSS agent masquerading as someone from the Department of Defense paid us a visit. He was accompanied by a military policeman."

"What happened?" Concern showed in Gerald's voice.

"Unfortunately, we had to eliminate them at the farmhouse."

"That *is* most unfortunate."

"We had no choice," defended Becker as he enjoyed his wine. He reached for the bottle and refilled his glass. "They were obviously onto us, so we had to do something. We had no time and no other option. We did what we had to do."

"I see." Gerald looked around the table and could see by the looks on the other men's faces Becker was giving an accurate account of the events. "And what of the two dead Americans?"

"It really doesn't matter now, does it?" Becker repaid Gerald's evasive comment a few minutes earlier regarding Gretel.

"No, I guess not." Touché, Gerald had to quietly admit to himself.

Langer joined the conversation. "Excuse me, but is it too much to ask that we discuss Berlin's orders? After all, that's why we're all here."

Everyone, including Jon, at that moment stopped eating and gaped at Langer for abruptly bringing up the elephant in the room.

"But of course, you're right," answered Gerald. "I was under the impression you were in receipt of Berlin's recent orders."

"That is correct," said Becker. "But, as our situation had become so volatile, we hardly had time to discuss them in detail."

"No matter," said Gerald in a nonchalant tone. "The orders have changed yet again."

All of the men were stunned, with Langer and Eric exchanging looks of disbelief.

"You must be joking," accused Becker, not at all finding Gerald's statement humorous.

"I'm afraid not. I received new instructions just this morning."

Becker wanted to protest, but knew it was fruitless to do so. Langer and Eric shared feelings of anger and more frustration with yet another alteration.

"And what is it Berlin wants us to do now? Blow up the entire Norden manufacturing facility?" Becker asked with intended mockery in his voice.

Gerald paused, realizing the eyes of the four men were focused on him. They could hardly contain their anticipation about what he was going to reveal. "Nearly."

"What do you mean, nearly?" inquired Eric. Becker shot him a glare—keep quiet!

"I mean damage the production facility for the Norden sight," explained Gerald.

"Isn't it enough to steal their engineering drawings and one of the devices?" asked Langer.

"Apparently not," answered Gerald. "They want us to do more significant damage to the manufacturing process instead. Herr Goering, in particular, has changed his position on the value of obtaining one of the devices. That alone will not relieve the Fatherland of the damage these evil things are doing. Even the over-confident Goering knows the Americans are winning the war, espe-cially in the air. The Luftwaffe is enjoying limited success at best and cannot shoot down enough of the American bombers. The Fuhrer is placing more pressure on him to achieve some meaningful results, and quickly. Stealing a copy of the engineering drawings and perhaps one of the devices will not stop the bombing." Gerald paused, allowing the news to sink in.

"And sabotaging the manufacturing facility will?" asked Langer.

"I understand the point you are making. Truly, I do. We all realize how America's manufacturing prowess is the true enemy. It would appear there is no end to how many planes, tanks, and bombs they can produce. While they continue to bomb our cities, destroying our valuable production capabilities, America has borne no such destruction. Their production continues on, stronger and stronger. Goering wants the production of the Norden sights stopped, even if for a brief period."

"How can that possibly help Germany now?" inquired Becker.

Gerald sighed, "Goering firmly believes a brief pause, or at least a temporary slowdown in the accuracy of the bombing, will allow him time to build up the Luftwaffe's former strength and power. The stronger the Luftwaffe, the more Germany will be protected."

Becker set down his glass and looked directly at Gerald, then the other men. "Forgive me, but this just doesn't make sense. My understanding from the beginning was this mission's objective was to obtain the drawings so we could begin producing our own accurate sights, for when we begin bombing America."

"Let's not be naive, gentlemen," said Gerald. "There is *no* hope of Germany bombing America . . . or even England again . . . ever. The war has not progressed as the Fuhrer has planned. On the contrary, it's just the opposite. Failure in Russia and now the nonstop American and British bombing has robbed Germany of the capabilities the Wehrmacht once enjoyed. We no longer have the resources to be the aggressors. Although too many in Berlin refuse to believe this simple fact, there are a growing number who realize we are now the defenders, not the pursuers. The best we can do now is to hold on until our enemies tire of losing their sons on European soil, and then hope for acceptable terms in a peace pact." He could see the unsettling news had dampened their enthusiasm.

Eric decided to bring up the obvious, yet still unmentioned, problem. "Does anyone in Berlin realize we spent a year preparing for a completely different mission? Langer and I have not trained for this. The odds of succeeding at this point seem nearly impossible."

"You may very well be correct," replied Gerald, "but Berlin sees it differently."

"So how much time do we have to prepare?" asked Langer.

"That is another problem," answered Gerald.

"I'm almost afraid to ask," said Langer.

"Berlin wants this completed on Christmas Day."

"Christmas Day?" replied Becker. "They can't be serious, that's just five weeks away."

"I am serious. And more to the point, so is Berlin. Especially Goering."

"Let me make sure I understand this correctly," interrupted Eric. "Four of us planned for a year to obtain a copy of the Norden sight along with a copy of its drawings. Berlin gave us six months to accomplish this already difficult, if not impossible, task once we arrived. We lose Kurt and Lars before we even get started. They reassign Mr. Becker and Jon here to become part of our team, even though we've not trained with them and have no idea what their particular skills are. We're discovered at the farmhouse, kill two Americans in order to escape, make it safely by some miracle to Indianapolis, and now they redirect our orders to something entirely different. Something we've not spent one day training or planning for. And rather than six months, we have roughly five weeks to get all of this accomplished. Is that about right?"

Eric's brief synopsis of the situation concisely revealed the full impact of their dilemma. The five men, although all extremely capable, were summarizing in their own minds the effect of Berlin's latest directive. Becker took the now nearly empty bottle of cabernet and poured the last of the wine into his glass. Langer stared ahead, lost in his own thoughts. Jon continued eating as though he had heard none of Eric's words.

After a moment of reflection Gerald broke the silence. "Yes, Mr. Keller. I would say you have summed up the situation well."

"Are we to assume Mr. Becker is still in charge or has there been a change there as well?" continued Eric.

"Mr. Becker and I will be in charge cooperatively. He is still in charge of your team. But here in Indianapolis I have the ultimate responsibility to see this through. Berlin believed, and rightly so in my judgment, that I am most familiar with the surroundings of the city and the plant where the bombsight is manufactured. It only makes good sense that I direct the strategy, leaving Mr. Becker to work out the details of how it gets accomplished."

"And what of *us,* if and when, and I emphasize *if,* we succeed?" asked Langer.

"There is no change from the original plan. We have agents who will meet you in Canada. From there you will receive new identity papers, then make your way to Halifax, and then home when the time is right." Langer seemed satisfied for the moment.

"Why Christmas Day?" Becker asked.

"For very good reason, actually. American plants are running around the clock to keep their military supplied and, for the most part, have done an excellent job. There are very few instances when plants are idle, the best time to conduct our operation. Christmas Day is one of those days, perhaps the best day for us to complete our task. The plant will be shut down that day, as workers will be home with their families enjoying the holiday. The fewer the people, the higher our chance of success."

The four men had to agree, that part did make sense. Becker was nodding.

"Gentlemen," said Gerald, attempting to put a positive face on their circumstances, "this can and will work. For more than a year we have been studying the Lucas-Harold company. We know the workings of their facility as well as, if not better than, they do. We know their key personnel, schedules, and more importantly, their weaknesses. It is true Berlin has made our job more difficult. But not impossible. I'm convinced we can make a significant impact at the plant, and escape with our lives."

"All right," said Becker, "assuming for the moment this plan has a chance, may I inquire as to how you were able to gain all of this information?"

Gerald smiled. "Of course. We have two agents who are employees at the company. One is highly positioned, and the other is a maintenance supervisor. They have been employed there for almost two years and have been a great resource for us. It is because of them Berlin believes we can quickly adapt to this variation. We will have full access."

"How will we have access?" asked Eric. "We're not employed there."

"Not now," answered Gerald, "but you will be."

"Please explain," said Langer.

"There are two maintenance crews working in twelve-hour shifts. Each shift has two men, one a supervisor. The individual working with our agent-supervisor is going to have an accident, opening up that position. There is an obvious shortage of qualified men, as most of them are serving in the military. Our agent is going to recommend an acquaintance for the job, someone who has recently moved to Indianapolis and is looking for work. That is you, Mr. Keller." Before Eric could respond, Gerald continued. "We prepared all the necessary paperwork for your employment prior to your arrival. The original orders had you infiltrating the plant as an employee, so this should come as no surprise."

"Yes, but I understood I was going to be on the line, not in maintenance."

Gerald nodded. "That's true, but this positions you much better for what the new instructions entail. With our agent-supervisor, you will have full access to every location within the plant. Maintenance personnel are, for the most part, invisible to everyone else working there. Workers are accustomed to seeing these workers without really *noticing* them. It is the perfect disguise."

"You said the current employee is going to have an accident. What did you mean by that?" Eric feared he knew the answer before he asked it.

Gerald looked at Jon. "I understand Mr. Kreuger has special skills in that department. Within three days from now, Mr. Kreuger will formulate and then carry out a situation where this worker will no longer be able to work. Whatever that may be."

"Wait a minute," interceded Eric, "what exactly do you mean? If that involves killing an innocent person, I must protest."

Becker looked at Eric with disdain. "Again, Mr. Keller, some innocents will need to suffer. Do I need to go over this one more time?"

Gerald was unaware of the argument Becker and Eric had engaged in at the farmhouse regarding Mary. "I'm obviously missing something. What's the problem?"

"The problem, Gerald, is Mr. Keller appears to value the lives of innocent Americans more than those of Germany."

"That's not what I mean, and you know it," replied Eric. "I understand the necessity of making this position available, but why does the poor man need to give his life for it? Doesn't he have a family? What about them? Have we become so ruthless and unfeeling that we now resort to needlessly taking lives when other options may work just as well?"

Becker was about to scold Eric once again when Gerald jumped in, showing a degree of sympathy for Eric's point. "Perhaps you are right. A death would certainly draw more attention." He looked at Jon. "Is it possible to fabricate an accident that will render this man unable to work without doing him permanent harm?"

All eyes focused on Jon. He continued chewing his food, totally unaffected with his new task. Without saying a word, he simply raised his eyebrows and nodded. Eric believed he was disappointed he wouldn't have another opportunity to use his knife or perhaps put a bullet into the head of another American.

"Very well," said Gerald, "that's resolved. I have a file on the maintenance employee illustrating in great detail his duties, family, where he lives, habits, etcetera. This should help you, Mr. Kreuger." Again, Jon nodded with no emotion.

"And what about me?" asked Langer.

"You and Mr. Becker are Canadian executives, visiting to replicate some of the manufacturing processes for your own new plant near Montreal. We have gone to a lot of effort with our other agent at Lucas-Harold to position both of you as respected and successful Canadian businessmen. You are expected next week, and the arrangements have all been made. Our Canadian agents have done a remarkable job providing a background paper trail that will fool even the most cautious of company security guards."

"What position does the other agent hold at Lucas-Harold?" asked Langer.

"He is the plant manager," answered Gerald, "a very high position in the company. And one that will not draw suspicion when he escorts two Canadian executives around the plant."

"Very thorough," stated Becker. "Once we're in, what are our instructions?"

"As businessmen you will naturally carry briefcases, a perfect transport for explosives. On Christmas Eve you will pay your last visit to Lucas-Harold and leave your briefcases at strategic places within the plant during your final tour. Timers will be set for early in the morning on Christmas Day." Gerald then looked over at Eric. "You will appreciate the timing of the explosives, as it will minimize innocent casualties." Eric nodded his approval.

"But won't that raise suspicion if we bring briefcases in and leave without them?" asked Becker.

"It would, yes, but our man inside will have duplicate briefcases there. You will take the copies and leave with those in hand. It will appear you left with the same cases you walked in with."

There was silence for a moment while each man contemplated the plan and their odds for succeeding. Becker downed the last of the wine in his glass, regretting the bottle's demise.

"It may just work," concluded Becker.

"Of course it will work," answered Gerald. "*If* we all do our jobs."

"Don't worry about us doing our jobs. You've done yours up to this point, and you can certainly depend on us." Becker glanced around the table, conveying his newly found confidence with the most recent instructions.

"So when do we leave Indianapolis?" asked Langer.

"Christmas Eve. We leave in two cars immediately after everyone returns from the plant. If anyone asks, we're just traveling to be with our families for the holiday. Each car will take a different route, which I've already planned out. We'll cross the Canadian border at different locations, and then meet up with our contacts there. Eventually all of us will leave from Halifax."

"And what of June?" asked Eric. Although he didn't look at Becker, he could feel his glare from across the table.

"Very simple. June will return to her family and continue her university work. Before this assignment, she was quite the student at Indiana University. June was studying music, and I believe she's anxious to return to her studies. She's entirely too valuable to us here to take with us. She'll lay low for a while but remain an asset should the need arise." Eric was relieved.

Gerald rose from the table and addressed the men. "I'm sure you're exhausted from your long trip. I suggest we all get a good night's sleep and meet tomorrow around ten to review some of the other details. You have plenty to think about for now. Please help yourself to the kitchen or anything else you need. Your visit here will be short, so make it comfortable. I'm very happy to have all of you here." He turned and disappeared up the staircase.

"Well," said Langer, "tomorrow it begins."

CHAPTER 5

JUNE

Eric stirred as the sun began to shine through his bedroom window. Following a wonderful meal the night before accompanied by two vodkas, he slept like a baby. The only sound in the bedroom was the ticking of the gold clock on the nightstand. He saw it was already half past eight and could not remember the last time he had slept past six.

The house was extremely quiet. Even with his door closed, Eric thought sure he would hear the others up and around, but he could not hear a sound. He sat up and lingered on the edge of the bed. He desperately wanted a bath and a fresh change of clothes; the last one he had taken was at the farmhouse several days ago. Not only would it make him feel better, but there was now an attractive female in the house—the thing he least wanted to do was offend her senses. He walked over and peeked out the window. The ground was white with frost. The trees limbs were exposed, their fallen leaves frozen like miniature statues scattered on the crisp lawn. He grabbed the toiletries from his suitcase and walked to the bathroom.

Twenty minutes later Eric felt like a new man. The hot bath and clean clothes were just what the doctor ordered! Now his stomach was demanding coffee and eggs. He walked down the stairs and entered the living room. It was empty, which he thought odd. Strolling through the dining room, he heard noises in the kitchen. He pushed open the swinging door, and there stood June, at the sink rinsing some dishes.

"Good morning," she said with a bright smile.

"Good morning." He thought she was actually happy to see him.

"The others have already eaten. May I make you something?" She took the towel and wiped her hands.

"How about some coffee, for starters. Then toast and a couple of eggs would be wonderful."

"Sure. Just have a seat." June took one of the coffee cups from the cupboard and filled it with coffee. She walked over and set it down in front of him. "Sugar's on the table. Do you like cream?"

"No, just black."

"How do you like your eggs?"

"Scrambled. Any chance you have some cheese?"

"Of course," June smiled.

"Perfect."

June went to the refrigerator and removed the carton of eggs and a small plate of butter. She set them by the stove. She reached for the cooking pan hanging from one of the hooks. "How many eggs?"

"Two."

"The paper's there if you'd like to read it. Supposed to be sunny all day." June turned on the burner and struck a match. The small rush of combustion could be heard throughout the kitchen. She sliced off a small section of butter and banged the knife on the edge of the pan. The butter immediately began to sizzle. She took the bread from the box on the counter and sliced off one healthy section and placed it in the toaster. She broke the two eggs and began scrambling them with a wood spoon. "Should only be a minute."

"No rush, I think I can make it," kidded Eric.

He opened the paper. The first article that caught his attention was a story about Allied bombers wreaking havoc on Berlin the day before. More than seven hundred British planes had participated. Authorities believed it to be the largest air raid of the war and in all of history. Berlin suffered the consequences. Thousands were killed, mostly civilians. Dozens of buildings were destroyed, including some all-important manufacturing facilities. Mostly, though, residential dwellings took the brunt of the damage. Few bombers had been lost.

Perhaps Goering and Gerald were correct. Was it really conceivable that Germany had overreached? Had their role really changed to that of defenders? If so, it would appear even as protectors of their own country, the German military was failing, and failing miserably. He read two more paragraphs before he could bear to read no further. He began to contemplate the destruction his countrymen were suffering. How was Germany going to turn the tide? Was it even possible to reclaim its once dominant military prominence? Eric had to admit Gerald may be right.

"Why the long face?" asked June. She warmed up his coffee, and then stirred the eggs to keep them from burning. The aroma of toast and eggs began to fill the kitchen.

"The news doesn't do much to spur on our hopes, does it?" Eric flipped to another page, doing his best to hide his disappointment with the words in the paper.

June placed two small bowls of jam on the table, strawberry and apricot. "Remember, it's an American paper. There's a lot of propaganda in there. I'm sure they do the same thing in Germany."

Eric looked up at June's smiling face. "You're probably right. Sorry for being so sour. It smells delicious in here."

"Thank you. It's just about done."

Eric decided to put down the paper and study June while enjoying his coffee. She dished up the toast and eggs and put them on a plate for him. "Where are the others?"

June placed the plate in front of Eric. "Let's see. Jon was up first. He didn't want anything to eat, then left without saying anything. He's a strange one. He left in your car with a file of papers. Then Mr. Kahn, Mr. Becker, and Mr. Langer were down about an hour later. They had some ham and eggs, and then drove off in Mr. Kahn's car.

They also had some papers with them. No idea where they went. Mr. Kahn just said they'd be back before lunch, and to let you sleep."

"That was good of him. Gerald's last name is Kahn?"

"Yes. Considering my position as housekeeper, he thought calling him Gerald was *too informal* for me." She rolled her eyes, kidding with Eric.

"By all means, you are obviously the dredge of society and probably shouldn't address him at all." He kidded her back. "Can you sit down a minute? I hate to eat by myself."

"Um, sure. Why not?" She took a clean cup from the counter and poured it half full of coffee. She walked over as Eric began to devour the eggs and sat down directly across from him. She was now studying him, noticing the pace at which he was consuming his breakfast. "Didn't they feed you before you got here?"

Eric stopped chewing and swallowed. "Sorry. I guess that's what happens when you're only around men for a year or so. Having a woman to share a meal with is a pleasant change. Hope you don't mind." He deliberately slowed down and began practicing the table manners he had grown up with. June noticed.

"Not at all." She sat back in the chair and began to relax, enjoying the company of a young, good-looking man.

"Are you at liberty to tell me a little bit about yourself?" Eric had not received any specific instructions to keep his distance from June. He was going to take advantage of that possible oversight and enjoy her company. At least for the moment.

June took another sip of her coffee, weighing just how much she should say. He would soon be leaving for Germany, so there was probably no harm in some meaningless small talk. "What would you like to know?"

"Gerald tells me you studied music at the local university."

"That's true, but I haven't attended any classes for over a year now. They called me for this job, and to refuse would not have been wise. I'll pick them back up when this is over."

Eric decided to ignore the "unwise" part of her statement and keep the conversation light. "What did you play?"

"The violin. Both my mother and father play, so I guess it was in my destiny to become a violinist."

"No kidding. Do they play professionally?" The eggs were gone, and now Eric was wiping up what little remained of them on the plate with his toast, relishing every bite.

"Yes. In Germany they played in the Berlin Orchestra for two years after they graduated. They were good, from what I understand."

"They must have been awfully young when they came here."

"I think so. They don't talk about it much. All I know is they quit playing professionally when they came to America."

"Well," concluded Eric, "if they're good enough to play in Berlin, they're good enough to play in any orchestra here."

June smiled. "It's good of you to say that. I keep telling them the same thing. But, they insist the professional part of their musical lives is behind them. It's a shame really. But who knows, they could go back if the conditions were right."

"For their sakes, I hope that happens."

June nodded. "Me too."

After a moment of silence and their continued study of one another, June decided it was her turn. "What about you? Is it against the rules to tell me a little about yourself?"

Eric shrugged his shoulders. "I don't think so. My story is pretty boring. I'm sure you don't want me to put you to sleep."

"Try me," said June.

Eric took a deep breath, wondering where to begin and how much to tell. "I was born in Remseck, a small farming village not too far from Stuttgart. Our farm has been in my family for generations. I have two older brothers and no sisters. My mother still lives there, but my father died when I was ten. If it hadn't been for my brothers, we would have lost the farm. My mother did the best she could to raise us. I never enjoyed farming, but I loved books, mainly about travel and faraway places. I wanted to see the world. That seemed romantic and exciting! I got a taste of America on a study-abroad trip I was selected for, where I briefly lived with a family in upstate New York on the Canadian border."

"Sounds like you got your wish."

"In a way, but I hoped for more. When Germany began asking for men, I joined the army, knowing it would get me out of Remseck. My mother wasn't too happy, but she gave me her blessing just the same. She knew I wasn't cut out for farming."

"Did your brothers join too?"

"Hans did, but the oldest didn't. He permanently injured a leg in a farming accident. He needs a cane to walk, so the army told him to stay on the farm and help my mother. It's just as well because she wouldn't be able to manage by herself."

"What will you do when the war is over?" asked June.

"Really haven't thought about it that much. Settle down back in Germany, I suppose. I can assure you it won't be in Remseck though. What about you?"

"Well, I know my parents would like to go back at some point. Not right away, maybe after things settle down a bit. They would want me to go with them. But I'm not sure."

"Really?"

June nodded. "I was born here. Even though I'm German this has always been my home. My studies are here. My friends are here. There's really not much for me in Germany. I'd be starting over. Not sure I want to do that."

Eric was surprised with her candor and sincerity. "I think I can understand that. How would your parents feel if you didn't go back with them?

"Much the same as your mother when you left the farm. Not thrilled, but in the end they'd let me do what I want. They want me to be happy."

"Good for them," agreed Eric. He decided to change the topic. "Can you share how you came to know Gerald?"

June paused, then stood up and took Eric's plate. "I'm not supposed to talk about that."

Eric realized he had crossed the line and regretted it. "I'm sorry. Didn't mean to push you, I was just curious."

She smiled, and then rinsed the plate in the sink. "It's OK. I'm only here temporarily. I'll follow my orders, then hopefully get back to my studies."

"I hope so too." Eric stood, realizing their conversation had come to an end. "Thanks, June."

"For what?" June asked with an inquisitive expression.

"For sitting with me and for the great breakfast."

"You're welcome. I enjoyed it too."

Eric had opened the swinging door to leave when June caught him. "Oh, Mr. Kahn left something for you on the dining room table. He said to start studying it."

"Thanks," said Eric.

He saw the manila envelope on the table with "Keller" handwritten across the top. After picking it up, he undid the clasp and pulled out two dozen sheets of paper, most of them typed. Also included were several floor drawings of a large building. The name Lucas-Harold was written on them. It was time for homework.

Eric chose one of the comfortable-looking chairs in the living room. He began studying the contents of the envelope. Among other things, it contained a variety of American identity papers: a driver's license, birth certificate, and a medical report showing him as 4-F, a designation rendering him exempt from American military service due to a physical or mental disability; in his case, curvature of the spine. Definitely 4-F. He continued to read and was impressed at the detail which had been fabricated about his fictitious life. Fortunately his name remained Eric Keller. At least there was one piece of information that wouldn't be difficult to remember.

Although many items relating to his new background remained the same from training, some had changed. The new Eric Keller was from Omaha, Nebraska. He had been working in maintenance for a small food-processing plant when he left for better opportunities in Indianapolis. He is now staying with a friend until he secures a new job. His mother and father were killed in an automobile accident when he was a child, and he has no other living relatives. He is on his own. There is no one alive in America to either verify or dispute his identity.

As Eric continued scanning the documents, he even saw a high school diploma from Omaha Central High School, along with attached grade cards from his junior and senior years. His grades were mostly Bs and Cs—not quite good enough to get into college, yet worthy of a responsible job in building maintenance. Gerald, and whoever had helped him, were thorough. There were even three positive job performance reviews in the file. Impressive, he thought. Nice touch.

The floor drawings of Lucas-Harold were detailed, with critical points of possible disruption highlighted. Also on the drawings were areas marked with a red "X," which Eric assumed were locations where explosives were to be placed.

There were schedules of production shifts, names of supervisors, security details, and even noted times of preventive maintenance on the machines that produced components of the Norden bombsight. Page after page. Finally there were a half-dozen photographs. Several were of the exterior of Lucas-Harold, but most showed the interior and specifically the production line. The last photograph was of a man about forty. Near the bottom of the black-and-white photo was his name and title written in pencil: James Redding-Maintenance Supervisor. Eric assumed, rightly so, that this was to be his contact and supervisor in the plant.

Eric had known some of this information beforehand during their training, but nothing to this level of detail. He would need to learn all of it. And it would take time. He decided to start with the first page and continue through the documents one at a time until everything was second nature to him. If someone had gone to this much effort to gather this information, then he was going to put forth the effort to learn it.

Forty minutes later June walked in from the kitchen with a small hand cloth and began dusting the large dining room table. Eric set down the papers he was studying, needing to take a short break.

"Is it always this quiet?" he asked.

"Almost," answered June, as she moved to the beautiful mahogany hutch and continued to clean. "Sometimes Mr. Kahn will be gone for days. Then it's just me in this big house. It seems such a waste to have all this room and no one using it."

"I know what you mean. Just the same, I'm enjoying the elbow room after my last address."

"Not quite this luxurious?"

"Not even close."

June noticed the stack of papers in Eric's lap. "I'm sorry, I didn't mean to disturb you. I'll go work upstairs."

"It's all right, I needed a break anyway."

Suddenly hearing car doors slamming shut, she turned her head toward the kitchen. "I think someone just pulled up." She walked over to the kitchen door, pushed it open, and saw through the window it was Gerald's car. "It's Mr. Kahn and the others. I'm sure they'll want to talk to you. I'll head upstairs so you can have some privacy." Without waiting for an answer, she excused herself with a bow of her head and made her way up the stairs with her cleaning supplies, just as Gerald, Langer, and Becker walked in.

"Ah, it's good to see you up. Did June make you breakfast?" asked Gerald.

"Yes, and it was delicious. You were right about her cooking."

"Did you have a nice conversation with her?" asked Becker in the same contentious tone he had used to confront him regarding Mary back at the farmhouse.

"Relax, she just made me breakfast. That's all." Eric wanted to avoid placing June in any position of suspicion whatsoever.

"I'll be down in a minute," said Langer. "I'm just going to grab my folder." He walked up the stairs, leaving the other three alone in the living room.

Gerald picked up a few of the documents Eric had placed on the table. "So, what do you think of our preparations?"

"I have to say, they're impressive," answered Eric. "The background we had in training was very good, but nothing compared to this."

Gerald smiled. "I'll take that as a compliment. Do you see anything that will cause you difficulty?"

"No. I should have most of this down in a day or so."

"Very good. You'll need to be ready for your new position at Lucas-Harold very soon."

"Oh?"

"Yes, I believe so. Mr. Becker informs me your friend Kreuger has always been . . . shall we say . . . *expedient* when carrying out his orders. If that proves to indeed be the case, then I expect within the next day or so the position at the plant will become available. Then you will have your opportunity to step in and begin your part of the mission. You must be ready."

"Jon is not my friend," Eric corrected. "He is only a member of our team. And I have no doubt he will quickly carry out his orders. I only hope he is not too zealous in completing his task." He shot Becker a knowing look. "Don't worry, I'll be ready."

Puzzled, Gerald glanced first at Becker and then back at Eric. "I'm not sure what you mean, but I trust you agree the end result will be to our advantage."

Eric nodded. "Of course. I'm as anxious to get started as anyone."

"All of us are," added Becker.

Just then Langer returned from his room with a similar envelope, noticing an awkward moment of silence. "Did I miss something?"

"No, nothing," answered Becker. "Now that you're here, let's get to work. Jon will be back soon, he can catch up later."

✠

As a group the four men spent the next few hours reviewing all the documents in each man's folder. Gerald believed it absolutely imperative each member of the team know the others' roles. He continually probed Becker, Langer, and Eric for their thoughts and, more importantly, asked them if there was any item of the plan that could be improved. There were a few minor suggestions, which were adopted. For the most part, however, the plan Berlin and Gerald had laid out was brilliant. All of them were beginning to believe their chances of success were good.

It wasn't long before Eric realized he had the easier of the four tasks. Even though he would be responsible for laying four timed charges along the assembly line in strategic locations, at least he did not have to impersonate Canadian businessmen. In his mind that would be the most difficult part of the mission. Any misstep whatsoever would jeopardize and perhaps doom their efforts. Jon's mission was both simple and clear—interfere with the current maintenance man so he would not be able to work, by whatever means necessary. After that Jon's mission was to provide any security required during their brief stay in Indianapolis. Eric secretly wondered if silencing June when the mission was concluded was part of his duties.

Around two o'clock Gerald suggested they take a break for a few hours. "I'm hungry, how about the rest of you?"

"Yes, I'm starved," replied Becker. He immediately rose from the chair to stretch.

"I'll ask June to make us some sandwiches." Gerald walked through the dining room and peeked his head into the kitchen, holding the swinging door open. "June, can we see you for a minute? I think we'd all like something to eat."

Gerald returned to the living room with June close behind. As always, June was accommodating, with a genuine happiness about her that all the men appreciated.

"Yes, gentlemen. What would you like?"

Gerald spoke first. "If we have any of that ham left, I'd love a ham sandwich with some pickles."

Becker looked at Gerald as though he had just requested liver. "I'll take the same . . . only without the pickles."

"Same here," said Langer.

Eric was thinking, wanting to order something different, even though a ham sandwich sounded delicious.

"And you, Mr. Keller?" asked June.

"Ham sounds good, but I don't suppose you have any soup, do you?"

June nodded and smiled. "Well, yes we do. I'm sure we have some vegetable soup still in the refrigerator. Would you like a sandwich to go along with it?"

"No thanks, soup is fine."

"I think I'll have some for myself after you're finished, if that's all right with you, Mr. Kahn." June was still looking at Eric, which the others noticed.

"Of course. We'll have it in the dining room."

"I'll have it ready in ten minutes." June turned and walked back to the kitchen, the men hearing the sound of the swinging door behind her.

Jon had driven the route between Lucas-Harold and the home of maintenance man Doug Fuller three times now. Jon had risen very early that morning with the purpose of arriving at Fuller's home before he left for work. Even though Gerald had marked out the exact route Fuller took each morning, Jon wanted to verify the information and then formulate his own plan accordingly.

At 6:45, however, a different car pulled up in front of Fuller's home and beeped the horn. The car, dull green in color with black rims, was nearly frosted over. Scrape marks to remove the frost could be seen on the rear windshield and side windows. Jon doubted they provided much visibility. White exhaust fumes began to envelope the back of the car. Jon could only see it was a man wearing a baseball cap behind the wheel. After a few seconds another young man opened the front door of the small bungalow house, and then kissed a plump young woman good-bye as she handed him a black lunch pail and large thermos. Jon compared the man coming down the walk to the photo in the file. It was Fuller.

Fuller trotted down to the car and got in, exchanging some type of pleasantries with the driver before the car drove off. Jon could see the woman in the doorway wave as the car began to fade in the distance. Car pool. This was a new wrinkle that suddenly made Jon's assignment more difficult. Now it would be two men involved in an unfortunate accident, not just Fuller. Jon silently cursed Eric and his do-good comment about not needing to eliminate Fuller once and for all his way. A quick bullet to Fuller's head, or perhaps a six-inch blade in the neck would be so much faster and require less effort and planning. And, to Jon's disappointment, deprive him of the pleasure of taking another American's life up close and personal. His dislike for Eric was growing.

Once the car reached a safe distance, Jon pulled out from his spot a hundred feet down the street from the bungalow and began to follow Fuller's car. They did indeed follow the route Gerald had marked out. There was little traffic, allowing Jon to easily trail their car while maintaining a safe distance with little interference from other vehicles. Neither occupant in the car ahead had any idea they were being followed. Fifteen minutes later, Fuller's car pulled into the driveway of Lucas-Harold. Jon slowed down and drove past, noticing the armed guard at the gate checking their IDs. Then their car proceeded through and toward the large parking lot.

Satisfied with the route, Jon drove it several times, making frequent stops at locations he deemed most likely to result in a serious accident. A place where investigators would immediately conclude a driver had become distracted and lost control. A place that would not raise too many suspicious questions of foul play. An accident that would result in great harm, if not death, to the unfortunate driver, or in this case, driver and occupant. A place where he could force an accident yet escape himself.

During his third drive of the route, Jon made his decision. After more than a dozen stops along the route to surveil different surroundings, he selected a location. It was perfect. It was five minutes into the drive to the plant—a fairly sharp curve heading down a rather steep hill, and then a sharp embankment ending at a fast-moving creek of cold, muddy water. There were numerous trees, which would hide the car from view to passersby. Jon figured the car would roll at least once before entering the creek. Yes, there would be no way to avoid serious injury, thus rendering Fuller and his unfortunate carpooler incapable of work. And if the poor occupants broke their necks, or perhaps even drowned, well, that's war. And all is fair in war. At least it was in Jon's mind.

＋

The four men had just finished their late lunch when June began clearing the table, holding their plates in each hand. As she walked through the swinging door into the kitchen she looked up to see Jon standing there, staring at her. It not only startled her but gave June a very unsettling feeling. She managed to force a smile.

"May I make you some lunch? The others just finished eating."

Jon did not answer and walked past her into the dining room where the men were still talking. All of the small talk immediately stopped when Jon entered the room. He looked at Becker and motioned with his eyes they needed to talk.

Becker rose from his chair. "Will you please excuse me?"

"Of course," answered Gerald. He then shot Eric and Langer a puzzled look.

Jon led Becker back through the kitchen, brushing past June. They stepped outside, and Becker closed the door behind them where they stood under the small awning. June looked up and could see their breaths in the frosty air but could not hear what was being said. Whatever it was, she could tell it was serious. Jon was obviously unhappy about something and was making his displeasure known to Becker. For his part, Becker was raising his arms attempting to reason with Jon, seemingly with little effect. She could hear Becker's voice continuing to raise in volume, still unable to determine what he was saying. Now she was sure Becker was angry. June tried to keep her eyes on the sink and the dishes she was washing, but the tone of Becker's voice and the apparent level of agitation was drawing both her attention and concern.

All of this was making June nervous. She was having second thoughts now on accepting this assignment, an assignment she didn't want in the first place. Her alarm bells began going off, signaling she could actually be in danger. She really wasn't even a spy, she was the daughter of spies. Her mother and father were the loyal Germans, not her. She considered herself an American. Her parents, on the other hand, had readily agreed to provide whatever information they could to their family back in Germany. They were doing their part for the Fatherland. Even though most of the information they furnished regarding America in the Midwest was useless in the eyes of German intelligence, they were convinced their efforts were making a difference.

June was taken into her parents' confidence and kept abreast of their spying activities once she reached the age of sixteen. At first she was shocked, and then angry. She felt they were betraying the America she loved, the America that had treated all of them so well, the America she called home. In her eyes they were all Americans now, not Germans.

She was quickly corrected on that line of thinking. The "reeducation" of June occurred at the dinner table each evening over a meal. It began harmlessly at first. Her mother and father began sharing their loyalist views. Germany was superior in every respect over every other country in the world. America was "second rate" compared to the Fatherland. France and Great Britain were mortal enemies, sworn to Germany's destruction at any cost. They defended the Fuhrer's aggressive attacks on Germany's neighbors. They believed Hitler was more than justified in his actions.

At first June could not believe what her parents were saying. She had read the American papers. She listened to her professors and other students. Her educated friends spoke about Hitler and the evil and needless violence he was spreading across Europe. He was leaving nothing but death and destruction in his path. He was destroying Germany. Why couldn't her parents see that?

In spite of June's fondness for America, they wanted to get her involved on Germany's behalf. Perhaps she could learn something useful from her comings and goings at the university. Even small details of everyday American movements were important, insisted her parents. June resisted at first, claiming she loved America. It was the only home she knew. She was happy in America and wanted to make her home here after the war. Her parents warned her more than once not to become too attached to Americans and their way of life. Americans were overindulgent and tolerated inferior races, more specifically Jews and Blacks. June reluctantly provided tidbits of intentionally useless information here and there. She was not going to betray "her" country.

Then six months ago a high-ranking official in German intelligence via a courier contacted June's parents. They were told about Gerald Kahn. He was a very important man and was heading up an extremely vital and secret mission right there in Indianapolis. The mission's success would save German lives, perhaps thousands of them. June's parents were both thrilled and honored they were asked to contribute to the cause. Mr. Kahn would be in touch with them soon.

Gerald called on June's parents a few days later about assisting him in purchasing a house on behalf of German intelligence, a house to be used in the upcoming operation. He would need a house located in an affluent section of the city, somewhere off the beaten path. A house where no one would dare suspect the enemy was conducting operations. And, he needed it soon.

June's parents spent nearly every waking hour investigating different areas of the city that fit Mr. Kahn's requirements. They would not fail. After two weeks they located the house where the four men, and June, now resided. Mr. Kahn thought the location and house were ideal for their intentions. The purchase was made, and Mr.

Kahn conveyed Germany's appreciation. Their efforts would not be forgotten. June's parents beamed with pride, expressing their desire to be of help wherever and whenever needed.

Several months later Mr. Kahn once again came calling. The German housekeeper who was brought in from Germany was not working out and was being sent home. They needed another house-keeper right away. Someone loyal to Germany who knew how to keep quiet. Would their daughter, June, be willing to take the job? It would only be for a short time, perhaps a few weeks. There would be no danger, and she would earn enough money during those few weeks to pay for an entire year's studies at the university. June's parents were again overjoyed they were being asked to help the Fatherland. Of course June would take the job. They assured Mr. Kahn she could and would indeed keep her mouth shut.

June was furious her parents promised her to Mr. Kahn without consulting her, and immediately declined to take the "assignment," as her parents called it. Even though the money was more than she could have imagined, June wanted no part of it. She might be young, but she knew full well the house would be used for war activities against America. Her America. How would she be able to reconcile betraying the country she called home? Her father pulled her aside and explained once German intelligence requested your service, it was required you comply. To refuse would be disastrous for not only June but for them as well. It was her duty, not just to Germany but to her mother and father.

June felt trapped. To participate in any capacity toward the harm against her adopted country made her angry and resentful. In June's mind, they might as well have asked her to betray her friends, the university, and the very way of life she loved. How could her parents ask her to do such a thing when they knew her true feelings? In the end, however, she made the gut-wrenching decision to side with her parents, at least this one time, for their protection. All she was being asked to do was keep house and remain quiet. It was only for a few weeks. The money would go a long way toward financing her studies.

After making her reluctant decision, June informed her mother and father over dinner one evening. The looks on their faces conveyed happiness and relief. Now they wouldn't have the dreaded and potentially deadly task of reporting back to Mr. Kahn they could not accommodate his request. Once again they would be in Germany's good graces. June made it clear this would be the only time she would be in Germany's services. Don't bother to ask her ever again.

Becker walked in the door, obviously upset. June could see Jon head toward the garage. A moment later she heard the car door slam shut, and the engine start. She did her best to ignore Becker and keep her focus on the sink and dishes that needed drying. Becker walked past without saying a word and entered the dining room where the three men still sat, discussing some other details of the mission.

"Is everything all right?" asked Gerald.

Becker pulled out a chair and sat down with a scowl on his face. "No, everything is *not* all right."

"What is it? What happened with Jon?" inquired Langer with concern in his voice.

Becker turned his attention to Gerald. "Did you know the maintenance man, Fuller, shares a ride with another worker to the plant?"

"What?" Gerald was truly surprised with this troubling revelation.

"That's right. Jon was waiting at Fuller's house this morning to verify the route he takes to the plant. It was quite a surprise when another vehicle pulled up in front of the house. Then Fuller got in and rode with another worker to Lucas-Harold. So now, instead of one worker, it appears there are two men who need to be . . . disabled."

"We followed Fuller for weeks," pleaded Gerald. "He either drove himself, or his wife drove him. There was never another vehicle involved. I swear."

"Well," said Becker, both skeptically and matter-of-factly, "there is now."

Gerald's mind was racing. He had been meticulous in his planning and thorough in observing Fuller's work habits, including the daily commute. "The only thing I can think of is either his car has malfunctioned or perhaps exceeded his petrol coupons."

"Coupons? What coupons?"

"As you can imagine, most of the petrol is being used for the war effort. The government began rationing tires for their rubber. Soon it spread to petrol, some foods, and other items deemed critical to the war. He would definitely be considered a "nonessential" driver, so he must watch his petrol consumption. It only makes sense to share his commute with someone else. "

"Great," said Becker.

"I assure you, he was driving himself just last week. This is a recent development."

"OK," said Langer, "so there's another person involved. Why does that make Jon's job so much harder?"

"Trust me, it does."

Eric was curious what the new plan would be. "What does he intend to do now?"

Becker looked around the table at the three men, and then spread his hands up as though he was reasoning with them. "He'll do what he always does. He'll take care of it."

Eric didn't like the sound of that.

Very early the next morning Jon was again waiting in his car a hundred feet down from Fuller's home. He thought it fortunate the days were getting shorter, allowing his plan to take place in the predawn light. The sun would not come up for another thirty minutes. All the better in Jon's mind.

Headlights appeared in Jon's rearview mirror. Right on schedule, the dull-green sedan approached Fuller's house. Just like the day before, the driver pulled up to the curb and beeped twice, waiting for the front door of the small bungalow to open. Seconds later the front door opened, and the same plump woman stood in the doorway holding the lunch pail and large thermos. Fuller was putting on his jacket as he stood in the doorway. He took the two items, then gave his wife a quick kiss on the lips. He then looked back and said something to her as he enthusiastically trotted down the steps. She laughed, and then nodded. She waited until Fuller was seated in the car and he closed the door.

Like yesterday, the two young men exchanged pleasantries. Then the car slowly pulled out onto the street on its way to Lucas-Harold. Jon allowed the green sedan to advance several hundred feet before pulling from his parking place. Following the sedan was easy. The car was going the posted speed limit and taking the same route as the day before.

As the green sedan approached the hill near the selected location, Jon increased his speed and closed the gap to about fifty feet. The green sedan crested the small hill and began its descent toward the dangerous curve above the embankment and creek. Jon noticed the sedan slow down, its brake lights glowing. The driver of the green sedan was obviously aware of the treacherous curve ahead. Now the sedan was just fifty feet from the curve and Jon was only twenty feet behind. He could see the driver of the sedan glance in his mirror, surely wondering why he was following so dangerously close. Just as the sedan began to make the turn, Jon sped up and hit the rear of the car.

Jon pushed the accelerator to the floor, immediately forcing the sedan in front of him through the curve and off the road to the edge of the embankment. Jon hit the brakes, stopping just short of going off the road himself. The green sedan's momentum carried it over the edge, and it began to slide down the hill toward the creek, plowing down several small trees in the process.

Jon pulled his car onto the side of the road where there was little danger of being struck by another vehicle. He opened the door and raced down the embankment to see the result of his staged accident. He pulled the revolver from his coat pocket, just in case one or both of them escaped the doomed green sedan. He wouldn't need his revolver today. The green sedan had indeed rolled over once and hit the fast-moving creek with a huge splash, teetering it onto its right side. Within a couple of seconds, the force of the water turned the sedan completely upside down. Shortly afterward, the sedan began floating down the creek. Only its underside and front two tires could be seen.

Jon knew at once no one would be able to survive such an accident. The shock and realization of their impending doom would startle the two men into inaction. The cold water would shock them even further, and hypothermia would set in almost immediately. Once saturated with water, their heavy clothes and winter coats would weigh them down like anchors. Suspended upside down in dark, moving water would completely disorient them, rendering the two unfortunate men helpless. They would be dead in less than a minute. He smiled, his mission complete.

Just then he noticed another car pulling up behind his. Satisfied the men would die shortly, Jon ran up the hill and grabbed the pistol inside his coat pocket. An elderly man got out of his car and ran to the edge of the embankment.

"What happened?" asked the old man in a near panic. He peered over the ledge and saw the bottom of the sedan as it began to vanish from view.

"The car in front of me was heading down the hill and lost control. It went right over the cliff."

"Oh my God, is there anything we can do?"

"I'll go for help," exclaimed Jon. "You stay here and help them if they get out. The police should be here soon."

"Yeah, sure. You better hurry!"

Jon nodded. He casually trotted to his still-running sedan and drove off, smiling. He wondered how long the old man would stand there before he realized no help was coming. No matter, he would be long gone by then.

✛

Eric had just finished another breakfast of bacon and eggs. June was more than happy to make him whatever he wanted. She had been looking forward to seeing him again, even if she was just serving him breakfast. Eric was studying June as she mindlessly busied herself with wiping up around the kitchen. She was indeed a very handsome woman. A hard worker as well, with a mind of her own and unafraid to share her thoughts and ideas. He liked that.

"So, what do you plan to do after you graduate?" asked Eric, hoping to initiate another pleasant conversation with the attractive blonde.

June turned and faced him with a smile. "I'd love to play for a symphony someday. If I were good enough, maybe even in New York or Boston. I hear they're the best. But that's probably not going to happen."

"Why not?"

June walked over and stood by the table. She was about to say something when Eric motioned her to sit down. She did, and was happy to do so. "The odds of that happening are pretty slim. I'm good, but not that good. They only take the best, and I'm not even close to being in that class."

"But you haven't finished school yet. Don't you think you're cutting yourself short?"

"Well, maybe. Guess I don't want to set false expectations only to be disappointed later."

"Sorry," replied Eric, "I'm not buying it. You don't really believe that, do you?"

"Well, why shouldn't I?"

He smiled. "Because I think you're the kind of person who can do anything you set your mind to."

"That's kind of you to say," she said with a grateful smile. "People do say I'm stubborn, so maybe you're right."

Eric felt more relaxed around June than he had around anyone else in the last year. He experienced a general good feeling in her presence. She seemed to have a calming effect on him. He liked it.

"June," he said sincerely, "I have this feeling you *are* going to play professionally, and in a large city like New York or Boston. Don't set your sights too low. I know you can do it. Who knows, someday I may even come and hear you play, perhaps when the war's over. Nothing would make me happier."

June chuckled, "You're more encouraging than my parents. All they do is tell me I'll be a failure as a musician if I don't practice more, study more, be more like them. It's nice for a change to hear some positive encouragement and faith in my abilities. But you haven't even heard me play."

"Not yet, but I'm sure you're wonderful. In fact, I'd love to hear you play. Perhaps you'd be willing to play for us one evening after dinner. It would give you a chance to practice, and God knows it would be a welcome change from spending more time talking about the war. If words were bullets, Germany would have won by now."

June smiled again, then shook her head. "Mr. Kahn would never allow it. I'll just wait for this job to be over and then take it back up again."

Eric was not going to take no for an answer. "Would you mind if I ask him?"

"I don't know. I don't want to get into any trouble."

"Let me handle it. I really want to hear you play, and it will do all of us some good."

"OK, but don't push him too hard. If he says no, please leave it at that."

"I promise . . ."

Just then Jon opened the door to the kitchen and walked past Eric and June. He looked at Eric sternly and then continued through the swinging door to the living room. They heard Becker's voice from the other room. "Well?"

Half a minute later Jon returned to the kitchen, walked back outside, and slammed the door shut behind him. Right on his tail was Becker. He stopped by the table where the two were sitting and looked first at June, then at Eric.

"Well, Mr. Keller. You better be ready. You start tomorrow."

CHAPTER 6

PREPARATION

Eric was nervous. Very nervous. He didn't like it and was even a little ashamed of himself for feeling so. All the months of training for this moment, all the dangerous travel, the improbable survival of just getting here, and finally all the pride he felt for doing something meaningful for the Fatherland was doing nothing to calm his nerves. Why did he feel this way? He was prepared and ready. He knew everything in the file Gerald had given him forward and backward. He had read and studied it so much it invaded his dreams. He had become Eric Keller the maintenance worker for Lucas-Harold.

He looked at his hands as he held the newspaper and hoped they weren't shaking. He prayed they wouldn't betray his anxiety. He sat at the kitchen table doing his best to scan the morning paper in a vain attempt to distract himself from what was going to be a difficult day. June busied herself in the kitchen, as always, preparing breakfast. She couldn't help but notice he was preoccupied; he barely acknowledged her this morning. She occasionally glanced his way, hoping to catch a smile. There was none to be had this morning. His mind was elsewhere.

Everyone in the large house was now aware Jon had made quick and deadly work of the poor young maintenance worker and his unfortunate friend, whose only mistake was providing a ride for his coworker. What of their families? Did the young men die quickly and without pain? Were their deaths really necessary? Gerald and Becker quickly and verbally concluded to everyone it was indeed necessary. They were unfortunate casualties of war. Nothing more. What was it to them if two Americans died when thousands of German civilians were dying each day at the hands of the indiscriminate American bombers? Becker could later be heard saying to Gerald, "With any luck, many more Americans will be dying. And soon. The more, the better."

"Are you all right?" asked June. She placed one of the large blue plates in front of Eric with two biscuits and delicious-smelling sausage gravy. Two slices of buttered toast accompanied the biscuits. Steam rose from the plate.

He put down the paper, folding and then tossing it to the end of the table. "Sorry, guess I'm not very good company this morning. It's my first day at the factory, and I have to admit I'm a little nervous. I don't want to make a mistake, so much is counting on me." He laid the napkin across his lap, then reached for the fork and blew on the steaming gravy before taking his first bite. June could hear him quietly moan with pleasure as he enjoyed the delicious meal she cooked for him.

She offered him that warm smile Eric always enjoyed seeing. June reached over and touched his left arm, her blue eyes sparkling from the morning sun peeking in through the kitchen windows. "You're not going to make a mistake. I've seen how hard you've been studying. Everyone has. You'll do fine."

Eric was enjoying his breakfast. June's gentle touch and reassuring words did indeed have a calming effect on him. He appreciated her encouragement. Of course she was right. "Who is encouraging who now?" he asked.

June chuckled. "Well, if you believe I can play in a professional symphony, then you can surely play an American."

He nodded as he filled his mouth with another piece of biscuit smothered in gravy. He gulped it down as though it were his last meal. "Well, we'll know soon enough if that's the case." He took the napkin and wiped his mouth.

June stood and walked over to the coffee she was keeping warm on the stove. She brought it over to the table and filled Eric's cup. "You know, it may be easier if you look at them just as fellow workers, and not the enemy. They're not the ones killing our countrymen. They're only trying to provide for their families. They're not that different from you and me."

Eric stopped eating for a moment and studied June. "It sounds like you're taking their side."

"That's not what I mean." June took the liberty of taking the chair across from him and sitting down. "Remember, I've lived here all my life. I've grown up in this country. They are not bad people. Most are hardworking, honest men and women who only want to do what's best for themselves and their families. I've made a lot of friends here and know them well. They have hopes and dreams just like ours. They worry about bills and other problems like we do. Many of my student friends have lost family members, neighbors, and coworkers in the war. They watch them leave with their youthfulness and enthusiasm, then see them return in a box or crippled for life. Sometimes they don't come back at all. Their mothers weep like ours. Trust me, they don't like it either. More than anything, they just want the war to be over so their loved ones can come home and get their lives back to normal." She paused for a moment. "All I'm saying is, don't hate them without getting to know them."

Eric continued to stare at her, feeling some appreciation for her thoughts and straightforwardness. She did have a point. Even so, he knew he was there for a specific mission. Lest he forget even for a minute, the Americans were the enemy, in spite of whatever feelings June had for them. He did hate them.

"You may have a point," he reasoned, "but remember they *are* the enemy. These people are making devices that are killing our countrymen. Like you say, you've been here all your life, so you don't realize how many German lives have been lost to American bombs. Hitler still makes claims of how well we're doing. It's a lie. He and other high-ranking officials claim this is only a *temporary* setback. But I've seen the devastation the bombing is doing. Our once beautiful cities are becoming sad and tragic skeletons of their previous selves. So much of what our country was is gone . . . probably forever. We have to do whatever we can to save what's left. It's our duty to do everything we can to stop them. If we fail, thousands more at home are going to die."

"Of course I don't want any more Germans to die. I don't want anyone to die, Germans or Americans."

"None of us would be here if their bombers weren't killing us. It's their own doing."

"Perhaps to a point. But surely you can't believe Germany is totally blameless in this war."

"What do you mean?" Eric was becoming uneasy with the direction June was taking, hardly believing his ears regarding her defense of America.

She realized she needed to tread lightly. The last thing she needed was for her only friend in the house to turn on her. "You know as well as I do Hitler struck first, invading Poland and then others without provocation. And he has his own little war against the Jews. German Jews, no less. They are our own citizens, yet he still has them rounded up and imprisoned or killed. What kind of person does that to his own countrymen?"

"I don't believe all that propaganda," Eric said flatly. "I know the Jews aren't popular, but Germans don't do that."

"Eric, this is not propaganda. Jews have escaped to Canada and America. They have told their stories, and they're horrible! Squads of German soldiers went out and rounded up the Jews just because they're Jews. Then they either killed them on the spot or made them dig their own graves before shooting them. Even women and children were shot! Sometimes hundreds at a time."

"That's a lie! I don't believe it."

"It's true, some have even produced photos. Not *everyone* can be lying, telling the same terrible stories. This group of soldiers, called the Einsatzgruppen, was formed for just one thing. Mass killings. Their only responsibility was to find Jews and kill them. Now what's worse are the rumors they've created death camps across Germany and Poland. They work the Jews to death. If they don't cooperate, they're executed."

To say Eric was skeptical was an understatement, but curious just the same. June was so confident in her accusations. "How do you know all of this?" he asked. He still could not believe his countrymen were capable of such deeds. Nearly everyone he had come in contact with in the military was honest and respectful. At least he thought they were. Jon, for sure, was one exception. Were there more like him at home? Could he really be that naive? Could June be right?

"Mostly from the university," answered June. "Escaped Jews have come to speak to us, and I went to hear what they had to say. I was curious. My parents didn't know, they would have been very upset. Needless to say, I was also shocked at first and didn't believe it. They had to be lying to gain American sympathy. But their stories were so compelling! No one can make up stories like that. Then they had photos. How can you argue with those? I struggled with what I heard for a long time. I thought the same thing you do now . . . Germans don't do that."

"I don't know . . ."

"I believe it's all about Hitler. He is the one to blame," June continued. "I know it's unwise and probably dangerous to be talking like this, especially to another German. But he has poisoned so many good Germans. Even my own parents."

Now Eric grabbed her hand and squeezed it. "Listen June, you can believe what you want. Maybe some of what you say is even true. But I would be very careful in this house. I think it wise to keep your thoughts to yourself. I care about you and don't want any harm to come your way. And with the others still devoted to the Fuhrer, they will take great offense and perhaps action. I especially don't trust Jon, so keep a wary eye on him."

"I know you're right. It breaks my heart this war is tearing us apart. I just want it to be over. Don't worry, I'll do my duty—"

Gerald pushed open the swinging door and entered the kitchen. June immediately stood up without completing her sentence and reached for Eric's plate, now clean. Eric wiped his mouth.

"Something smells delicious!" Gerald exclaimed. "Is there any left, or did Eric manage to consume it all?"

"Good morning, Mr. Kahn," said June, hoping he hadn't heard their conversation; it could be the end of her if he had. "No, there's plenty left. May I prepare you a plate?"

"Yes, that will be most appreciated. Thank you."

Gerald took the chair across from Eric at the table. June took down another blue plate from the cabinet and began filling it with two biscuits and then gravy from the simmering pot on the stove. Gerald glanced at June, then studied Eric. "Well, today is a big day for you. Are you ready?"

"Yes, I think so," replied Eric.

"Think so? I certainly hope you *know* so. You have a very important role. Without you, any success we have will be greatly diminished."

"Yes," Eric answered, looking with all sincerity into Gerald's eyes, "I'm ready. You needn't worry about me."

"Good."

June walked over carrying the steaming plate in one hand and a cup of coffee in another. As she placed them down in front of Gerald, she exchanged a quick look with Eric. Had Gerald heard any of their conversation? How would he have interpreted it if he had? "May I bring you anything else?" she asked. She noticed her hands were trembling, so she quickly hid them in the pocket of her apron.

Gerald surveyed the food on the plate and slightly nodded his head in approval, offering a smile of thanks. "No, June, this looks wonderful. Thank you." June turned and was about to place the lid on the pan when Gerald interrupted her thoughts. "Oh, June?"

It startled her. Perhaps he did hear something. "Yes?"

Gerald was busy with his knife and fork, cutting off a slice of biscuit and dabbing it through the gravy. He looked at Eric with incriminating eyes. "Will you please allow Eric and I a few moments alone?"

"Of course. I need to gather up the laundry anyway." She stirred the gravy one more time, placed the lid on the pan, and then turned down the burner to its lowest setting. She removed her apron and placed it on the hook next to the swinging door. Then she turned and offered the two men a smile before exiting through the swinging door into the dining room.

After a moment Eric asked, "Is everything all right?"

Gerald finished his mouthful of food and took his time answering, as though he was giving considerable thought to his answer. "To be completely honest? No, everything is not all right."

Now Eric was more than a little alarmed. "What do you mean?"

Gerald put down his fork and gave Eric his full attention. "I received a call last night from an … *associate*. There's a possibility we have been compromised."

Eric was shocked at that piece of news. "Compromised? What are you talking about?"

"Well, I'm not exactly sure. At least not yet. As you can imagine, I am not the only active intelligence operative in the area. In fact, there are quite a few of us over here, and have been for some time. You may also be interested to know we had hundreds of spies here in America even before the war. Then after the war began, that branch of the Third Reich, the Abwehr, began infiltrating their own highly trained people in more strategic locations. They proved more effective in many areas of … well, espionage. There are currently several of the Abwehr here in Indianapolis." Gerald paused to confirm he had Eric's full attention, which he did.

"Go on," said Eric.

"One of the Abwehr's many responsibilities is to look after one another. They determine if one of their fellow Germans may be in trouble, perhaps discovered by American officials—policemen, military personnel, or especially, the OSS. You do know about them?"

"Yes, Becker filled us in."

"Good. Unfortunately one of the other tasks of the Abwehr is spying on each other."

"I don't understand."

"I know, it doesn't *seem* to make sense at first. But it does indeed make sense, very good sense. It shouldn't come as a surprise, some of our people here have turned, changing sides to help the Americans. Not many, but it has happened. They spend enough time here that they become comfortable with the American way of life. Next thing you know, they share American ideals and, eventually, their sympathies. They make friends and are influenced. It's at that point they become vulnerable to America's own intelligence efforts. You may say they become Americanized."

"What happens then?"

"It depends," answered Gerald. He stuffed another bite of biscuit into his mouth.

"On what?"

Gerald took his time chewing and then swallowing. "On how much damage they can do to us."

"Meaning . . ."

"Meaning, Mr. Keller, if it's determined they can do considerable damage by providing the Americans sensitive information, they will be neutralized."

"You mean killed."

"Yes, I mean killed. That's obviously the last option we want to pursue. But sometimes we're left with no choice."

Eric realized those who turned were traitors and could not be allowed to betray the Fatherland any further by revealing sensitive information. Perhaps death was indeed the only safe option for Germany.

"I think I understand. So, what does that have to do with us now?"

"Recently one of the Abwehr became alerted to some troubling information. Information that leads us to the conclusion someone knows of our mission. Someone who has been working off and on with our intelligence for some time. This person knows the workings of what we do and has gotten wind of our operation here. I think you would call them a double agent."

Eric felt a surge of adrenaline shoot through his veins, and it nearly made him nauseous. "Do they know who?"

Gerald shook his head in disappointment. "Unfortunately not. The Abwehr believes this person to be an otherwise loyal German with a history of serving the Fatherland. If we knew who this individual was, we could take the appropriate measures. At this point, we're not even sure the report is accurate. Even so, we must assume it is and take every precaution. The smallest mistake or careless indiscretion will endanger our mission, and our very lives. My request of you is that you be even more diligent of your surroundings as you begin your task at Lucas-Harold."

"Of course. Should I be looking for anything specific?"

"I can't really say at this point. Just be on your guard for anyone who appears to be watching you at the plant. We have many people working for us here, most of them civilians. Their only job is to observe and report. A few even work at the plant in menial positions. Their job is to report anything unusual at the factory. The double agent could be one of them."

"Why don't you tell me who they are?" asked Eric.

"I don't think that is necessary at the moment. You need to focus on your specific task, not tracking down possible traitors. Leave that to us. The Abwehr is secretly undergoing their own investigation of these individuals to determine if there are conflicting loyalties. That will, of course, take some time. That said, be aware of anyone befriending you, striking up needless conversation to learn more about you, where you're staying, that sort of thing. If anyone appears overly nosy, please tell me immediately."

Eric nodded in agreement. "Any idea how long this person has known about us?"

"No, I'm afraid not," answered Gerald, again disappointed and frustrated with the lack of more definite information. "My source believes this person knows about us as well as the mission itself, another troubling development. We're confident they're unaware of our timetable. With any luck, we will complete our task and be long out of town before they take any action."

"Maybe we should lay low for a while until you know more."

"Absolutely not. Too much is riding on our success. Not only that, but there are many others involved in helping us escape after we're finished here. Everything has been set on very detailed timetables. To change any of those now would only disrupt very thought-out plans. No, I think our only option is to proceed, and hope the Abwehr can locate and then terminate this person or persons. The quicker we accomplish our mission, the better. Right now time is on *our* side, not theirs."

"What? You think there's more than one?"

"I don't know, but that would be my guess." Gerald saw the forlorn look on Eric's face. He didn't like it. "Don't be discouraged. Carry out your part of the mission just as you've prepared. If I'm correct, this person will be working at the factory. Eventually they will make themselves known, *if* you're alert to them. Act like any other young man, happy to have a job. Be friendly, but not too friendly. Don't draw any attention to yourself. Be suspicious of anyone who makes an effort to know you better or asks a lot of questions. Do you understand?"

Eric nodded. "Yes, of course. I'll do my best."

"I know you will." Gerald seemed satisfied.

"Do the others know?" asked Eric.

"I told Becker last night, and I believe he informed Jon. I'm planning to tell Langer next."

"I'll bet Becker was upset."

"All he said was, 'It figures,' then immediately agreed the mission must go on. This is our only chance."

"Yes, I believe you're right."

"I know I'm right. Now," said Gerald, changing the subject, "what were you and June talking about?"

Eric did not miss a beat. "I was encouraging her to continue her violin studies when she's finished here. I was hoping she may be permitted to play for us one evening. It would allow her to practice and give us a chance to enjoy some German music. She didn't think you would allow it."

Gerald smiled. "Violin in this house? What a splendid idea! A minor distraction may do all of us some good. I'll talk to her about it. Very thoughtful, Mr. Keller."

⁜

Twenty minutes later, Gerald drove Eric to the plant following a similar chat with Langer in the living room regarding the Abwehr's news. Now everyone, except June, was aware of the very likely possibility someone knew who they were and what they were up to. But who? How many were there? Questions that, for the moment, had no answers. Gerald was employing every possible, available resource to find them. Until he heard differently, all of them would proceed as planned. With any luck, it was a false alarm by an overzealous member of the Abwehr. Gerald knew, however, the Abwehr was extremely thorough and rarely made mistakes.

The fifteen-minute ride was, for the most part, silent. Gerald asked a few general questions about their homeland, Germany. Eric was honest and blunt about the current situation. He could see the news greatly bothered Gerald, and then regretted he had shared the tragic situation as it was. He liked Gerald, in spite of his ruthlessness, and felt remorse for upsetting him when so many other troubling issues were on his mind.

As the plant came into view, Eric's stomach began churning itself into knots, his adrenaline doing its unpleasant job. He detested the feeling, but realized it heightened all his senses. He could see people in other cars pulling into the lot, stopping at the guard shack and showing a pass before entering the grounds. Many cars would briefly stop in the small driveway running parallel to the plant, let a passenger out for a shift at the factory, and then take off to make room for the next car. Workers would walk to the gate, show their pass to the guard, and then make their way to the factory entrance. This is what Gerald and Eric would be doing every morning for the next few weeks.

Gerald pulled up just behind the car in front of them, a black four-door sedan. It stopped and three men exited, grabbing their lunch pails from the car. The man who had been sitting in the front, turned and blew a kiss to the woman driving the car. The other two men made some jabbing, yet friendly, comments at the man. He raised his middle finger at them in response, and then all of them laughed and walked up to the guard shack. Eric knew they were the enemy, every bit as much as the soldiers fighting on his home soil. Even so, he appreciated the camaraderie between them. Was June right? Were they really like Germans? No matter, he was going to complete his mission.

Gerald pulled up next and came to a stop. Eric turned to open the door, and just before he stepped out, Gerald grabbed his arm. Eric looked back.

"Good luck. Remember what we talked about," reminded Gerald.

Eric forced a smile. "Don't worry, I'll be fine." Encouraged, Gerald nodded and waited for him to shut the door. As soon as he did, Gerald pulled out and vanished over a rise. Eric was on his own. There was no one there to help him if he ran into trouble. Would the guard think he's German? Would he innocently slip and say something to immediately incriminate himself? Did he look nervous? He could feel small beads of sweat forming on his forehead. He forced himself to walk slowly and deliberately toward the guard who was checking passes.

Eric bravely took his place in line behind the others reporting for work. He noticed the ominous chain-link fence surrounding the factory and its grounds. It stood more than fifteen feet tall, possessed a cold and impersonal appearance, and screamed, "Stay away, you're not wanted!" Looking down the long fence, he saw two other army guards in the distance walking the perimeter. Both had army rifles slung across their backs.

The guard shack standing next to the gate was the only way onto the Lucas-Harold grounds. It was nothing more than a small gray building composed of concrete blocks and windows that allowed visibility from every angle. One guard was in the building surveying the workers, while the other stood at the entrance checking passes. Eric stood behind two dozen men and women as they slowly made their way to the guard and the entrance. Each would stop and quickly show a pass to the guard, and he would briefly glance at it and wave them on. It seemed to Eric the guard knew most of those passing through the gate. Sometimes they would exchange greetings, even a chuckle or two. Day after day of the same routine resulted in the guards recognizing familiar faces.

Only six workers away, he noticed the guard was about thirty, rather large, and securely carried a US Army-issue Colt 1911 .45 caliber pistol in the holster on his belt. Eric looked over and saw the guard in the shack studying him with a serious expression. Eric forced an innocent smile and then turned his attention back to the entrance, trying not to draw any unnecessary attention to himself. Only two workers in front of him now, and he hoped no one could see or hear how hard his heart was beating. Again he was ashamed of himself for feeling so nervous.

The guard quickly looked Eric over. "Pass?" he asked seriously.

"This is my first day. I'm supposed to report to Mr. Redding, the maintenance supervisor." Eric was relieved his voice didn't shake, as he was shaking inside.

The guard turned to his partner in the shack, "Joe! New employee, will ya call it in?" He waited for his partner to acknowledge the request, and then he motioned for Eric to walk over to the shack. The guard didn't want to waste much time with Eric and thus hold up the rest of the workers who were anxious to be on time.

"See Joe in the guard shack. He has to call it in to make sure Redding is expecting you. Then he'll give you a temporary pass. Should only take a minute." The guard immediately turned his attention to the next person in line, a young, attractive woman about twenty. The guard recognized her and smiled. "Good morning, Ruth, you look pretty today."

She smiled back. "Thank you, Ed. I'm sure you say that to all the girls."

"Nah, just you. Have a good day. See ya tomorrow." He quickly glanced at her pass, not really examining it. He knew it was authentic. Eric thought his task would be much easier if he were a young, good-looking woman, like June back at the house.

He stepped out of line and walked over to and inside the open door of the shack where the other guard was waiting for him. The guard was all business. He removed a clipboard hanging on the wall and prepared to write. "Name?"

"Eric Keller."

"Position?"

"Maintenance."

"Superior?"

"Jim Redding."

The guard finished writing down the information, and then reached for the phone on a small desk. He dialed three numbers and waited. Eric looked around the shack. It was the size of a small bedroom. The desk only had three items on it. A phone, which the guard was now using, and two large thermoses. On the far wall next to one of the large windows was a key rack with four or five large keys. Below one of the windows was a gun rack with four Army-issue rifles and two machine guns. Several unopened boxes of ammunition were neatly stacked beside the guns.

"Yeah, this is Sergeant Evans out front. I have a new employee here. Name's Keller, Eric Keller." There was a pause as he listened. "He's not on our list out here," the sergeant said as he continued to scan the clipboard. Another pause. "That's correct, says he's to report to Jim Redding." The guard was becoming slightly agitated. He nodded his head a couple of times, then turned toward Eric. "They have to call Redding. Seems he didn't notify the personnel office you'd be starting today."

Eric shrugged his shoulders innocently. "No problem, I can wait."

"I'm afraid you'll have to. No one gets in without the proper authority, *especially* guests and new employees. This is a very secure facility, you understand."

"Of course. Probably just a mistake."

"I'm sure it is," reassured the sergeant. "Just the same, if they can't get it straightened out inside, then you'll need to come back when they do."

"I understand." Eric was now frustrated and nervous. How in the world could Redding fail to notify the proper authorities in the plant he was starting today? If they gave Redding a difficult time due to some technicality, Eric would have to leave and come back tomorrow. Furthermore, Gerald was long gone with the car, so he wouldn't have a ride. Becker would be furious. Eric knew he would be the one to catch the blame.

He was fighting a growing feeling of panic that stirred in his stomach. He had to get out of the shack and away from the guard, lest he recognize the fear on his face that was increasing by the second. What if, inside the plant, they already knew he was a German spy sent to blow up their facility? What if the Abwehr was correct? What if Redding had been discovered and confessed their plot? He glanced at the array of guns on the rack, wondering now if one of them would be used on him. It took every ounce of his emotional strength to remain calm and dispel those disturbing thoughts. He was at the gate, he was committed. There was no turning back. To do so could possibly tip his hand and reveal that something indeed was wrong.

Eric decided to do something normal, to give the impression he was relaxed and not bothered in the least. "Is it all right if I step outside and have a smoke?"

The guard didn't look at him, still scanning the clipboard as though Eric Keller's name had to be there, simply hidden from his view. "Sure. Sorry this is taking so long."

Eric managed to force a smile. "Don't worry about it, it's not your fault. I can always come back tomorrow if there's a problem." He didn't wait for the sergeant's reply. He walked outside the guard shack and reached for the cigarettes in his coat pocket. He could see his breath in the cool morning air. The line was much smaller now; only a few workers were left. He removed one of the cigarettes and placed it between his lips. He noticed the guard watching him. Eric held up the pack, gesturing his offer to share one with the sergeant. The guard politely shook his head and rolled his eyes, signaling his helplessness to speed things along.

Eric had nearly finished the cigarette when he saw the sergeant talking on the phone, nodding his head and writing something down on his clipboard. After a few moments, he turned and motioned for Eric to enter the guard shack.

Eric entered the shack and could hear the sergeant speaking with some irritation into the phone. "I'll send him through, but you're supposed to tell us when new employees are reporting for work. Otherwise we have to call you. Now this poor guy is going to be late." One more pause. "I see. OK, he's on his way."

The guard put down the clipboard and opened the top desk drawer. He pulled out a bright yellow tag with a clip on it. He handed it to Eric. "OK, Mr. Keller. Sorry about all the confusion. Seems Mr. Redding failed to mention you were starting today. Typical screwup. Anyway, here's your temporary pass. Wear it at all times. Just clip it on your pocket." The guard handed it to Eric, who clipped it on his breast pocket. The guard nodded his approval.

"OK, you're good to go. Just walk through the main employee entrance over there and Mr. Redding will meet you. I'm sure they'll make you a permanent pass sometime today, then you won't have to go through this again."

"What do I do with this one?" asked Eric.

"Leave it with Mr. Redding when you get the new one. He'll take care of it. You better hurry, the clock starts in a couple of minutes."

"Thank you. Didn't mean to be so much trouble."

"Not your fault," replied the guard. "Shit happens, if you know what I mean."

"I do."

"Good luck. And welcome to Lucas-Harold. This is a pretty important place, you're lucky to be working here."

"I know, and thanks."

Eric nodded at Sergeant Evans and exited through the open door. He showed his guest pass to the other guard and then walked to the factory entrance. The building was much smaller than he had anticipated. His superiors in Germany had given the impression Lucas-Harold was housed in an enormous building. On the contrary, it was a redbrick two-story structure of moderate size with few windows, and even those windows had been frosted over with some type of coating that allowed light to penetrate but concealed the activities within.

He could feel his heart beating stronger now, wondering if anyone would stop, point their finger at him, and yell at the top of their lungs, "Guard, guard! There's a spy! Stop him!" But no one said a thing. In fact, he went unnoticed. If the Abwehr was right and someone was aware of his mission, then he could be walking into a trap. Maybe their plan was to allow him access into the factory where they would arrest him there. Then they would interrogate and perhaps torture him until he finally relented and gave up everything they wanted to know. He would be the weak link. He would be the one who failed. He would be responsible for the continued bombings in Germany. With great effort, Eric forced those thoughts from his mind.

He walked through the door and was immediately met by a man in gray coveralls. Eric recognized the man from the photographs in the file Gerald had given him. He was a small man, about five foot five and balding. Eric thought he looked nervous.

"Mr. Keller?"

"Yes," answered Eric.

"I'm Redding. Sorry for the screwup. Welcome to Lucas-Harold. Follow me."

Langer and Becker were preoccupied. They had been sitting at the dining room table most of the morning preparing for their roles as two Canadian businessmen. Little, however, was really being accomplished; Eric was on their minds. The entire mission, including Eric's role, had changed much since their training in Germany. And most of it within the last few days. None of them had the luxury of adequately preparing for their new assignments, and Eric the least. Berlin badly needed a success, and if it required their agents to assume more risk to achieve one, then so be it. Their lives were expendable. If they failed, then they failed. But they would fail trying. Berlin, however, expected them to succeed. Changes in the plan, inadequate time to prepare, and the loss of team members along the way were no excuse. You adapt and move forward. It was your duty. No delays or attempts to alter Berlin's directives would be tolerated. Failure, as their superiors were fond of saying, is not an option. And now Eric was the first of the team to enter the unforgiving jaws of the enemy target. If he did not perform, if he made a mistake, if he simply clammed up and was overcome by a fatal dose of stage fright, then the rest of their efforts were doomed.

June politely interrupted them every thirty minutes to check their coffee. She easily concluded their minds were elsewhere, and she knew exactly where. Everyone was thinking of Eric. He was the first to enter the factory of Lucas-Harold. He was the first one on the firing line. He could also be the first to be discovered and detained. Even her own thoughts were with him this very important morning, noticeably more than usual. In spite of her best efforts not to, she had become fond of him and cared for his safety, more than she wanted to admit. June had sworn she would never allow herself to become friends or otherwise involved with any of those in the house. She was going to serve as the cook and maid, nothing more. It would make her job easier and provide the needed detachment from whatever they were planning to do to *her* America. She constantly reminded herself she was only doing this for her parents she truly loved but believed wrong in their defense of Germany.

But it was too late. She had become involved with Eric. True, there had been no open expression of affection or secret intimacy.

Still, there was a definite connection of two young souls troubled by their duties; a connection they felt in their private conversations, occasional touches, and finally, in a discreet communication between them when their eyes met. A sense of anxiety for each other's welfare conveyed more than mere comradeship. They genuinely cared for one another.

June quietly reprimanded herself for vocalizing her opinions earlier and secretly hoped they were heard only by Eric. If Gerald had overheard even part of their conversation, he gave no indication of such. Just the same, she would be more on guard and exert more caution when speaking.

"May I bring you anything?" asked June. She knew the answer before she asked. The silence was depressing. Perhaps her voice would break the shroud of impending doom that seemed to hover over the two men.

Langer put down the paper he was studying and looked at June with worried eyes. "Thanks, but no."

"How about you, Mr. Becker?"

"Nothing for me either. I don't think we'll be needing you until lunch."

She smiled, relieved she could attend to some of her other duties. "Very well. I'll just tidy up the bedrooms." The two men nodded.

They waited for June to leave the dining room table and head to the stairs. Once she was out of sight, Langer closed his file and stared blankly at Becker.

"How do you think he's doing?" asked Langer.

"Eric? I think he's doing fine. No one studied the material harder than he did. I quizzed him several times and he never made a mistake. Not once. He's as prepared as anyone can be."

"Then why are we so anxious?"

"Because," answered Becker with both reason and consolation in his voice, "there is much at stake. And at this very moment, whatever's happening is out of our control." Becker paused a moment, gathering his thoughts. "The only thing one cannot truly prepare for is the ultimate pressure when everything is hanging on your performance. You can practice all you want, but when you're onstage, nerves, doubt, and fear of what could go wrong invades one's thoughts. It's that very invasion that has the ability to negate all of your previous efforts."

Langer nodded in agreement, realizing Becker had accurately described the situation. "I've trained with Eric for nearly a year. We've been through some difficult times, and I have no doubt he will carry out his duty without falter. Of all of us, he was always the rock, the one who would not only keep a cool head but encourage the rest of us to as well. He'll do his job, of that I have no doubt."

Becker smiled and nodded his head in agreement. "I'm sure you're right."

"Even so," said Langer, "it does drive me a little crazy with all this waiting around."

"On that we agree," replied Becker. "Let's go back to work on each of our parts." With that, they both picked up their files.

CHAPTER 7

THE FACTORY

Gerald was waiting in the car line when Eric exited the plant. He walked calmly through the gate and past the guard shack on his way out. He was wearing a new red pass, indicating he was a permanent employee. He nodded his head as he passed the two guards. Both nodded back in return, and he noticed they were different men from earlier that morning. Without thinking, he naturally wondered how long their shifts were and what time the change occurred. Did they follow the same pattern every day, and with the same rotation of guards? His time in the military, especially in German intelligence, trained him to automatically consider such things.

It was five o'clock and the bright orange sun was already kissing the horizon, clearly visible through the leafless trees. There was a chill in the air, and he noticed a nearby pond on the grounds where steam was rolling off its calm waters. He had never understood how that phenomena occurred. Just the same, he thought it beautiful as the steam filtered upward into the sun's remaining beams of light, casting an eerie, yet mesmerizing, spell as it enveloped the neighboring trees. He glanced around and thought he was the only one who had taken notice of Mother Nature's beautiful display. Their loss. It was as though she were saying, "Good-bye and have a good evening." He decided to take it as a good omen.

Eric quickly spotted Gerald's car and trotted over. He opened the passenger door and got in, setting his lunch pail between them. Neither one said a word for several minutes, until Gerald could stand it no longer.

"Well? How did it go?"

"Fine," replied Eric emotionlessly.

Gerald sternly looked over at him; that answer was simply not going to do. "Fine? What do you mean, fine? You're going to have to do better than that!"

Eric paused and looked out his window. He was tired and really wanted to have a few minutes to gather his thoughts from all the day's activities. It had been one of the most stressful days he could remember, including the raft experience his first night in America. There had even been a few moments during the day when his mind went completely blank and he could recall nothing from the file he had been studying for days. Fortunately it all quickly came back.

"Other than Redding not being prepared for me today, everything went according to plan." He continued to look out his window.

"What?" asked Gerald in disbelief.

"You heard me," replied Eric. He now returned a stern look at Gerald. "Redding was not ready for me. He thought it was next week. I wasn't sure I was going to make it inside the plant today."

"I don't believe you." Gerald was shaking his head.

"Well, don't believe me if you want, but it's true."

"Please explain."

"For starters," explained Eric, "I show up at the gate and my name's not on the list. So they keep me waiting there while they try to confirm with Redding I'm actually supposed to start today. It takes them nearly ten minutes to track him down, and then he makes the comment to the personnel department that he just plain forgot. I guess they chewed his ass a little, as he looked pretty down-in-the-mouth when I finally got in and met him."

"I can't believe it. He was fully briefed . . . on several occasions. True, the plan has changed several times over the last week or so, but he knew full well you were coming today."

Eric chuckled. "No, he obviously didn't. Somebody screwed up somewhere."

Now Gerald was upset. "We'll just see about this. This is completely unacceptable. Mistakes like this can get us caught . . . or worse, killed! Berlin would be livid if they knew. I'll speak with Redding later tonight."

"Forget it," said Eric. "There's nothing we can do about it now. I'm confident everyone there thought it was a legitimate mistake. Once they got it straightened out, everything went fine. If you put Redding on the hot seat now, he may get even more nervous and make more mistakes. More *serious* mistakes. Let this one pass."

Gerald paused for a moment, then slowly nodded in agreement. "You may be right." He looked over again at Eric. "You are very wise for your years, Mr. Keller. I see now why Berlin has so much confidence in you. You were able to take a potentially disastrous situation and turn it into a success. You're to be commended."

"It wasn't that difficult," said Eric, downplaying his efforts. "You just have to adapt. Both Redding and I did that today. You know as well as I do complicated plans like this never go exactly as planned. Changes always occur."

"Yes, you're quite right. Just the same, job well done."

Eric smiled and looked out his window as the sun's final sliver dipped out of sight. "If you say so. I sure hope June has something good on the stove. I'm starved!"

June did indeed have something good on the stove. Eric and Gerald walked into the kitchen to the delicious aroma of simmering tomatoes and garlic, setting Eric's grumbling stomach on a much faster pace. He saw June leaning over the stove, stirring the large pot of tomato and meat sauce. She turned and gave him that innocent, warm smile he was so fond of. He was becoming accustomed to seeing her around the house, and he liked it; he even liked it a little more than he wanted to or thought he should. Still, he was going to enjoy her company as long as he could.

At that instant and for a lingering moment, Eric allowed himself the all-too-infrequent luxury of imagining life under different circumstances. He would walk into the kitchen, sneak up behind June, gently lower the collar of her shirt, and then softly kiss her on the back of her neck. She would slowly turn and throw her arms around him, planting her warm, moist mouth on his. He would hold her tightly, and she him. He couldn't wait to hear her tender voice, and the soothing feeling that came from hearing it. They would sit down to dinner and she would ask how his day went, and then tell him about hers. June could say anything, as long she would gaze into his eyes with that intoxicating smile. After dinner and a glass of wine, they would leave the plates soaking in the sink. He would lead her by the hand upstairs to their bedroom. There they would share the enjoyment of each other's bodies with a passion like no other. Afterward they would lay in the darkness, sheets barely covering their still-naked bodies, and talk about the future and their dreams. Anything would be possible at that moment. Time would stand still. The two would be as one, and nothing would be impossible. It would be heaven, or at least as close as they could come to it on earth. If only. Perhaps in a different time.

Eric realized that all his anxiety from the day's events, his high blood pressure, and his worries, evaporated upon seeing June. He also recognized in her eyes her relief to see him as well, knowing he had safely returned. True, she didn't know the details of their plan, but surely she knew all of them were in danger. He couldn't talk with her now with Gerald there, but would look for an opportunity later.

"Smells like spaghetti," stated Eric, smiling broadly at June.

"It is. I hope you're hungry because I made a lot of it. Mr. Becker requested the spaghetti. He thought everyone would be up for something a little different."

Eric walked up to June, glancing first at the large pot, then gazing into her eyes. "It's perfect."

Gerald studied the two young people. Something was going on, and he was going to keep an eye on them. "I'll call the others." He walked through the swinging door looking for Becker and Langer.

June had set the dining room table for four instead of the normal five. She had also taken the liberty of using the good china, expensive silver, and even the beautiful crystal from the dining room cabinet for the night's dinnerware. She wanted dinner to be special, even if the meal was spaghetti. It was Eric's first day, and she believed if she went to this effort, Eric would surely return safely.

Eric desperately wanted to get a bath and clean up. But first things first. He poured himself a generous portion of vodka and then took two large gulps. As always, it burned a little on the way down. It didn't matter; it was just what he needed. The growing pangs in his stomach reminded him again he needed to eat soon. He noticed the table was one place setting short, and he was immediately curious who would be absent. As he stood next to the cabinet enjoying his cocktail, June began bringing in the food. First the pot of tomato and meat sauce. Even with the lid on to retain its warmth, he could see steam escaping around the edges. She placed a large ladle next to the pot, and next to that, a saucer and small folded dishtowel to prevent the white lace tablecloth from getting stained. On her next trip she brought noodles in a beautiful antique bowl with a pat of butter on top, which immediately began to melt.

Eric heard footfalls on the stairway and looked up to see Gerald, Langer, and Becker approaching. For an instant, he thought Langer and Becker looked just as happy to see him as June did. No doubt they had a lot of questions. Gerald looked at the table and clasped his hands together. "Let's eat!" All took their normal places.

Just as they were ready to begin, June brought in one more basket wrapped in a red-and-white checkered dishtowel. "Thought all of you would like some garlic bread to go with your spaghetti." She set it on the table and gave Eric a quick glance to see if he was pleased. He was. "Is there anything else I can get you?"

"This is quite magnificent, June," exclaimed Gerald. "You really outdid yourself this evening. And I'm so happy you used the good china for a change. Thank you."

"You're welcome," replied June. It was good to be appreciated, which seldom occurred at home with her parents. "Well then, if there's nothing else, I'll have my dinner in the kitchen." And without waiting for a response, she excused herself with a nod of her head and walked through the swinging door back into the kitchen.

The four men quickly filled their plates while the food was still warm. Eric didn't miss Jon's company, but was curious about his absence.

"Where's Jon?" Eric asked as he looked toward Becker.

"I'm afraid that's my doing," answered Gerald. "I offered Jon's services to the Abwehr in the hopes he may have some success in locating the person we're looking for."

"He's the man for the job," chimed in Becker.

"Indeed he is," added Eric. He wondered what cruel pleasure Jon would derive from his new undertaking. There was no doubt in Eric's mind Jon would go to whatever lengths necessary to locate and then abduct this person, whomever it may be. He pitied not only the poor soul who knew of their activities, but also anyone else who got in Jon's way. And if, perhaps, this individual did turn out to be a traitorous German, well, may God have mercy on him. Jon would not. Whatever happened, sooner or later there was sure to be a trail of dead bodies.

"Well," said Becker, "are you going to tell us what happened today or not?"

Langer was growing weary of Becker's continued directness. "Can't you at least let him finish his dinner?"

Becker ignored Langer's remark. "He can talk and eat at the same time." He looked back at Eric. "Let's have it. What happened today?"

The three men at the table observed Eric with eager anticipation. Even Gerald, to whom Eric had already revealed some of the day's events, was waiting for him to speak. Eric took his time and casually finished chewing his food before swallowing. He calmly set down his fork and took another sip of his vodka. The other men slowly continued to eat in complete silence. The only sound was the clicking of utensils on their plates.

Finally Eric spoke. "There are numerous locations for concealing explosives. More than one can imagine." He took another sip of his vodka and slowly put down the glass.

"Do you think," asked Becker with a hit of frustration in his voice, "that you could indulge us with perhaps a little more detail than that?"

"I would also like to know," added Langer.

Eric looked around the table, realizing he had their full attention. "The maintenance supervisor, Redding, is unfortunately not as reliable a resource as I was hoping for. He's an extremely nervous person. I hope he can see this through."

"What do you mean by that?" asked Becker.

"For starters, he forgot to let the personnel director know I was starting today."

"You're kidding, right?" asked Langer, believing that had to be a joke.

Eric shook his head. "I wish I were. There's no doubt he's committed to our mission, but he's so nervous, I fear he may make a mistake that could reveal our true identities."

"Go on," prompted Becker as he gave Gerald a worried glance.

"Once I made it past the guards and into the plant, I met Redding. He took me to the personnel department where I met the director. A very direct and cautious man by the name of Lewis. The three of us spent nearly an hour going over company policy. He scolded Redding about the infraction of failing to let them know ahead of time about the change of today's start date. In his own defense, Redding came up with a plausible excuse. He said next week was the original date, but that he was backed up with equipment problems and needed me right away. He was so busy completing maintenance paperwork, he became distracted and forgot to turn in the new date; the office memo was still sitting on his desk. He took the blame, and Lewis bought it."

"Well, that's a relief," sighed Becker.

"Lewis spent the next hour going over company rules and things of that nature. He's very detailed and double-checks *everything*. He even went through my file while I was there, asking me to verify most of the facts." Eric looked at Gerald. "You and your men did an excellent job on the background. Even Lewis seemed to be pleased with the completeness of it. Everything he needed was there . . . and in order. Any more, and he might have thought it too complete. It was just right."

Gerald nodded. "Good, and you're welcome."

"After that Redding and I waited for another thirty minutes for my new identity pass, which I must wear to gain access to the plant." Eric reached in his shirt pocket and pulled it out, showed it to them, and then passed it to Langer. He then handed it to Becker, who carefully examined it. Eric continued, "Without a pass, you are not permitted to enter. If you do, the guards will contact your supervisor to clear you first. Forget your pass twice, and you're relieved of your position. No exceptions."

"What did you think of the plant?" asked Langer.

"I was impressed. Their facilities are every bit as good as ours. And the workers seem very dedicated to their duties. The assembly line is well laid out, and I can see now how a few properly placed explosives would greatly disrupt production."

"Yes," replied Becker, "but will you have the *opportunity* to place them without being observed?"

"Yes, I believe so. Redding gave me a thorough tour of the plant. Although the workers saw me with Redding, they really didn't notice me. You may say I was invisible. And that's the way I prefer it. I saw numerous locations where even a small explosive would create a significant disruption to the line. There are also areas where the sights and other components are stored. I'm sure we could put something there, and that would destroy both the sights and the components that go in them."

"What about the offices?" asked Langer. After all, his job was to leave explosives in that part of the building.

"Other than Director Lewis's office, I didn't see much. Sorry."

"Don't worry, Becker and I will get a chance to see them soon enough. Good job, Eric."

"Yes," added Gerald, "a good job indeed. Other than Redding's little hiccup this morning, I'd say it was a very productive day. I'm sure he'll settle down after a day or two. Besides, his only job now is to show you the maintenance routines so you can become more familiar with strategic locations for our explosives."

"I'm sure he'll do that quite well," said Eric.

Then Becker asked a question no one had anticipated. "Do you think there is any possibility of obtaining one of the Norden sights before we complete our mission here?"

"Do you mean a complete, functioning sight?" asked Eric in disbelief.

"Yes, a complete sight."

"What are you talking about?" Gerald interrupted.

"What I mean," said Becker, "is why can't we expand our mission to obtain one of the sights and sneak it back to Germany? Our superiors would be thrilled."

"Yes, I'm sure they would be," answered Gerald, "but that is not our mission."

"You realize we always have the ability to expand our mission if we deem it realistic and beneficial to Germany. Can you imagine how valuable one of the sights would be to Goering? *And*, that was our original mission."

"Yes, I know it was. But that is *not* our mission now. We discussed this earlier. Germany has no real use for the sight. There is no possibility of them bombing either England or America now. Those hopes are long gone."

"That is the thinking today. What if their thinking, their strategy, changes six months or a year from now? Would you not agree the Norden sight would be a huge advantage?"

Gerald sighed. "Perhaps. But our superiors have spoken, and they have said—no, they have *directed* us—to destroy America's capability to produce the sights, not steal one."

"Yes, but—"

"And what about the increased risk to our current mission?" interrupted Gerald, now becoming irritated with Becker. "What if we fail our current orders attempting to fulfill your desire to obtain one of the sights? What then do we tell our superiors? That we took it upon ourselves to deviate from their direct orders to do what *we* thought was best for Germany? No, I think not. Our mission is quite clear, *and* risky enough as it is. Believe me, if Herr Goering truly believed having one of the sights in his possession was that important, our mission would be obtaining one of the sights. But he doesn't, and it isn't."

Becker focused his attention on Eric. "You've been in the plant. What are the possibilities of securing a sight and stealing it from the plant?"

"This is quite enough!" exclaimed Gerald, now at the point of exasperation.

"Answer the question, Mr. Keller," persisted Becker.

"Anything is possible, but Gerald is right. The security is extremely tight. Plus the workers are fully aware they are producing one of the military's most highly guarded secrets. It's almost as though the entire workforce is part of the security."

"But is it plausible?"

Eric slowly shook his head. "I'm just not sure. I've only been there one day. Besides, I agree with Gerald. The increased risk would most certainly jeopardize our primary mission. And if we fail as a result of our own . . . aspirations, then I fear our superiors will show no mercy with our future, whatever that may be."

"I think it's a bad idea too," added Langer.

"There," concluded Gerald, "it's settled. We will continue with the mission as directed. No deviations."

"It is *not* settled," countered Becker. "Gentlemen, we only have this single opportunity to obtain one of the sights. We will never again be this close. It's now or never. To simply blow up the plant is one thing, but to take one of the sights from under the noses of the Americans will not only help Germany, but also demoralize the arrogant people here in this country. We don't have a choice."

"You are correct about that," argued Gerald. "And the choice is not to expand our orders on your say-so."

"May I make a suggestion?" pleaded Eric to break the growing hostility between Becker and Gerald.

"What is it?" demanded Becker.

"Look, it's just my first day. Give me a week to become more familiar with the plant. By then I'll know more about the security and any possibility of stealing one of the sights, or even a part of a sight. At that point you can contact our superiors with this information, then they can decide if we should expand our mission."

Becker leaned back in his chair and folded his arms. He realized this was the best option for the time being. He also knew the other three men at the table were not going to proceed on stealing a sight without Berlin's approval. He made up his mind a sight was indeed going to be stolen, even if he had to do it on his own; then all the glory and accolades from their superiors would be his, and only his.

"Well, Mr. Keller," said Gerald, grinning, "again you have impressed me with your wisdom on a delicate situation. I believe your idea to be an excellent one."

"As do I," added Langer, unwilling to take on any more risk than necessary.

"Mr. Becker?" Gerald looked for Becker's agreement.

Becker leaned forward and looked all of them in the eye, conveying his obvious contempt for their lack of vision and their cowardice. "Very well. One week then." With that he pushed back his chair from the table. "Good evening, gentlemen. I must prepare for my own meeting at the plant next week." He turned and left the room, heading up the stairs to his bedroom. A few seconds later they heard his door slam.

"Don't they call that pouting?" asked Langer.

"Indeed they do," answered Gerald.

"I think another drink is in order." Eric walked over and poured himself another vodka. "By the way, I think it would be a great idea for June to play her violin for us some evening. It would do all of us some good. Even Becker."

Gerald was beginning to take a genuine liking to Eric. "Another splendid idea. I'll talk to her about it."

Eric waved a friendly good-bye to Gerald the next morning when he dropped him off at the gate of Lucas-Harold. He wouldn't normally wave to a fellow intelligence officer but believed it important to keep up the illusion for the factory workers. For all they knew, Gerald was a friend, father, or brother—preferably anyone other than who he really was. Gerald smiled and waved back before pulling out of the limited drop-off area.

It was an overcast morning, the cold gray clouds moving briskly across the sky. The sun was conspicuously absent. Snow flurries were swirling in unison at a steep angle, appearing to do anything within their power to avoid meeting the ground. Soft, muddy footprints from the day before had frozen overnight into hard concretelike formations. Workers pulled their coat collars up around their necks as high as they could stretch them. Most of the men pulled the flaps of their fur-lined hats down to cover their ears. The women equally bundled themselves in warm coats, colorful scarves, and knitted hats for protection against the bitter breath of late November. All the workers stuffed their hands deep into their coat pockets and their lunch boxes under their arms. Without hands to hold them, some clenched their cigarettes in their lips, puffs of smoke immediately disappearing into the strong wind along with the frosted breaths of those who had refrained.

Eric stood in line, reaching for his pass to show the guard who was standing outside the gate entrance. As he advanced toward the guard shack, he noticed the same two soldiers as the day before. After a few moments, the sergeant in the shack made eye contact with Eric and recognized him. Eric smiled and held up his red pass, signifying it went well the day before. The sergeant smiled back and nodded his head. The guard mouthed the words, "Good for you." Then he looked the other way and took a drink of his coffee.

Two women stood in front of him, slowly making their way to the entrance. Eric couldn't help but overhear their conversation. They were complaining about the weather, the absence of their boyfriends overseas who were fighting who knew where and, most of all, the damn war. When would it end so everyone could come home? Two young men walked up behind Eric and took their place in line. Even though baseball season was long over by now, the two men were arguing over the World Series. More specifically, how could *The Sporting News* not give Stan Musial the Player of the Year award? Even though the Yankees won the Series, Musial possessed the best overall statistics. One of the men believed it was given to Spud Chandler because the Yankees won the Series. None of it made any sense to Eric. He hoped they wouldn't involve him in the conversation, asking for his opinion. He kept looking forward and displayed his pass as he walked by the guard.

Once inside, Eric moved with the others over to the wall where the time cards were stored in gray, metal slots, one for each worker. Sorted in alphabetical order, he pulled the card marked *"KELLER, E"* and quickly inserted it into the time clock, invoking a distinct "click" that let him know his card had been stamped with the current time. He quickly removed the card and placed it in an identical rack on the other side of the time clock. Each worker took a turn, so the process repeated every few seconds. The repetitive click, click, click sound dominated the time clock area twice a day, where a soldier stood watching.

Eric walked down the long hall, then turned right, past a line of more than twenty worktables. Workers took their places like actors in a play. Most of the employees in this first section were women. He could see them exchanging pleasantries, placing their lunch boxes under the tables, and hanging their coats on the backs of their chairs. Eric did his best to remain invisible, avoiding all eye contact. He walked past another soldier with only a sidearm, no rifle or machine gun, who was surveying the group of workers for irregularities of any kind. Even though he smiled at many of the workers, mainly the women, he was all business. The soldier gave Eric a quick glance, checking the ID clipped to his shirt. Eric dipped his head in acknowledgement. The soldier did not return the gesture and immediately turned his attention back to the tables and the carts placed beside them that contained parts.

So far he had seen four soldiers, excluding the guards walking the perimeter of the fence surrounding the factory: two at the guard shack, one at the time clock, and one at the assembly worktables. Lucas-Harold was taking security seriously! Becker was fooling himself if he believed they had any realistic chance of stealing a complete Norden sight.

He continued down the large hall where the concrete-block walls were painted a dull, lime-green color. Very practical, but ugly in his opinion. He passed a large overhead door where the main assembly line was located. He could hear machinery clanging along with other sounds of mechanical movement, mostly gears grinding against one another. He stopped for just a moment, realizing production in America was not unlike that of Germany; at least, the way it used to be. The workers were already working with beelike efficiency, working the machines as though they were an extension of their bodies. This section was staffed more by men than women. The foreman was walking up and down the aisles, occasionally stopping to check work or converse with one of the workers. The rapport appeared to be quite amicable. Just before Eric moved down the hall, he noticed yet another military guard. Again carrying a sidearm. Again all business. That made five.

He immediately recognized the obvious pattern. An armed military guard was stationed in each section of the factory. There would be no conceivable way to avoid them during his maintenance rounds, which were to begin today. Caution was going to be paramount. Finally he walked to the end of the hall where there was no worker activity and the sounds of a busy factory quieted. There, with "MAINTENANCE" painted in large black letters on a door, he found the maintenance department—his department. He was relieved there was no guard or any other activity in this part of the building. It would at least provide a small level of privacy. He and Redding would be able to converse out of range of probing ears and eyes.

Eric walked in and saw Redding eating what looked like a piece of cake with only his hands. He was sitting at a tattered, gray, metal desk that faced the wall. A large corkboard hung on the wall in front of him. The corkboard was chock-full of pinned papers of all sizes, most bearing the serious header of "MEMORANDUM." On the desk were dozens of handwritten scraps of paper with dates and other numbers on them. Eric thought it a complete and disorganized mess. This would never do in Germany. Neatness is the key to a clear mind, and thus the efficiency of work.

"Good morning," said Eric. He walked up to Redding, doing his best not to startle him.

Redding put the slice of cake down on a napkin and reached for his coffee. "Good morning. Are you ready for your first real day?"

"Yes, I think so."

"Good. Grab that chair over there and let's talk a bit before we get started."

Eric took a few steps over to the other tattered, cluttered desk. He set his own lunch box on it and took hold of the chair, turning it where he could face Redding.

"Let's get one thing straight right now," said an irritated Redding as he peered into Eric's eyes. Eric had no idea what prompted his cross attitude or where this was going. "Fuller was a good kid," continued Redding. "He did his job and never complained. He was always at work on time and did whatever was asked of him. Not only that, he was a damn good mechanic. Could fix anything. Why in the hell did you guys have to kill the poor guy? He never hurt anybody. Now his wife is gonna have to raise that baby all on her own!"

"Baby? We didn't know he had any children."

"Not yet, but his wife is six months pregnant."

Eric sighed. "We didn't know." Now he hated Jon more than ever.

"You could have asked me. I would have told you!"

"Killing Fuller was not the plan. The instructions were to *disable* him, just enough to prevent him from working for a few weeks. That's all."

It was obvious Redding wasn't buying it. "Well, your plans don't hold muster. How is running him off the road in a frozen creek not gonna kill the poor sap? And then you kill two men, not just Fuller!" Redding held up two fingers. "Is this the way you people do everything?"

Eric did his best to be contrite. "No, it's not the way we do everything. I'll admit, the plan with Fuller did not go well. You have to believe me, we were not trying to kill him. It was an accident." Even saying those words, Eric knew in his heart Jon had planned to kill the innocent Americans despite what he and Gerald had agreed on. Jon took pleasure in it. Jon's only regret was that two Americans were murdered that day, not more.

Redding studied Eric. He seemed to be telling the truth, but Fuller's death was completely unnecessary. He took some more sips of his hot, black drink, peering at Eric over the top of the cup, steam gently rising into the air. Redding knew there was nothing he could do. Fuller was dead, and he was committed to this mission, even if halfheartedly now. To back off from helping these German agents even in the slightest would not only mean certain death for him, but more than likely for his family too. If they could kill Fuller without a second thought, they would surely kill him and those he loved just as quickly and easily. He had no option other than to see this through.

"Well, I'll just have to take your word for it."

"I guess so," answered Eric.

Redding turned and grabbed a small, red, ringed binder with large white letters on the front marked "SCHEDULED MAINTE-NANCE." He tossed it on the desk between Eric and himself. "This is where we're going to start." Eric stared at the binder, having no idea what it was. "I've given it a lot of thought," said Redding. "The best way to show you all the potential areas for completing your mission is by inspecting areas we're responsible for. Everyone expects us to complete these inspections, especially management. If a machine breaks down and they see we didn't do our regular inspection, our asses get chewed out. And believe me, they will not hesitate to chew them out. The first thing they'll do if something breaks is go through this log and check the last time we did our regular maintenance inspection. If there is no record of it being inspected, there's going to be trouble. Workers, management, and even the guards are used to seeing maintenance men walking the plant, poking and probing about. It's our job. No one is going to suspect anything unusual."

"Makes sense," agreed Eric.

"Of course it makes sense. It's the only way for you to see every part of the plant without interference. It's the only way you're gonna be able to place your little device without being noticed. *Trust me*." Redding could not help adding the last comment.

Eric smiled. "I really don't have a choice, do I?"

"No. Now let's get started." Both of the men studied each other, realizing they had reached an understanding. Satisfied, Redding grabbed the binder and flipped open the book to a section marked "CRITICAL COMPONENTS." He pointed to the first item. "This may be the most vulnerable part of the factory. We'll start here."

Before the two men left the maintenance room, Redding pointed to a group of five lockers, one of them with a piece of tape over the handle that simply read "KELLER." Eric changed into the company-provided protective clothing, which fit well considering no one had taken his measurements. Earlier that morning Redding had merely guessed Eric was Fuller's size and had picked out one of his many pairs of available overalls for Eric to use. Redding had hung them in Eric's assigned locker before he arrived for work. Eric noticed the name "FULLER" was still taped on the locker next to his. He correctly presumed Redding had left it there as a reminder of the team's ruthlessness. He knew the reminder would greet him every morning as he changed his clothes.

Once changed, Redding led Eric toward their first stop, deep into the factory past dozens of workers. Eric held the red binder under his arm while Redding grasped a clipboard with attached checklists. Both looked official, like they were on a mission—a mission to do nothing more than insure the mechanical efficiency of the very important production line.

For the most part, the employees largely ignored them. Some would quickly look up from their work to see who was walking past, but just as quickly lower their heads back to the task at hand. Even the guards gave them only a passing glance, realizing their importance and the necessity for them to be there. They were the "grease" to keep the all-important production line moving.

This was how the military guards saw them as they fit into the factory: Germany was the enemy, they needed to be destroyed, American bombers were destroying the enemy, the bombers were doing it with the help of the Norden bombsight, the bombsights must be produced, and maintenance kept the line moving to produce the sights. Simple. It wasn't complicated. Let maintenance do their job, do not bother them. They were helping win the war.

As Eric continued to walk through the plant with Redding, he realized more and more how brilliant Gerald's plan was. He and Redding had full and unencumbered access to every nook and cranny in this critical facility. Even all of Lucas-Harold's company security, all the military guards, and all the loyal Americans who were working the production line, weren't enough to stop him. A German intelligence officer was walking among them, unnoticed and invisible. The enemy was in the hive and bent on destroying them, and they didn't even know it. Perfect.

They arrived at one of the larger pieces of equipment near the far end of an enormous room. Eric guessed thirty to thirty-five employees worked in this area. Redding stopped and placed his clipboard on a table next to the machine, acknowledging the worker operating it. Redding walked over to the worker and raised his voice to be heard over the sound of the machine. "You can keep working. We just need to check the grease fittings. Don't want them to run dry." The worker nodded he understood and immediately went back to his specific task.

Redding motioned for Eric to join him as he leaned down beside one of the rear panels, out of sight from the worker. Eric got down on one knee and waited for Redding's instructions. Redding took a small screwdriver from his overall pocket and began removing the screws holding the panel in place. The panel was approximately three feet square and, despite its size, it was not heavy; one man could easily remove it. From the other pocket, Redding withdrew a flash-light and pointed with its beam of light. It revealed a compartment about the size of two refrigerators that contained all sizes and shapes of gears, rods, belts, and even two chains. All were moving at a frantic pace and making a loud noise. A misplaced hand, finger, or even an overall sleeve could spell disaster for whoever ventured too close to the moving parts.

Redding knew it would be impossible for the worker to hear what he said above the noise of the machine. "This is where the device should go," he said to Eric. He moved the beam around to a small ledge inside the large machine where a small package could easily be placed. Eric studied it a moment, formulating in his mind a proper bomb size and how he could secure it. The machine's vibration would be a problem; much care would be required to keep the bomb in place. He memorized the location and shape of the small ledge. Eric signaled to Redding he had seen enough. "Let's put the panel back on and move to the next one."

Redding nodded, and the two men screwed the panel back on the machine. Once finished, Redding stood and walked back over to the worker. He motioned for Eric to join them. Once the three men were together, Redding explained to the worker what was going on.

"There's enough grease to last another week or so, but it is running a little low." The worker indicated his understanding. Redding continued. "This is Fuller's replacement. He'll be doing the maintenance next time, so he'll be the one filling the grease cocks." Again the worker acknowledged. Then they were finished. Redding looked at Eric, and he nodded his understanding. Very smooth and logical. He would be able to place a bomb in the machine right under the nose of the worker. Eric thought it almost humorous that the worker may be more alarmed if he didn't show up again than if he did show up with a device to be placed in the machine. How ironic. This was too easy!

Over the next few hours, the two men made inspections on eleven other machines. Not all were good candidates for explosives. Redding was correct about the first machine. Even so, there were at least five or six other machines that would accomplish two things: first, easy access and ample room to place a device; second, locations that would prove devastating to the production of Norden sights. This was an excellent start, and Eric felt encouraged about their prospects.

Prior to their lunch break, Eric and Redding stopped back in the maintenance room. No one else was there, and it was remarkably quiet considering how close they were to the noisy factory.

"Is it always this quiet back here?" asked Eric.

"Usually," answered Redding. He tossed the clipboard on the desk. "Well, what do you think of the machines we looked at this morning?"

Despite his initial feelings about Redding and his competency to fulfill his part of the mission, he was impressed with the thoroughness in which Redding had completed his job. At least up to this point.

"I'm not a mechanic, but it looks to me like you've done an excellent job with your selections. What does that first machine we looked at do?"

Redding smiled. "In my opinion, it's the Holy Grail of the entire plant."

That piqued Eric's interest. "How so?"

"Well," replied Redding, "it produces two very important components. One is the gyroscope, and the other is the trial arm. The sight is pretty much worthless without those two items. Put those two out of commission, and well . . ."

"Very good. How long would it take them to make repairs and bring the line back up?"

Redding thought for a moment. "I'm not really sure, but I can safely say it would take weeks, if not months. Perhaps longer. One thing I do know, if you can take even that one machine out, you're gonna cause a lot of pain around here."

Eric folded his arms and leaned back in his chair, his mind still working on what kind of explosive to use. One that was not only reliable but would also do the most damage.

Redding interrupted his thoughts. "You better eat your lunch. This afternoon we'll be busy doing regular maintenance duties. You may as well go through the motions."

Eric smiled. "I agree." He reached for his lunch box, curious to see what June had packed for him.

CHAPTER 8

THE PROBLEM

Ten days had passed since Eric's first day at Lucas-Harold. He had set two objectives for himself thus far, and he had accomplished both. The first was to simply blend in, which he did, even more easily than he ever could have imagined. By the end of the first week, he could see that most of the workers recognized him in his familiar gray overall, always with the maintenance binder under his arm. He did look official and was only doing his job. The second objective was to select the locations for the explosives, and then become acutely aware of everything around them. That included maintenance schedules, guard rotations, workers, foremen checks, and, most of all, the ability to place the bombs out of view of curious, prying eyes. That he also accomplished.

With each day that passed without incident, Eric became more confident in their mission and its ultimate success. His nerves were beginning to settle, allowing him to think more clearly and act more deliberately. In the beginning he was extremely wary of the very real possibility someone might be watching him. Someone who knew who he really was and what he was doing there. Someone waiting for the right moment to pounce. Someone who would sneak up behind him, stick a gun in his back and state with authority, "Mr. Keller, you're under arrest." It never happened. He especially kept his eyes on the military guards; even though they did their best to be cordial with the workers and management, they took their job seriously. Eric could not afford complacency. Not now. To do so could result in failure, imprisonment, or even death. He didn't have the luxury of letting his guard down. Not even for a minute.

Redding, on the other hand, was becoming more nervous with each passing day. He realized the day was approaching when the German intelligence officer would place the bombs, set the timers, and totally destroy the all-important production lines. The group of agents did not inform Redding of the actual day; they decided he was a liability, perhaps a minor one, but a liability nonetheless. Divulging that important detail to Redding was unnecessary and dangerous. Not that Redding would intentionally disclose such an important detail to the authorities, but rather let an innocent slip-of-the-tongue derail everything the agents had been planning. This was too important. Redding would be kept in the dark.

Every night June had dinner either on the stove or in the oven by the time Eric and Gerald arrived back at the house. And every night Eric and June exchanged gazes filled with mutual attraction. Both were cautious to prohibit their emotions from getting the better of them. Several times both had resisted the temptation for a secret rendezvous. They continued their conversations, each refraining from becoming too personal. One thing could lead to another. Even so, they both felt the undeniable pull of attraction.

Gerald continued to drive Eric to and from work. It would not look right if a new, young employee had his own car, especially when so many were making sacrifices. Most would have dismissed the appearance of such a luxury, but it only took one curious person to raise suspicions and begin asking questions. It was a risk Eric and the others were not prepared to face. When some of the workers asked him how he was getting to work, Eric replied a friend was helping him out until he could afford his own vehicle. The story seemed to work, and then it was forgotten.

Eric walked into the kitchen once again after a long day at the plant. Gerald was still in the garage getting something out of the car. June was in the kitchen peeling potatoes. She looked up and thought Eric looked more tired than usual.

"Long day?" she kept peeling.

"It was. This maintenance thing is harder than I thought. I assumed it was going to be easy, the maintenance part. But my supervisor works very hard and keeps me busy. Even so, I'm enjoying it. I've actually learned a few things about machines and mechanics. I think my mother would be proud."

"Are you trying to say you're not manly like your brothers, who can fix anything?" June smiled as she kidded him.

"I don't think manhood has anything to do with whether or not you can work on machines," replied Eric in a feigned attempt to defend himself.

"Uh-huh. If you say so," continued June with the mock debate.

"Well, there are more important areas where one can prove himself to be a man."

"Oh, and what would they be?"

Eric walked up to the counter where June was standing. He leaned over, deliberately close so he could smell her, and reached above in the cabinet for a glass. He slightly brushed his arm across her shoulder as he did so. He could barely feel her soft shoulder through her blouse. A very slight gesture, but the closeness, the subtle touch, was slightly erotic, perhaps partly due to Becker and Gerald prohibiting any contact at all with June other than what related to the mission. The fact their increasingly intimate contact during Eric's brief stay at the house was forbidden, made even the slightest touch, accidental or not, exciting.

June immediately recognized what Eric was doing. She could smell him as well and, as much as she wanted to deny it, his scent aroused her. He wanted to be with her, and not in the kitchen. And she with him. The tension had been building to a much higher level in the previous days. Both of them knew in another situation, in another life, they would be confidants and lovers, perhaps forever. The chemistry, the desire, was clear and undeniable. What brought them together here and now, under the dangerous and stressful environment of this mission, was cruel and regretful. Why couldn't they have met under different circumstances? Was there any possibility of being together after the mission? Would Eric even survive? At the moment, all options appeared fruitless and unkind. Getting involved had no possible chance of a positive outcome.

"For example," answered Eric as he backed away and leaned against the counter, holding the glass in his hand, "when in the presence of a beautiful lady such as yourself—"

Gerald flung open the door in a near panic. "Mr. Keller! Please come with me!"

Eric threw June a puzzled look. Without saying a word, he turned and quickly followed Gerald outside and into the garage. "What is it?"

Gerald had opened the trunk of the sedan and was pointing to some plain brown boxes inside it. "What do you see?"

Eric stared at the brown boxes. The lids were removed, revealing some electronic devices inside with their colored wires tangled in a disarrayed mess. Other than that he noticed nothing out of the ordinary. "Just tell me what's wrong."

Gerald sighed. "These are the timers for the explosives. They have been tampered with."

Eric took a harder look at the boxes. "What are you talking about?"

"What am I talking about?! I'm talking about someone sabotaging the timers for our explosives! Can't you see that?"

Eric leaned over and took a closer look. Even with the trunk light glowing, it was so dark it was difficult to see much detail. It did indeed look like the wires had been pulled apart from the small clocks in the boxes. But without further examination it was impossible to be sure. "Let's take them inside where we can see them better."

"This is a disaster!" Gerald was more upset than Eric had ever seen him.

"Calm down." Eric reached in and grabbed two of the four boxes. "Help me get them inside. Even if they've been tampered with, we may be able to repair them."

Gerald realized he was correct and appreciated his calmness. Gerald again confided to Eric how impressed he was with Eric's wisdom and pragmatic thinking. Perhaps they could be repaired. He took the other two boxes and slammed shut the trunk. He followed Eric into the kitchen where June was putting the potatoes on the stove to boil.

She looked concerned, noticing the two boxes he was holding. "Is everything all right?" Then she saw Gerald storm in behind Eric carrying two more boxes. She thought he looked panic-stricken. This could not be good.

Eric shook his head, conveying bad news. "We may have a problem, but I'm sure we can fix it. Can you put off dinner for a little bit?"

"Of course," she answered. June immediately turned down the burner on the stove to the lowest setting. Knowing she couldn't be of assistance, she wanted to ask anyway. "Is there anything I can do to help?"

"No," answered Gerald, trying to regain his composure. "But thank you. Let's put off dinner for an hour or so, that will be help enough." He didn't want to alarm June any more than necessary. It was too late for that, however. She knew something was terribly wrong, and it made her uneasy.

Eric and Gerald walked past her and into the dining room. They set the boxes on the table, which June had already set for dinner. Both of the men began moving dishes, glasses, and silverware to one end of the table, clearing a large section to further examine the devices. As they removed the contents from the boxes it became obvious, even to the most novice of intelligence officers, the important timing mechanisms had been tampered with, and perhaps irrevocably destroyed.

Eric stared at the tangled mess of wires, his eyes conveying what he desperately did not want to believe. Many of the wires were cut and deliberately damaged beyond any hope of salvaging. He could hear the sound of Gerald letting out a large breath of despair and hopelessness. His shoulders drooped, and a look of defeat and confusion spread across his face. Eric thought he looked pale, as though Gerald had just received news of his own death sentence. And perhaps, in a way, he had.

Becker had been sitting in the living room examining some papers. He heard the commotion and strode over to the dining room. He saw the boxes and tangled mess in a heap. "What's all this?"

Gerald was not able to speak, too dejected to offer an explanation. Eric waited for him to reply. After a few seconds, it was clear Gerald was not going to say anything.

"Our timers have been sabotaged," stated Eric flatly.

"Sabotaged? What do you mean, sabotaged?" Becker was in complete disbelief and perplexed at the same time.

"Just what I said," continued Eric. "Someone has tampered with our explosive timers and rendered them useless." He picked up one of the timers by its tangled web of wires and held it out for Becker to examine. Becker took it from him and began to look at it more closely. Gerald, in the meantime, walked away and looked out the large window, hands on his hips.

Becker looked over at Gerald. "How did this happen!" he demanded.

Gerald turned from the window and eyed the two men standing at the table. "I have no idea. I've been in possession of the car most of the day. Someone, somewhere must have been following me and gained access to the trunk when the car was unattended."

"Well," persisted Becker in an agitated voice, "think. How many times did you leave the car alone?"

"I'm thinking!" snapped Gerald.

"Let's all just calm down a minute," said Eric, as he raised his hand to part the two angry men. He studied Gerald. "Just take your time and retrace your steps. First of all, when was the last time you saw the timers before just now in the trunk?"

Gerald walked over to the table and sat down. He placed his hands on each side of his ashen face, searching his mind to make some sense of when the damage could have occurred. "It was last night, after Langer and I assembled them and then placed them in the trunk. It was around nine o'clock. We had just finished the last one and decided to go ahead and put them in the trunk instead of keeping them in the house."

"Why the hell would you do that?" asked Becker, still annoyed.

"Langer and I were afraid June might find them. We didn't want to take the chance of her moving them or perhaps becoming a little too curious."

"Why would you think June would have any interest in them?" asked Eric.

"That's not what I mean. She's a very thorough housekeeper and has access to every room in the house. We were afraid she would stumble across them and try to move them while cleaning. Langer and I thought it best to put them in the trunk until we had an opportunity to explain to her these boxes were to be left alone and not moved under any circumstances. We needed a safe place to hide them in the house. Somewhere where they could be hidden, where June did not have access. She had already turned in for the night. It was only going to be for one day."

Becker was becoming more and more agitated by the minute. "I think you'll agree it was one day too many!"

Eric was becoming annoyed with Becker and shot him an unmistakable look signaling him to again calm down, or else. Becker understood the meaning and walked to the liquor cabinet and reached for the bottle of scotch. He knew Eric was right, of course. Now was not the time to let emotions interfere with logic and deductive reasoning about how to resolve the current setback. It was obviously important to determine how the timers were discovered and destroyed. Even more important and imperative was how to replace the timers.

Footfalls could be heard on the staircase. Langer heard the raised voices and came down from his room to investigate. He walked into the dining room and saw the four boxes and clump of wires and analog timers on the table, the same ones he and Gerald had assembled the night before. They looked different, much different.

"My God, what happened?" Langer asked.

Before either Becker or Gerald could answer, Eric reached for one of the damaged timers and handed it to Langer. "Someone has tampered with the timers."

Langer looked first at Eric, then at Becker and Gerald for further explanation. None of them were forthcoming. Finally he began to studiously examine the timers, shaking his head in denial. "I can't believe it. How did this happen? We just finished assembling them last night."

"Can you repair them?" asked Eric.

Langer continued to study the damaged devices, turning them over in his hands. "I don't know, whoever did this wanted to make sure they couldn't be used. They may have succeeded."

Gerald walked over next to Langer and studied the timer he was holding. "Do you think there's any chance of salvaging at least some of the parts?"

Langer's mind was racing, pushing his brain to come up with a solution. "Perhaps. We may have to disassemble all of them and save what parts we can. At best we may be able to get a few of them working, but not all. Too much damage has been done. I'm really not all that concerned about the wires. The mechanical timers themselves are the problem. If those have been broken, we're cooked."

Becker joined the group once again with scotch in hand and composure regained. "Gentlemen, please sit down. I think we have another, and perhaps, even larger problem." The men sat down in their usual seats.

"And that would be?" asked Langer.

Becker leaned forward and opened his hands. "Someone definitely knows not only who we are, but where we're living. I believe it's a reasonable assumption they also know where we go and when." Becker looked at Eric. "We have to assume they know you're working at the plant." That sent a chill down Eric's back. Becker continued, "Someone knew we placed the timers in the trunk, and then had access to the car. How that can happen without us knowing about it is disconcerting. What else do they know about us and our movements?" Becker had everyone's attention. "We are in serious danger right now, gentlemen, and we need to consider making some drastic changes to our plan if this person or persons can't be found *and* neutralized quickly. Very quickly."

Gerald was nodding his head. "Yes, I think you're right. We could be heading into a trap. They may even know our schedule for setting off the charges. I don't think we can wait until Christmas Eve to set them off."

"Hold on a minute. I'm not yet sure any of them can be saved," added Langer.

"Just what are you saying?" asked Eric.

Becker was taking a moment to formulate an answer before responding. "If Langer can save some of the timers we should move up our plan. In my mind, we should set the explosives within the next few days. Otherwise our entire plan may come tumbling down around all of us, and we may end up in a military prison . . . or dead."

"You're kidding," quipped Eric. "I'm just now becoming familiar with the machines. Don't you think it's a little premature to go to this extreme? Think of the added risk."

"Yes, I know," agreed Becker. "It does increase the risk, but so does waiting around for another setback to occur. The next one may be more serious."

Gerald was watching Langer handle the timers, carefully dismantling the wires. "I must agree with Mr. Becker. We have obviously been compromised. Waiting any longer only exposes us to further risk. We may be on the eve of discovery and even apprehension. Waiting at this point is foolhardy in my opinion."

"Don't we have a duty to inform Berlin?" asked Eric. Anything to buy more time. Secretly, and ashamedly so, he didn't want to leave June so soon. He had been looking forward to two more weeks.

"I'll be honest," answered Becker, "there may be a traitor in the communication chain with Berlin. I don't know how many hands our communications must go through to reach them, but it surely goes through many. One of those hands may be dirty. One of those hands may be the person we're looking for. I've suspected it ever since the farmhouse. I don't have proof, it's just a feeling. But I fear I'm correct in this assumption. I don't think we can trust them right now."

"So, you're suggesting we act on our own, institute our own change to the original plan?" questioned Eric.

Becker paused once again. "Yes, that's what I'm suggesting."

"You know," added Gerald, "if we change Berlin's instructions and fail, there will be no help from Berlin, or anyone else for that matter, when we make our escape. We'll be on our own."

"In my mind," said Becker, "we're already on our own."

The table was quiet for a few moments while the four men contemplated their predicament and possible fates. None of their options offered much hope. They would need luck, a lot of luck. Eric had felt the mission was doomed from the moment they left the submarine. Everything that occurred since that terrible night had worked against them. All of their luck was bad up to this point. Then he corrected his thinking. June was the only positive thing to happen during this entire ordeal. That alone, in his mind, made it all worthwhile. The thought of never seeing her again saddened him deeply.

Eric addressed Becker, focusing his thoughts once again on the plan. "What about Jon? Has he had any success identifying this person? We haven't seen him in days."

"As you know," explained Becker, "he has been busy working with the Abwehr. I spoke with him last night. It seems they have questioned several people, all of them former German loyalists. All but one has been eliminated from any suspicion."

"And what of that person?" asked Gerald with much interest.

"That individual is still being questioned, under some duress, I may add, to force him to be more forthcoming with his answers."

"You mean tortured, don't you?" asked Eric.

"Call it whatever you like. It produces results."

"I'm sure it does. My concern is that it produces accurate results," added Gerald. "We don't have the luxury right now of proceeding on inaccurate information. Have they produced anything we can use?"

"The only piece of information obtained with any regularity is the very real possibility our person of interest may be a woman." Revealing that information made Becker smirk, unwilling to believe it himself.

"A woman?" Skepticism was obvious in Gerald's voice.

"Yes, I know. My guess is, if a woman's involved, she's working at the plant and has been watching Eric closely." Becker turned his attention to Eric. "Have you noticed anything, anything at all from a woman at the factory?"

Eric thought. "No. But there are so many women working the assembly lines, it would be nearly impossible to single out just one."

"Well, you must be on your guard now more than ever," cautioned Becker.

Langer grabbed two of the timers. "I may be able to save these two. Not sure yet, but I think it's possible."

"How long will it take before you know for sure?" asked Gerald.

"I'll get started on them right away. I need to concentrate, so I'm taking them to my room. Should know more by morning." Without saying another word, he headed toward the staircase and his room with the timers. The others nodded, hopeful in Langer's ability to salvage what he could.

"I'm still confused how anyone knew the timers were in the car, and then was able to gain access and damage them. Why didn't they just take them?" asked Gerald.

June peeked her head through the swinging kitchen door. "Do you want me to wait longer on dinner?"

"No," answered Gerald. "We're all hungry, you can bring it in. You'll need to serve Langer in his room tonight." June nodded her understanding. As soon as she disappeared back into the kitchen, Gerald began gathering up the rest of the damaged timers along with the clump of wires and forced them into one of the remaining boxes. "She doesn't need to see this."

"Even if Langer can repair the timers, I don't see how we can get them in place and properly set within the next couple of days," complained Eric. "There's too much risk."

"I don't see where we have a choice now," responded Becker.

"You're not the one taking the risk."

"We're all at risk, you know that."

"Perhaps," persisted Eric, "but it's my ass in the factory. I'm the one who has to get them inside the machines. Without getting caught."

"What are you saying? Are you afraid? Are you refusing to carry out your mission?"

"Of course I'm afraid. I'm not an idiot."

"I didn't say that."

June inadvertently interrupted the argument by re-entering the dining room and setting the hot bowls of food on the table. She was acutely aware something was amiss. Something serious. She dared not ask any questions. Eric, Becker, and Gerald remained quiet for a moment while June was in their presence.

"June?" asked Gerald.

"Yes?"

"Have you noticed anything unusual around the house lately? Perhaps someone lurking around, or perhaps some unexpected workmen? A nosy neighbor, that sort of thing?"

June looked up from her dinner duties and paused for a second before answering. "No, not really. Is something wrong?"

"No, my dear," answered Gerald. "Just wondering."

June smiled, but knew her answer disappointed not only Gerald, but Becker and Eric as well. She turned to fetch the biscuits from the kitchen when she looked back at Gerald. "It's probably nothing, but the neighbor's dogs were barking wildly late last night. They woke me up. I got up to see what the commotion was about, but there was nothing I could see, so I went back to bed."

"Which neighbors?" asked Becker.

"The garage side," she answered. With that, she exited through the swinging door and out of sight of the three men. They all looked at each other.

"I think we'd better have a look around the garage," said Becker.

All three men got up from the table and walked through the kitchen past June. She was surprised to see them, knowing they didn't have time to even begin eating, let alone finish their meal.

"Is there something wrong with dinner?"

"Of course not," replied Eric. "We just need a minute to check on something. We'll be right back. Everything's all right, don't worry." But Eric was doing just that. Worrying. So were the others.

"June, where's the flashlight?" asked Gerald.

"In the second drawer by the door," she immediately answered. Concern was growing on her face.

Gerald rushed to the drawer, found the flashlight, and then quickly clicked it on and off to make sure the batteries still had power. Satisfied, he nodded at the others, and then the three men grabbed their coats in the mudroom by the door and walked out the side kitchen entrance. They quickly approached the detached garage just twenty-five feet from the house. Gerald clicked on the flashlight, pointing it at the ground. They walked together around the front and then to the side where there were two windows. Gerald walked up to them and pointed the flashlight as he and Becker examined each one closely to see if they had been broken or damaged. They hadn't been. Then they continued around the back of the garage toward the small service door. It was closed, but upon closer examination, Becker discovered deep gouge marks near the lock.

"Shine your light here," pointed Becker. "Look at this."

Gerald and Eric looked closer and also saw the obvious gouges and chunks of wood missing around the simple and inadequate lock. Eric pushed on the door and it creaked open with little effort. The lock had obviously been jimmied and was no longer any use.

"That's not good," said Eric.

They walked into the garage where only the one sedan was still parked. Jon had the other. Eric found the light switch and turned it on. Gerald clicked off the flashlight. The concrete garage floor was dirty. Since none of them had been using the small rear service door, it was apparent to all of them someone had walked in and made himself at home.

"Well," said Becker in a capitulated tone, "this is how they gained access to the car. They must have been watching us from nearby. They had to have seen you and Langer carry the boxes out here. Was the garage door open when you placed the timers in the trunk?"

Gerald looked ashamed and his voice revealed the same. "Unfortunately, yes. We shut the door once we entered the garage, but someone could have easily seen us carry the boxes in here. That is my error, and one I must apologize for."

"Well," observed Eric, "that explains the barking dogs. They must have seen or heard whoever it was breaking in the back door last night."

"I think you're right," agreed Gerald.

Becker opened the trunk and was looking inside for any type of evidence that could still be there. There was just one empty box. Something struck him as odd. He reached down in the trunk and examined the box, then put it back.

"Wait a minute, "said Becker. "Didn't you say there were five timers altogether?"

"Yes," answered Gerald.

"But there were only four of them on the dining room table."

"Ah, that's right. Why?" Gerald began looking in the trunk with Becker and Eric. It only took a moment for all of them to realize one of the timers was missing.

"They took it," Eric quickly deduced.

"I'm afraid so," agreed Becker.

"Why would they do that?" asked Gerald.

"To know what they're dealing with," answered Eric.

"What do you mean?"

"Let's go inside, it's freezing out here," suggested Eric. Without waiting for an answer, he walked back and closed the rear door. As it could not be locked, he found an old wheelbarrow and propped it up against the door so no one could enter without a lot of effort. Then he approached the garage door and opened it, looking back at Gerald and Becker.

"Are you coming?" he asked. Then he exited the garage toward the house. Becker and Gerald were close behind, Gerald closing and locking the garage door.

Once inside they walked directly past June and into the dining room where they sat down and remained silent for a few moments. June could do nothing but stare at the men as they walked by. Something was obviously wrong; they wore their troubled faces like signs of doom. No words were needed. Even Eric's familiar reassuring look had vanished. This was really serious.

Eric stood up from the table. "Langer should be here." He walked to the bottom of the stairs and called his name.

Langer appeared at the top of the staircase. "What?"

"You better come down here," answered Eric.

Langer joined the other three men at the table. "OK, what is it?"

Becker held up the empty fifth box he had retrieved from the trunk a few minutes earlier. "How many timers do you have in your room?"

"Four."

"And how many boxes are on the table?"

Langer quickly counted. "Five. So where's the last timer? Did you discard it?"

"Hardly," replied Gerald.

"Then where is it?" Just then Langer began to surmise the problem. Before anyone could answer, he replied to his own question. "It's gone, isn't it?"

"I'm afraid so," confirmed Gerald.

"Is anyone going to tell me what happened?" persisted Langer.

"Someone stole it out of the trunk last night. We found the back door had been broken into," explained Eric.

Langer lowered his head, searching for some kind of explanation. "Any idea who could have done it?"

"We don't know," answered Becker in a very agitated voice. "Enough of this. The timer is gone. Someone knows we're here and what our plans are. We need to do something now!" He looked directly at Langer. "How many of the timers can be saved?"

"I'm not sure yet, maybe three. For sure two. I need more time."

"Well, we don't have any more time," declared Becker.

"Just wait a minute," reasoned Eric. "We don't know if they know our plans or not. Yes, they know we're here. They know we have explosives. But we don't know for sure if they are aware of what, when, and where we're going to use them."

"Mr. Keller," asserted Becker, "again you amaze us with your naivete with such matters. Do you really believe anyone who can get this close to us, and even abscond with one of our timers, doesn't know the details of our mission?"

"Then why don't they just arrest us?"

"That I don't know."

"I believe it's because they don't know. At least, know for sure." Eric looked over at Gerald for some support.

Gerald glanced at Becker, whose face was turning red. "He may have a point. They may be waiting for us to show more of our hand. I agree, they know about us and where it's going to happen. After all, they've surely followed Eric and me to Lucas-Harold. Even so, I seriously doubt they know *when* we intend to act."

"As I stated before," said Becker with more certainty than ever, "we must move up the schedule."

"How soon are you talking about?" asked Langer, alarmed. "I need more time with the timers."

"Can you have them ready in a day or two?" asked Gerald, now resigned to Becker's line of thinking.

"Perhaps, but I can't guarantee it."

"Just do what you can," said Becker. "If you will focus on the timers, we'll start preparing a new plan." Then he looked at Eric. "I think tomorrow you should plant the explosives themselves. You can attach and set timers just as soon as they're ready."

Eric did not like it. Not one bit. He did realize, however, that the group had been compromised. Perhaps fatally. Now they had one chance, and only one chance, to complete the mission. And Becker's idea was the only plausible one, as much as he hated to admit it. Even at his young age, he knew mistakes happen when in a hurry. Careless mistakes, deadly mistakes. And now they were in a hurry. Then, as before, his thoughts turned to June. He had precious little time with her. Then, he would never see her again. For the first time he hated the mission and what it was doing to him and June.

"OK," said Eric resignedly. "It appears we have no choice."

Becker and Gerald nodded their approval. Langer just stared at Becker, fully aware of the great risk all of them were taking by diverting from the plan. Their training had taught them diversion was to be avoided at all cost. Now the pressure was on him to get the timers functioning properly. He didn't want to contemplate the repercussions if they failed. Berlin would have all of their necks!

Eric addressed Becker. "Just where the hell is Jon, and why hasn't he provided us any useful information? If he was half as good as you claim, odds are none of this would have happened."

Becker placed his hands flat on the table to demonstrate his firmness. "What Jon has been doing the last few days is none of your concern. It is mine, and mine alone. He is doing his duty and following orders. That's all you need to know."

"None of my concern?" angrily replied Eric. "It concerns all us! Our very lives are at stake."

"Let me worry about Jon. You worry about getting the explosives into the plant tomorrow. And Langer will worry about getting as many timers ready within the next few hours as possible. We'll go over final details in the morning." Becker got up and left the table before anyone could reply.

Gerald lifted the lid to one of the pots still sitting on the table. "It's cold," he stated. "I'm starved. Let's see if June can warm some of this up."

+

Eric couldn't sleep. He rolled over and saw the barely luminous hands on the clock indicating exactly 1:07. He laid on his back, hands behind his head. Fully awake, his mind was playing and replaying everything that had occurred within the last few hours, and what would take place in the next forty-eight. He was nervous and, yes, frightened. He realized his anxiety would sharpen his senses. It would also increase his heart rate. The increase could, if he were not careful to control it, betray him as well.

He was surely being watched at the plant. By whom and where were questions for which he didn't have the answers. The only thing he did have the answer to was that the Americans were onto them. There was no doubt about that now. How long had they known about them and their mission? How long had they been following them and tracking their movements? Was it possible they knew which machines he had selected to place the explosives into? Questions, questions. And no answers.

The mission should have been aborted immediately after Lars and Kurt were lost coming ashore. Becker and Jon should never have been assigned to their team. The two Americans should never have been killed at the farmhouse. The accelerated time frame Gerald proposed should never have been approved by Berlin. And now Becker wanted to move up the schedule once again! These disturbing thoughts kept circling on and on in Eric's mind until he finally thought to himself that he would have little, if any, sleep tonight.

Eric threw back the covers and got out of bed. He quietly opened his bedroom door. He walked into the hallway and realized how quiet the house was. All the bedroom doors were closed. He finally heard snoring coming from Gerald's room. How could anyone sleep, he pondered. Was he the only one with a brain that fully understood how dangerous and foolhardy Becker's new plan was? They were all going to end up in prison, or dead.

Eric needed a drink, and badly. He quietly walked down the stairs and over to the dining room cabinet where the liquor was stored. He leaned over, opened the small door, and found the vodka. Medicine for the troubled mind. He took the bottle and walked to the kitchen so he wouldn't wake the others. He set the bottle on the kitchen table and found a small glass in the cabinet where a few hours earlier he had brushed June's shoulder.

He pulled the chair out and poured his vodka, just enough to take the edge off, but not too much. He didn't want to impair his judgment the next day. He sat in the quiet and nearly dark kitchen. The only light came through the side kitchen door from the small yellow bulb attached to the garage itself. It only permitted Eric to see outlines. There, in the quiet and low lighting, he began finding peace and comfort. He sipped the vodka and began thinking of home, and how much he wished he were there at that moment. If only his family knew where he was and what he would be doing the next couple of days. They simply wouldn't believe it! They all thought he was in occupied France with Rommel, relatively safe from any danger.

Eric heard a door creak. The sound came from the back of the kitchen near the side door. That was June's room. A moment later June cautiously emerged from the room. She was wearing a flannel nightgown and strained to see who was sitting at the table. She recognized Eric, even in the dim light.

"Eric? Is that you?"

"Yes."

"Is everything all right?"

He sighed, wanting to avoid troubling her with his problems. But he couldn't resist and wanted to share some of his apprehension with someone. She was the only person he really trusted in the house. "No, everything is not all right. I just needed a nightcap to calm myself a little. Sorry I woke you. I'll be quiet, you can go back to bed."

June walked over to the table and sat down. She looked at the glass and then into his eyes, as much as she could see them in the darkness. "I know you're not supposed to talk to me about your job here. But please, tell me what's bothering you. I promise no one will know. Getting it off your chest will help you."

He smiled. "You may be right, but you know I can't talk about it."

June reached for his hand and squeezed it. "I'm very proud of you."

He chuckled. "Me? Why?"

"Because you're so conscientious about everything. I can't help but notice how everyone looks to you when something goes wrong. I'm not blind; I know something's happened. Something bad. I just hope you're not in more danger. I'm not sure I could bear it if something happened to you."

He would need to remain cautious about how much he should say. She was right though. Not even a blind person could ignore the fact there was more tension as well as raised voices in the house the last few days. And after tonight, it was more than clear something was amiss. One could cut the negative atmosphere with a knife. It was naive to think she wouldn't notice.

"How much do you really know about us? About what we're doing here?" he asked.

June thought for a moment before answering. "I know all of you are on some kind of mission for Germany. Mr. Kahn said as much before he hired me. It doesn't take a genius to know it's dangerous. I also know you'll be leaving soon. After you're gone I'm supposed to leave this house and never come back. That's all I know."

"It's probably best you don't know more. You could be in danger if you did."

She remained quiet for a moment. "Are you going to die?"

"Well, I hope not. But it's possible if things don't go right."

With that June felt a twinge creep down her spine. Even in the darkness, Eric could sense her concern and sadness.

"Why don't you leave now, before whatever it is begins?"

He squeezed her hand. "You know I can't do that. How could I leave the others behind?"

"Well, maybe they would leave too if they see you're gone. Maybe they would give up whatever they're planning and just go back to Germany."

"Berlin would have all of us killed. They don't tolerate failure very well."

"Killed?"

"Surely you already know that. Wasn't it you who said Germany was murdering its own people, especially the Jews?"

"Yes, but—"

"June," he interrupted. "Our military leaders are ruthless, and they expect success. Germany is finding herself on the ropes these days. They need to land a blow, a decisive one. One that truly hurts the Americans. And soon. If they don't, well then, that's bad for Germany."

June desperately wanted Eric to agree with her. She wanted him to take her away, just the two of them where they could be together forever. She had fallen for him and fallen hard. Her feelings were unmistakable.

"I don't suppose I'll ever see you again," she said resignedly.

With help from the faint beam of light outside, Eric's eyes began to adjust to the darkness. He could now see the sadness on her face, and it saddened him as well. His heart was breaking.

"No, I don't see how that's possible. And for that, I'm truly sorry. It's the one thing I regret about this whole damn thing. There are times I wish someone else had been standing at the stove that first night we walked in; then it would be easy to leave. That very night, I knew you were special. I can't really explain it, but there was a feeling

I had when you turned around and smiled at me with those beautiful blue eyes of yours. I think I fell a little in love with you that night." He regretted saying this as soon as the words left his mouth.

June leaned over and kissed him softly on the lips. He didn't resist. Their lips parted slightly for a moment, then joined together again with more passion. This night, the long-awaited and mutually restrained attraction was more than either one could control. It could be their last moment together, and they wanted to share each other's affection in spite of what anyone else thought or ordered. The feelings of prohibited arousal they had experienced were heightened by the stress, danger, and even the finality of their situation. There was no turning back now. They had crossed a line of mutual capitulation to each other's bodies and the comfort they provided.

June parted first, standing and softly grabbing Eric's hand. She pulled it toward her as she stood. She could see confusion on his face. He stood, following her silent instructions. She turned and slowly led him toward her bedroom door at the end of the kitchen. Eric stopped at the door and looked back toward the dining room and the stairway leading to the rooms upstairs. Then June pulled once again on his hand.

"It's all right," she said softly. "They're sleeping, they can't hear anything down here." Then she pulled him into her room and slowly closed the door. She walked over to the bedstead where a small nightlight glowed beside an end table. Eric thought her more beautiful now than ever, the soft yellow light glowing off her face. She sat on the edge of the bed. She reached up behind her head and untied the small ribbon holding her hair in place, as she did every night when she turned in. Then she began unbuttoning her nightgown. Eric was mesmerized by her beauty and confidence.

June threw back the covers. "Come on, let's get in bed."

Eric walked toward the bed, unbuttoning his shirt. "Great idea."

✦

Eric and June lay in bed, delightfully exhausted. Their sexual tension had been building like an overwound watch ever since Eric arrived. The spring had been released. Both discovered complete escape and ecstasy in each other's bodies and tender affections. Never before had either one felt such fulfillment in another person. There was now a completeness to their forbidden relationship. While making love, neither felt the pressure of Germany, timers, misguided parents, and even the inevitability of their permanent departure. They were truly living in the moment. It was wonderful! Why did it have to end?

June's head rested on Eric's chest. She gently stroked his chest, while he softly played with her hair. He dropped his head slightly and took a deep whiff, his nose taking in the fragrance of her natural smell. He couldn't remember anything so sweet. He would remember it forever, he thought. And miss it forever as well. There must be some way to be together. But how? That was yet another question he didn't have an answer for.

He stroked her arm. "I don't think I've ever felt anything so soft and smooth."

"I bet you say that to all your lovers."

"You're my only lover. I just wish we could be lovers forever."

She turned her head and looked him in the eye. "Me too. I wish it didn't have to end."

Eric sighed. "War really is hell."

"I guess we can blame Hitler for all of this. But then again, in a way it was Hitler who brought us together."

"Hmm ... I guess you could say that. If that's true, it may be the only wise thing he's ever done."

She chuckled. "No disagreement here."

As much as he didn't want to, Eric leaned over and noticed the clock. 2:13. He knew Becker would be up early, laying out the final details for planting the explosives. Eric didn't want to be caught sleeping in June's room when he came down for his coffee.

June sensed a change in Eric's body; it had tensed up. "What's wrong?"

He held her tight again. "I guess I'm a little angry."

"About what?"

"About Becker, about this reckless mission, and most of all, about having to leave you and this inviting, warm bed. That enough?"

"Yes, it sure is. Can you stay a little longer?"

"I'd like to stay forever. What's the worst they can do to me now?"

"I don't think they can do anything."

"Maybe not to me, but they could make it difficult for you."

"How so?" she asked. "We're just two young lovers enjoying each other's company."

"Something tells me they really won't care about that."

"I'm sure they have other things on their minds right now."

"Yeah, you're probably right about that," he agreed.

June reached down and tugged on the covers. Eric helped her pull them up and over her shoulders. It was cool in the room, the cold December night reminding them winter was just around the corner. Now that the body heat they had generated minutes earlier had dissipated, she wanted to cover up.

"May I ask you something?"

"Of course," answered Eric.

"I know you can't, but if you *were* able to leave tonight with me, where would we go?"

"Someplace warm," he kidded.

She gently elbowed him. "No, really. Where would we go?"

He thought a moment, giving it some serious thought. "I miss home, but we definitely couldn't go back to Germany. They would eventually find me, and I don't even want to think about what they'd do to us. Staying here would also be too dangerous, maybe even suicidal for me. I don't know, maybe Canada or South America. Somewhere far away where we could be left alone." Even though he realized such actions were impossible, he was enjoying the speculation. "What about you?"

"You know I love it in America. But I also know it's impossible for you to stay here. You would be in danger for a long time, at least until the war is over and perhaps even longer. No, we'd have to go far away. Canada, maybe. But I would prefer to go somewhere near a large city. I've always wanted to see Paris, that could work. *And* they have a great symphony. I could get a job playing for them."

"Paris? Hmm … now that's a possibility. My French is a little rusty, but I know I could pick it back up in no time at all."

June lifted her head and looked at him. "You've been to Paris?"

"Many times, mostly when I was younger. My mother has some family there and we would take our summer vacations visiting them. She loved the city, even though the French and Germans don't usually get along all that well. I think she secretly wishes she were born French. She loved all the art on display. She also had a fondness for the French way of life. More casual, not too serious. After my father died she thought about moving us there."

"Why didn't she?"

"She couldn't leave the farm. It was her only means of livelihood. We had no money and my brothers loved farming. She stayed because of them."

"What about you?"

"I was more like my mother. I could have been happy in France, but the farm was fine. And my mother felt she was fulfilling her sense of duty to my brothers."

"Paris it is then," said June with finality.

"Paris it is," agreed Eric. He would say anything right now to keep the intimate moment alive and, more importantly, June happy; if only for a brief intermission in their real and tragic situation.

He kissed her on the top of her head, sneaking another whiff. He didn't want to leave but knew he had to. The longer he stayed, the more difficult his departure would be.

"I really have to go," he said with false determination.

"I know. I don't like it, but I know."

"Don't get up, the floor will be freezing. Stay in the bed. It will be easier for me if you don't follow me out."

June didn't say a word. She realized he was right. She remained in bed under the covers while Eric slid out from under the blanket, doing his best to stay strong. He walked over and found his shirt and pants on the floor, piled in a heap. He put his shirt on first, looking down to avoid eye contact with June. He didn't want her to see how sad he was. Then he reached for his pants. As he did so, the lighter fell out of his pocket and clanged on the floor. He grimaced, as he wanted to remain as quiet as possible.

"Sorry," he said. June shook her head, indicating it wasn't important.

He knelt down by the dresser where the lighter had fallen and somehow bounced under the edge of the dresser. June immediately sat up.

"Just leave it, I'll get it in the morning."

"It's OK, I got it." He leaned down a little closer to the floor and saw his lighter. As he was reaching for it, he saw something else. Something that nearly stopped his heart. He stared at it, disbelieving what he saw. He froze, time standing still for a moment. There, not more than a few inches from the lighter, was a mess of wires. And attached to them was one of the timers. A flurry of emotions and thoughts rushed through his head. He extended his hand and pulled the wires and timer out from under the dresser. He stood up and held them out for June to see.

"What's going on? What is this doing here?"

June turned white. Fortunately Eric couldn't see her ashen face in the dim light. She could not answer. June looked directly at Eric with pleading eyes.

"June, what are you doing with these?" His voice was agitated.

"Eric, please sit down." She patted the bed.

"I don't want to sit down. Answer me! What is this doing in your room? Please tell me you didn't know this was here."

"If you sit down, I'll explain."

Eric stood still for a few seconds, unable to move. He was still in a state of shock. What was she doing with the timer? Was she the enemy spy all along? Had she played him? Again, more questions with no answers.

"Please," she pleaded. "Sit down."

Eric gradually moved toward the end of the bed and slowly sat down with the timer in his hand. He laid it on the bed.

"OK. Now tell me what's going on. Did you take the timer out of the trunk?"

She nodded, tears forming in her eyes.

"Did you sabotage the other ones?

She nodded again.

"But why?" he asked.

"I had to."

"What do you mean, you had to?"

"I didn't want any part of this, but I didn't have a choice."

"I don't understand. What do you mean? Do you know the others would expect me to kill you right now for this?"

"Please let me explain, it's not what you think."

"Well, right now I'm thinking you're the American spy all of us are looking for."

"I'm not a spy, but I am working for the American military."

Eric looked up at the ceiling in disbelief. "Damn! I can't believe it. All along I thought you were really interested in me, that we had something! It was all a lie. You've been playing me."

"It's not a lie! That was real, you know it was." She reached over and pulled her nightgown on.

"I'm not sure of anything right now."

"Just listen for a minute, then you can decide whatever you want."

"You have one minute." He could not believe he had made love with this beautiful young woman just thirty minutes earlier. He was sleeping with the enemy. How could he be so blind, so stupid?

June was formulating her thoughts. "Do you remember when I told you how Mr. Kahn came to our house? And that he asked my parents to provide some help for German intelligence?"

"Yes, so what of it?"

"If you remember, my parents were pressuring me to take this job, even though I didn't want to do it. I was worried about it. So much so, I confided in a friend at college. A couple of days later I was approached by two men who work for the American military. Some special group, OSO or something like that. I really don't remember. They asked me to take the job and report what happened in this house to them on a daily basis."

"Do you mean the OSS?"

"Yes, that's it."

"Shit."

"What? Do you know about them?"

"You may say that. They've been on our tail ever since we arrived. Go on with your story." Eric wanted to believe her. To give her the benefit of the doubt. To convince himself she had genuine feelings for him all along.

"Well, these two men were very persistent. They said they knew my parents were sending information back to Germany, and that they could be thrown in prison! Then they said if I would help them on a small job, they would look the other way and not arrest them."

"Those SOBs, if they had enough evidence on your parents, they would have arrested them already. They were lying to you."

"Maybe, but I couldn't take the chance. My parents would not do well in prison. It would be the end of them. So, I said I'd do it."

"What did they ask you to do?" asked Eric, still very agitated with her.

"They asked me to report when you left the house, when you came back, and where I thought you may be going."

"And how did you let them know?"

"Every morning when I fetched the mail I would leave a note in the mailbox with a red cross on the corner. I used lipstick. I think the postman was working for them, but I never saw him."

"My God, this is so simple it's embarrassing."

"I'm glad *you* think it was simple. I was always scared to death one of you would see me or catch on and know what I was doing."

"Trust me, we never suspected you. You played your part well. So what about the timers?"

June reached for a small glass of water sitting on the end table and took a sip. Eric noticed her hands were trembling. She really was nervous.

"Two days ago when I was making up the rooms, I stumbled across these things you call timers in Mr. Kahn's room. He had them hidden under his bed, not a very good hiding place. I had no idea what they were, but it was obvious they were something important. I was told to report anything suspicious, so I let the two Americans know in one of my mailbox notes. The next day when I was at the market, one of the men was there and told me to try and get one, if I could do it without getting caught. I told him I didn't think I could do that, but he kept saying it would help my parents if I could get one."

"I can't believe these cowards asked you to do something so dangerous."

"Well," added June, "I felt the same way, but I didn't think I had a choice. Then he said to destroy it if I couldn't get one out of the house. I think they wanted to examine whatever it was."

"I'm sure you're right about that. So you took one and damaged the others?"

"Yes. I saw Mr. Langer and Mr. Kahn take the boxes to the garage. It only made sense to take them when everyone was asleep."

"Why did you break in the back garage door? You know where the key is."

"I know," she answered, "but I wanted it to look like someone else took them. If there was no sign of a break-in, they might suspect me."

Eric nodded. "Good thinking."

"I looked around the garage for a few minutes and couldn't find the boxes, so I checked the car. The keys were on the seat. I opened the trunk and that's where I found them. There were so many, I couldn't take them all. Besides, the two men from the . . . OSS, they only wanted one. I had to take one for them and try to damage the others like they told me to do. I just started pulling wires and hitting them against one another. I didn't know what I was doing, the dogs were barking, and I was scared to death. What if Mr. Becker or that terrible man Jon would have walked in on me? I knew they would probably kill me on the spot."

"Yes, they would have. I know Jon would."

June bowed her head and began crying. She put her hands to her face, attempting to hide her tears and console herself at the same time. She was in terrible danger and she knew it. The last few weeks had been terribly stressful, resulting in sleepless nights and overjittery nerves. For the last few days, she had convinced herself the men in the house were onto her. It was only going to be a matter of time before Becker or Jon would surprise her in her bedroom holding a gun and put an end to her employment—permanently. She especially feared Jon. He was always studying her, looking at her with an air of suspicion and overall distrust. His glares and perpetual silence frightened her. Something was sinister about him.

She was in love with Eric, or at least she thought so. How was it possible to be in love with the enemy? If she were completely honest with herself, he was the enemy every bit as much as the others. And then again, he was different. The last few days she could sense he was souring on the mission and even on Germany's leaders and their ruthlessness. He had been reading the papers and was becoming enlightened, even persuaded, by America's perspective on the war. On several occasions he had confided to her he did indeed like the Americans he worked with at the plant. He appreciated their hard work and honest ethics. Many of them had asked him if he needed help. Most offered a smile and a wave each morning as he made his rounds at the plant. He was beginning to appreciate the American people. He shared his feelings with June over coffee or the occasional glass of wine late in the evening when they would get a few minutes alone together. Perhaps Eric was no longer the enemy after all. It was obvious he had conflicted feelings.

And what now? He finally knew the truth about her. She was working for the American military. Her job was to spy on them, and if possible disrupt their mission. She may have succeeded in accomplishing that task. Although it was not her intention, Eric had to realize the information she provided to the OSS was endangering him, possibly resulting in his capture or death. Of course he would believe she was playing him, using her attractive looks and innocent charms to lure more information out of him. Information that would be used against him and the others.

Eric moved closer to her on the bed. He gently reached up and took one of her hands away from her face, revealing the redness around her normally beautiful blue eyes. He was angry, yet sympathetic to her predicament. She was trapped. June had been coerced into helping the OSS. Those OSS bastards had taken advantage of a naive young woman, using the parents she loved as leverage to suit their own needs. What options did she have? Could she be blamed for protecting her family? Was it her fault for doing what she believed was the right thing to do for the country she held so dear? In spite of her parents' loyalty to Germany, Eric knew all along June's feelings for America. Yes, she was doing what she had to do. June had no choice, and Eric realized it.

June looked into Eric's eyes. "You must think I've betrayed you, and in a way, I have."

Eric sighed. "I know. But you didn't have a choice. I would have done the same had I been in your shoes. Just tell me you're telling the truth."

June nodded, wiping her eyes with her free hand. "It's the truth, I swear."

Eric knew it was. "I know."

"I'm so sorry. It was killing me to spy on you. I have to admit I really didn't care about the others. But you, you were special. I didn't want to hurt you. I love you."

Eric placed his forefinger to her lips as a sign to be silent. "I think I've known that for a while now. I have the same feelings for you." He let go of her hand and embraced her, holding with all he had the woman he knew he was in love with.

"What are we going to do?" asked June.

Eric released her and stared at the wall, his mind again racing for a plan of escape. "I really don't know. One thing's for sure, we have to get you out of here, and soon."

"OK. But there are some things I need to tell you that you don't know."

His eyebrows raised. "Like what?"

"The two men from the OSS, I think they know a lot more about your plan than you realize."

"What do you mean?"

"I mean I overheard them one day on the phone when they were telling me about the timers. They know you plan to set off some bombs at the bombsight factory, Lucas-Harold."

Eric couldn't believe it. He had been right all along; he and the others were walking into a trap. "I suspected as much. If that's true, why didn't they just arrest us here?"

"I don't know for sure, but I did hear them say they think there could be others, many others involved. They were playing for more time in hopes more enemy agents would be discovered."

"Do they know when we intend to strike?"

"Not exactly. They know it's soon, but not sure how soon. They thought before the end of the year, perhaps around the holidays when a lot of people are off at the plant."

The Americans weren't quite as dumb as Gerald and Becker thought. The OSS had obviously been doing their homework and managed to be on target for most of the details.

"Do you know how they plan to capture us?"

June nodded again. "They want to take you and the others at the plant. They want to take you alive but won't hesitate to shoot if they have to. That's why I wanted so desperately for you to leave—for *us* to leave—tonight! It's not too late. We can leave right now, the keys are still in the car. We can make it to Canada before morning and be safe across the border before they know we're gone. I'm ready, and—"

"June," he said as he stroked her face, "I would love nothing more than to get out of this mess, especially with you. But it just won't work. Becker and his assassin are ruthless and will do nothing short of hunting us to the ends of the earth to kill us. Berlin would expect nothing less. No, that's not going to work."

June thought a moment as they sat quietly on the bed, contemplating their apparent and unfortunate fate. Then she looked up with a hopeful expression. "There may be another way."

CHAPTER 9

ZERO HOUR

Eric came down from his room at half past six, just as he had every morning for the last two weeks. Becker and Langer were already seated at the dining room table. Becker was eating a large portion of scrambled eggs, while Langer was helping himself to a modest bowl of oatmeal covered in syrup. Neither meal looked all that appetizing to Eric. His stomach was already turning in knots, and his appetite was conspicuously absent. He would need to eat something, preferably light and bland.

"Good morning," greeted Eric with little emotion.

"Ah, Mr. Keller. I hope you slept well," said Becker in a feigned attempt to be friendly.

"Well enough," Eric lied. He looked at Langer. "How did you manage with the timers?"

Langer finished his mouthful of oatmeal before answering. "Only two of them could be salvaged. And I can't guarantee them for sure, but it's the best I can do under the circumstances."

Eric became more direct than usual, taking both of the men by surprise. "Are they going to work or not? I'm not risking my life for 'the best I can do.'"

Langer stared at him for a moment. This was a surprising outburst from Eric, but understandable. "Yes, they are going to work."

"Good. That's all I wanted to know." He sat down and reached for the paper, scanning the headlines. He was only going through the motions, his mind elsewhere. Langer looked over at Becker and shrugged his shoulders.

June walked in through the swinging door. "Oh, good morning. May I make you something for breakfast?"

"Any chance I can just get some toast with butter and a small glass of juice?"

"Of course." She turned her attention to the other two men. "Gentlemen, is there anything else I can bring you?"

"I could take some more coffee," requested Becker.

"I'm fine, June," added Langer.

"Very well. I'll be back in a few minutes."

"Thanks."

As soon as June left the dining room, Eric put down the paper and leaned forward in his chair. "Where's Gerald?"

"He ran a short errand," answered Becker.

"At this time of the morning?"

"If you must know, he's paying one of his contacts a visit to see if they have any more timers. He's also picking up the explosive material."

"I hope he remembers he's supposed to take me to work."

"Don't worry, he should be back any time. If not, I'll take you."

Eric nodded. "So what's the final plan? Are we still going for today?"

Becker put down his coffee. "I don't see how we have any other choice. The OSS is closing in. If we delay, if we hesitate, we're doomed. I don't like it any more than you do, but we must act. Waiting will insure failure. Surely you can see that."

Eric knew Becker was right. On Langer's face, Eric saw a look of reluctant acceptance of the new plan. If any one of them refused to go along, then all of them would fail. It had to be a team effort. The odds of success were now greatly diminished, even if all of them played their new roles with near perfection. They had come so far that to give up now would let their superiors down, and all of Germany as well. They had to try, in spite of the new danger.

Eric, of course, knew all along he would go with the new plan and do whatever was necessary.

"Yes, I suppose you're right."

"Good," said Becker with a slight nod. "As we discussed last night, I want you to place the timer in the machine you deem most critical."

"You said timer. Do you mean just one?"

"Yes," confirmed Becker. "As there are only two functioning timers, you will take one. Langer and I will take the other."

"And where are you going to leave it?" asked Eric.

"One of two locations. We have not yet decided."

Eric searched Langer's face, looking for a more definitive answer. "Don't you think you should know before you enter the plant?"

"Well," explained Langer, "we have decided on a primary location. Should it not be possible to place it there, we will go with our backup."

"May I ask where that is?"

"What does it matter? Just concern yourself with your own task. Let Langer and I worry about ours," replied Becker.

Becker's answer agitated Eric. Rather than initiate an argument that he realized would produce little if any positive outcome, Eric remained quiet on the subject. There was another concern, however.

"Fine. Can you at least tell me how we're to escape and then make it to Halifax if we're not communicating with anyone right now?"

"We will drive for the Canadian border tonight after we finish at the plant. By the time the explosives go off, we should be safely across the border. Once there, we'll make contact with our agents up there. Then they'll hide us until things quiet down."

"And what time are we to set the timers for?"

"Gerald and I thought it best just after midnight."

"And what of civilian casualties?" asked Eric.

"We knew that would be a concern of yours," answered Becker. "Only a small crew of janitorial and security workers should still be in the plant. It's the only time we believe the fewest number of workers will be exposed to risk of injury."

"Or death," added Eric.

"Yes, perhaps death." Becker was not going to allow himself to be drawn into another fruitless discussion on the merits of innocent, yet necessary casualties. It had to be done.

"And that will allow us enough time to cross the Canadian border?"

"Yes, ample time. Gerald assures me we can be at the border within four to five hours. Plenty of time."

Eric indicated his approval with a slight nod. He looked at Langer, who had finished his oatmeal and was studying the two men.

"What do you think?" Eric asked Langer.

"I don't like it. But under the circumstances, I think it's the best option."

"What are our chances?" asked Eric, resigning himself to the probability they wouldn't make it out alive.

Langer thought for a moment. "Fifty-fifty at best. Zero if we wait."

Just then the three men could hear a door slam in the kitchen. A few seconds later the swinging door opened and Gerald walked in, out of breath.

"Sorry I was detained, gentlemen," apologized Gerald.

Becker ignored the comment. "Well, did they have any more?"

Gerald shook his head. "Unfortunately, no. They could get more if they had more time, but it would take entirely too long for our purposes."

"What about the explosives?" continued Becker.

"They're in the trunk right now. Plenty of them."

"Good," said Becker. "Two timers will have to do." Becker then motioned for Gerald to sit down, which he did. "Any news?"

"Yes," answered Gerald. He quickly glanced at his watch. "Before I get to that, Eric and I should leave in the next twenty minutes. I just want to make sure he gets the timer in his lunch pail before we leave." Then he looked at Eric. "You'll need to wear the heaviest coat you have today. We'll stuff the explosives in the pockets. I don't think there'll be enough room in the lunch pail for both the timer and explosives."

"That's right," added Langer. "The timer will barely fit, so the pockets will have to work."

"OK," confirmed Eric.

"Are you sure on the connections and the time?" asked Becker.

Eric replied in a sarcastic tone, "Yes, I think I got it."

"Good." Becker turned his attention back to Gerald. "OK, what of the news?"

"Well, it seems Jon has had some success in working with our local agents. As you know, they picked up an OSS agent and were able to question him at length."

"And?" prompted Becker.

"It appears the person we've been looking for is a woman."

With that information, Eric nearly fainted. Adrenaline shot through his veins with that moment's realization that June had most likely been discovered. He was sure June knew nothing of the captured OSS agent and the extraction of this very important information. Her life was now in more danger than ever before.

"A woman?" asked Becker in disbelief.

"I know, it's not what we expected. But if you think about it, it's quite brilliant. None of us would ever have suspected a woman."

Eric was in a near panic and was struggling to control his emotions. He wanted desperately to leap up from the table, grab June in the kitchen, and escape in the car. If any one of the men tried to stop them, Eric knew he wouldn't hesitate to kill him. Leaving now, however, would only thwart the plans he and June had made the night before. No, he would leave the critical revelation to settle for the moment.

"Are you going to tell us who it is?" asked Langer.

Gerald paused. "We don't have a name yet, but Jon is working on it."

"You mean torturing the American until he produces a name," said Eric, again disgusted with the means these men were willing to take.

"Unfortunately, that's our only tool at this point. We're out of time and we need that information soon. Very soon. If we can discover who it is, she can be neutralized. If not, well . . . we may all be doomed as we sit here."

"All right," persisted Eric. "Even if Jon can produce a name, using whatever twisted method he uses, how do we know it's reliable information? Won't anyone say anything if they're under enough duress?"

Becker was becoming annoyed. "Again, you fail to understand what we're up against. What other method would you recommend for extracting this name if you want to avoid making someone uncomfortable?"

"There's a big difference between torture and 'uncomfortable.'"

"As you say, but that doesn't answer my question," argued Becker.

"I wish I had an answer you'd accept, but I don't believe I do."

Becker seemed satisfied with winning the argument. "Then all we can do is hope Jon can determine who this woman is before they make their move."

"He seemed to think it was one of the workers at the plant. But he's not sure. The only thing I am sure of is that he will get the name, sooner or later. Let's just hope it's sooner," said Gerald.

June walked in, realizing she had interrupted something. "I'm sorry. I just wanted to see if Mr. Kahn wanted something for breakfast."

"No thanks, June. I won't be eating this morning. I think it's OK to clean up."

June smiled and nodded her head. Then she went back into the kitchen, the door slowly swinging behind her. Becker was quiet, obviously deep in thought about something. His eyes followed June.

"What about her?" Becker motioned with his eyes toward the kitchen.

"You mean June?" asked Gerald in disbelief that Becker would ask such a thing.

"Oh, come on," agreed Langer. "She's just a kid. It's not possible."

Eric was feeling sick to his stomach. If Becker pressed June, she may break and confess she was indeed working with the OSS. If that happened, Becker, or even worse, Jon, would kill her. He could not let that happen.

"You really are stretching, aren't you?" asked Eric with sarcasm in his voice.

"Why not her?" Becker asked. "She's been here the entire time, has access to every room in the house, knows our schedules, and even has access to the garage." Becker's last comment was directed at the discovery and damage of the timers.

"That's just not possible," chided Gerald. "Her pedigree is strictly German. There is absolutely no disloyalty in her or her family. On that I bet my life."

"You may be doing just that if we don't at least consider her," added Becker.

"So," said Eric, "the Americans were able to recruit a girl barely out of her teenage years, and from a family with German ties above reproach. They trained her in all the skills she needed to be a successful spy at her young age, placed her in this house, and then trusted her with the security of the Norden sight." Eric was really enjoying pointing out Becker's faulty reasoning and hoping it would work. "Yes, I'm sure it's her. Why don't we call her in right now and ask her some pointed questions. Not that we'd reveal what we're up to in the process."

Langer, Gerald, and Eric all stared at Becker, telegraphing their amazement with his ridiculous accusation. Becker had to admit it wasn't plausible. Not even the Americans were that careless.

"I guess you're right. Let's move on." Becker placed a file in front of Langer. "Let's go through our visit one more time together."

Langer nodded, and Eric hoped no one could see the blood rush back to his face after it had all drained to his feet just moments earlier. June was safe, for now.

⊕

Right before leaving for Lucas-Harold, Gerald opened the trunk of the car with the garage door still closed, exposing the prepared explosives. Eric noticed four bundles, more than enough explosive power to do some major damage. All were neatly packed and very familiar to him from his training. It was perhaps the only thing that occurred during the mission he was even remotely acquainted with from the year of preparation for this day. Everything else, to his chagrin, had been unexpected and in many ways a disaster. Per their arrangement, he reached for two of the bundles and placed one in each of his coat pockets. He quickly surveyed the heavy bulkiness of his coat but concluded it wouldn't draw attention. Gerald nodded with approval.

Gerald closed the trunk and got in behind the wheel, as he did every morning. Eric was about to open the garage door when he walked up beside Gerald and said he wanted to double-check something on the remaining explosives that he thought looked odd. Gerald handed him the keys. Eric opened the trunk, and watching him from the rear-view mirror, Gerald could see Eric leaning over. A few seconds later Eric slammed the trunk and opened the garage door. He sat on the passenger side and handed the keys back to Gerald.

"Everything all right?" Gerald asked.

"Yes, my mind was playing tricks on me. I just wanted to check some of the wiring. Everything is fine!"

"Good. Here we go."

The men were quiet in the car on their way to the factory, both obviously preoccupied. So much was at stake today. Would the bombs go off as planned? Where would all of them be tomorrow at this time? Would all of them be alive? Only tomorrow would tell. Before leaving the relative safety of the house, Eric and June had exchanged knowing looks as he walked through the kitchen. No words, however, were spoken. June's eyes told the story, communicating both her concern and hopefulness. Eric returned the same look. Both wanted desperately to stop what they were doing and hold each other, as they each realized they might never see one another again. This could very well be the end. It took all the strength June possessed to hold her emotions together and refrain from sobbing. She loved this man and understood, after just one night of true pleasure with him, their relationship might already be over forever. She would be strong for him. And he for her. There was no other way. Not now.

✦

Twenty minutes later they approached the familiar drop-off lot at the plant. As their car approached, Eric could feel his pulse quicken, just as it did his first day. Gerald pulled forward and stopped. He reached over and grabbed Eric's arm in a show of professional affection. "Good luck. I'll be here to pick you up after work. Your *last* day of work." He offered up a smile.

Eric reached over with his right hand, offering it to Gerald. Gerald released his arm and shook his hand. "Just in case," said Eric.

He opened the door and, immediately after shutting it, shook his coat to make sure the explosives were securely resting in the depths of his pockets. As he did every morning, he held his ID badge in his hand, ready to show it to the guard before he walked through the gate. He was more than a little surprised by how nervous he felt as he approached the guard shack. He noticed the same two guards. They recognized him and gave him a familiar nod as he approached. He reached into one of his pockets where the explosives were hidden and reached for a pack of cigarettes he had placed on top. He pulled out the pack and hit the top of it with his hand, ejecting one to pull out.

Every once in a while, he offered a cigarette to the guard in the shack if he wasn't already smoking. This morning the guard wasn't, so he lifted the pack and raised his eyebrows, signaling he would share a cigarette if the guard wanted one. His reasoning was simple. It would help his own nervousness and eliminate any suspicion on the part of the guards. They wouldn't be expecting an enemy to offer them a cigarette, especially on the day planned to set off a bomb. The guard smiled and nodded. Eric walked up to the door of the shack. He opened it just a few inches to prevent what little heat the shack had inside from escaping. Eric held up the pack and the guard reached out and took one.

"Thanks, Eric," said the guard.

"You're welcome. See you tomorrow. Stay warm."

"I'll do my best." He closed the door and reached for the matches in his desk drawer.

Eric waited in line with the others for his turn to pass through the gate. The guard was motioning people through as he chitchatted with one of the female workers. He glanced at Eric's badge as he approached and motioned him through with his hand, turning his attention back to the attractive young woman. Eric wondered how the guard's superior would feel if he saw the fraternization.

Five minutes later he had clocked in and walked the daily route back to the maintenance room. Redding had his feet up on his desk, drinking a cup of coffee and reading the morning paper. If only he knew what was going to happen later that night!

"Good morning," said Eric. He walked over to his locker, carefully removed his heavy coat, and hung it on the hook. He grabbed his gray overall, then closed the locker door. Better to keep the coat from Redding's prying eyes. He slipped on his overall and walked over to his desk.

"Freezing out there today," said Redding.

"No kidding. I had to wear a larger coat today." What a convenient reason for wearing that large and uncomfortable thing.

"Yeah, me too. My wife even made me wear a scarf. I hate scarves."

"I'm sure this cold spell won't last long, then you can throw it back in the closet."

"Yeah," agreed Redding, "right where it belongs."

Eric grabbed his cup. "Hey, I forgot my thermos. Can you spare a cup?"

"Sure, help yourself," answered Redding, not looking up from the sports page he was reading. "What are ya gonna work on today?"

"The gyroscope machine is acting up again. One of the workers stopped me on the way in. I think the new toggle bolt we put in has worked its way loose again. I'll head down there in a few minutes." It was a lie, of course. No worker had stopped Eric. The previous fix was working just fine. The loosening bolt was a great excuse to gain access to that critical piece of equipment. It took nearly an hour the last time he made the repair, so he would have plenty of time to plant the timer and explosives if he needed it.

"How about I go with ya?"

"Thanks, but I can handle it. If I run into a problem, I'll come back and get you."

"OK, but don't screw it up." He kept reading the sports page. The last thing Redding wanted to do right now was get up and do some actual work. Eric, likewise, did not want Redding following him around. Especially today.

"I won't. Think it's OK if I finish my coffee first?" He wanted Redding to believe this was an ordinary day. Nothing special. No changes. Eric wanted to appear relaxed and unhurried to start his work. As far as he knew, Redding thought the bombs would be planted in a few weeks. Not today, for sure.

"Sure, why not. Waiting a few minutes won't kill them."

A poor choice of words, Eric thought. He sat down and reached over for a section of the paper Redding wasn't reading. The front page highlighted President Roosevelt's visit to Malta where he presented a scroll dedicated to its "people and defenders," expressing the admiration of the American people for Malta's contribution to democracy. It was nice to read about something other than the pounding that the American bombers were continuing to give Germany.

Eric finished his coffee and laid down the paper. Why put off any longer what had to be done? He stood up and walked over to the worktable where the toolbox was kept. He opened the box to make sure he had room to place both the timer and explosives inside. He did, just barely. All he had to do now was wait for Redding to leave. He would need less than a minute to move the devices from his coat to the toolbox.

Redding was a man of habit, and Eric began memorizing those habits on his first day at the plant. He knew at approximately eight o'clock Redding would take his paper and disappear into the bathroom for at least ten minutes. That would be Eric's opportunity to make the transfer. He walked back to his own desk and began reviewing some maintenance reports—anything to look busy for the next fifteen minutes. As Eric appeared to look busy leafing through the stack of papers, he stole an occasional glance at the clock hanging on the wall.

Right on schedule, at one minute before eight Redding did indeed stand up. He took a final sip of coffee, folded up the section of the newspaper he was reading, and stuck it under his arm. He walked past Eric's desk.

"Back in ten. Don't keep them waiting too long at the gyro."

"Yeah, I better get going. I'll make the normal rounds when I'm finished."

"Good idea." And with that, Redding walked over to the gray door marked "MEN," stepped inside, and closed the door behind him. Here, there were no bathrooms for women. Only men had ever worked in the maintenance area.

As soon as Eric saw the bathroom door shut, he took the toolbox and set it on the bench in front of his locker. He carefully opened the locker door, doing his best to keep the otherwise clanging metal latch quiet. He raised the lid to the toolbox and moved a few of the tools over to one side to make more room in the center of the box. He gently reached for his lunch pail on the locker shelf and set it on the bench. He opened the lunch pail and studied the timer before he removed it. He was still surprised by how heavy it was. The timer was nothing more than a modified clock with a black face, with a small knob in the back for winding and another for setting the time. A small battery was attached to the back of the device. Wires and clips were protruding out of the top of the clock and the battery, which would attach to the explosives.

Eric took a rag from his locker and placed it on top of the tools. Then he gently placed the timer in the box, making sure it was secure and wouldn't roll from side to side. Satisfied, he removed another rag from his locker and placed it on top of the timer. He reached inside one of his coat pockets and removed one of the explosives. Each bundle of explosives was a series of four small cylinders roughly the size of dynamite bound in three places by red tape. One end also had several wires protruding with clips. Eric knew, from demonstrations during his training, this type of explosive was more powerful than dynamite. Also more volatile. He had to be careful. With one more rag he covered the first bundle, then he removed the other one from his remaining coat pocket and placed it on top of the other devices. Again he gently secured them to make sure they would not move around in the box.

He leaned back and took another look at the clock. Redding had been in the bathroom for three minutes. If he exited now, he would plainly see what Eric was doing. Then there may be a problem. And right now that was one problem Eric did not want to deal with. He closed the lid to the toolbox, then as before, he gently closed the locker to quiet the clanging latch. He was sure Redding heard nothing. With care, Eric securely grabbed ahold of the toolbox handle. He also took the binder for the rest of his rounds. First stop was the gyro machine.

Back at the house, Becker and Langer were upstairs in Becker's room, sitting at the desk assembling the timer and explosives. Langer was in charge of accomplishing this task, and Becker was looking on wearing the unmistakable mask of anxiety.

"Relax," said Langer. "I know what I'm doing." Langer was quite adept at assembling the bomb, and the task took less than five minutes to complete.

When finished, Becker reached under his bed and pulled out a leather briefcase. He set it on the bed and opened it, emptying its contents near the pillow. "Let's hope they fit," said Becker.

"They'll fit." Langer took the bomb from the desk and set it on the bed next to the briefcase. He opened the case and peered inside. "Better get one of the small towels from the bathroom. I don't want it banging around on the bottom of this thing."

"Good idea," agreed Becker. He walked across the hall and quickly returned with several hand towels. He handed one to Langer.

Langer folded the towel and handled it just as carefully as he would the bomb. He placed the towel on the bottom of the case then took the bomb and adjusted it on the towel to gain the most support possible. Then he took one of the remaining towels and covered the bomb, carefully tucking the edges around it, making certain it was completely protected. Last, he carefully packed the timer. He then judged they were safely packed for their trip to Lucas-Harold.

"I think that's it," concluded Langer. He closed the bag and snapped shut the lock, resulting in a crisp-sounding click.

"Good," replied Becker with a sigh of relief. He looked at his watch, then placed his hand on Langer's shoulder. "We should leave in twenty minutes. Any longer and our contact will become worried."

"You're sure he's ready for us today? This new schedule is a big deviation from the original plan."

"I know, but Gerald was able to get a message to him we have to do it today. He wasn't too happy about it but said he would do whatever was asked."

Langer nodded. "I just need to pack a few things, then I'm ready." He rose from the bed and walked to the door. He stopped and turned. "And you're sure we can make it to Canada before these go off?"

"I'm sure. The map Gerald gave us will take us to the crossing in Ontario. After that, we'll make our way northeast. There we'll get in touch with our people. I'm not nearly as worried about that as I am these charges. I know you did your best, but if they don't go off—"

"They'll work," said Langer.

Eric did his best not to look back over his shoulder as he walked the route to the gyro machine, even though he desperately wanted to see if anyone was following him or perhaps studying his movements. He avoided all eye contact, stopping occasionally to check his clipboard, in an illusion to mask his true intention. The full impact of the mission was taking its emotional toll on his normally calm and controlled demeanor. He could feel his pulse quicken, and just like his first day at the guard house, he did not like it. Stay focused, he told himself.

The toolbox was heavy. Much heavier than he expected. He transferred it from one hand to the other every thirty seconds or so, being extremely careful not to drop it on the hard concrete floor. To do so would not only attract attention but could possibly set the sensitive and powerful bombs off.

He passed two guards, and both of them barely noticed him. They were accustomed to seeing him now; he was part of the regular crew. He was supposed to be there, even expected to be there. If they knew who he really was, what his true intentions were, they weren't showing it. Still, Eric was relieved to slip by both armed men without incident. Just fifty more feet and he would arrive at the gyro machine.

He nodded at the worker, who gave him a polite smile. "What's the problem, everything seems to be running fine."

"It is now, but we put a temporary hose clamp on last week until the new one came in. If I don't replace it now, you'll have problems later. I only need about five minutes."

"Yeah, you better take care of it then. I'll just take my break now."

"I'll be quick, I promise."

"Take your time, it's no trouble," said the young male worker. "I think I just saw that cute redhead walking toward the break room." He winked at Eric.

"Got it." Then Eric walked to the back of the important machine. He squatted down and looked around to make sure no one saw him. He gently placed the toolbox on the ground next to the rear access panel. He opened the box and removed a small screwdriver. It only took a minute to remove the four small screws, and then the panel easily detached from the machine.

Next Eric took a small flashlight from his overall pocket. He turned it on and set the light on a small shelf inside the back of the large machine. He knew from previous visits exactly where he was going to place the bomb. He turned back to the toolbox and carefully removed the top rag, revealing the timer and explosives. He took the explosives first and carefully placed them on the shelf next to the flashlight, making certain they were secure and wouldn't vibrate off the shelf. Satisfied, he then removed the timer and placed it on the same small shelf next to the explosives.

He began to wind the timer. Langer was very specific; exactly ten full turns. That would run the timer for sixteen hours, more than enough time. Any more, and the damaged timer spring may not work properly. Eric wound the timer, counting out loud with each turn. There was no danger of anyone overhearing him in the loud factory. After the tenth turn, he opened the glass face of the timer and set the time, checking his watch to make sure it was correct. Closing the timer face, he reached for the two wires that would attach to the explosives. He attached the green one first into one clip on the explosives. Then he took the red wire and was about to attach it when he paused.

At first Eric wasn't sure why he hesitated. He kept staring at the red wire. It seemed symbolic of something much larger than himself, a line that would forever sever him from June. He thought of all she had said about the Americans and her love of this country she called home. He recalled their precious time together just hours earlier in the warmth and comfort of her bed. He was in love with her, there was no doubt. How could he love her yet set out to destroy part of her country, part of something she held dear and loved? His conflicted feelings nearly overwhelmed him. Eric realized he was making a choice—a choice to betray Germany, or June.

Eric needed to make a decision. His five minutes had already expired, and the worker would return at any moment. Seconds later he backed out of the rear access opening and reached for its door. He positioned it over the holes, then backed it off just enough to see the loose, unattached red wire hanging over the shelf. He quickly screwed the panel back on and reached for the toolbox. No sooner had he walked around the machine than the worker walked up.

"All set?" asked the worker.

"All set," Eric answered.

✦

Becker and Langer pulled up in the dark sedan in front of the guard shack at Lucas-Harold. Sitting on the front seat between the two men were two briefcases, one larger than the other. Becker would take the smaller case, Langer the larger. Langer's case held the timer and explosives. Becker's held nothing but some meaningless yet important-looking papers in a binder. They knew from Ed Stevens, their contact inside and the plant manager, the cases would not be examined. Very careless, thought Becker, but it will work to their advantage. Stevens had already called the guards earlier in the morning to notify them of the two men's arrival. Stevens had an identical case that Langer would walk out with, so as not to raise any questions or suspicions.

The same guard Eric had offered a cigarette to earlier that morning remained on his post at the gate. Becker slowly came to a stop next to the guard shack where the armed sergeant stood erect, studying the car. Becker came to a stop and rolled down his window, cold air rushing in.

"Good morning, sergeant," greeted Becker with a forced smile. His stomach was churning inside, and he hoped it didn't show.

"Good morning, gentlemen," replied the stone-faced guard. "May I ask the purpose of your business?" The sergeant began a visual inspection of the men and the inside of the sedan. He was all business.

"Of course," said Becker. "We're here to see your plant superintendent, Mr. Stevens. Mr. Langer, here, and I are from Canada. He's giving us a plant tour today, as we are constructing a similar plant in Ontario to help with the war effort. We're hopeful we can learn some valuable insight as to how to set up our own factory up north."

"Yes, sir. Do you have any identification?"

"We do." Becker reached for his wallet, and Langer his. Both produced official-looking Canadian drivers' licenses and handed them to the sergeant. He took the two licenses and studied them carefully. Satisfied with the fake documents, he handed them back to the two men after writing their names on a list attached to his clipboard.

"Will you please wait here while I confirm your visit with Mr. Stevens?"

"Yes, of course," said Becker.

"Thank you, sir. It will only take a minute." With that, the sergeant turned, walked into the guard shack, and picked up the phone.

Becker looked at Langer, who he thought was turning white. "Relax, this is normal procedure. Gerald has already made all the arrangements with Stevens. There's nothing to worry about."

"I'm fine. Even so, I'll feel a lot better once we're inside."

Becker smiled. "Me too."

A minute later the sergeant returned with two yellow badges. "OK, Mr. Stevens confirmed your visit. Here are your visitors' passes. Please put them on and wear them at all times." Both Becker and Langer nodded, indicating they understood. The sergeant pointed to the parking lot up ahead through the gate. "Proceed through the gate, then make a left turn. There's a sign designating guest parking. Take any open space. Then proceed to door number five. Mr. Stevens will meet you inside. Are there any questions?"

"No, I don't think so," answered Becker.

"Are these the only two items you're taking with you?" asked the guard as he pointed to the two briefcases.

"Yes, just these. Would you like to examine them?"

"No, sir. That's not necessary. I just need to make a notation on the roster. Be sure you leave with just these two cases."

"I understand."

"Good day, gentlemen. I hope you enjoy your visit." With that, the guard motioned with his hand for them to move forward as another car pulled up behind them.

Becker rolled up his window and drove the sedan slowly through the gate, then made a left turn as the sergeant had instructed. Langer saw the sign first.

"There it is," he said pointing to a fairly large white sign with bold red lettering on it.

Becker found an open parking space and pulled in. Both men grabbed their briefcases and exited the car. Becker led the way to door number five with Langer two steps behind. It was just a little over one hundred feet from their parking space. Both men forced themselves to walk slowly, almost nonchalantly. Twenty feet from the door, Ed Stevens walked out and greeted the two men as though they had known each other for years, even though none of them had met before.

The sergeant watched the two strangers and Stevens as they walked into the plant. Something didn't seem right, but he couldn't put his finger on it. Then he looked over at the sedan. Something struck him as familiar. He walked into the guard shack and stood near the desk where the other guard was sipping his coffee.

"Did you notice anything unusual about the car that just went through?"

The guard, still holding his cup, looked in the direction of the parking lot. "What do ya mean?"

"I've seen that car before, but I'm not sure where."

"So?"

"So, these two guys who just came through have never been here before, yet I know I've seen their car. Don't you think that's a little strange?"

"I think you've been stationed here too long. That's what I think."

"I'm not kidding. Take a look."

The guard set down his cup, realizing the sergeant was serious. He stood up and walked to the window for a better look. "Hmm ... it does look familiar." He thought for a moment before speaking. "If

I didn't know any better, I'd say that's the same car that drops Keller off every morning." Both guards were now standing at the window gazing at the dark-green sedan.

✦

Eric was walking back to the maintenance room when he took notice of Becker, Langer, and the plant manager at the other end of the corridor. He stood for a moment as he saw Stevens pointing out something to the two guests. Becker just happened to look up, and he saw Eric standing there. He motioned with his eyes that he wanted to talk to Eric. Eric pointed to the men's restroom which was halfway between the two men. He could hear Stevens tell Becker they would be waiting around the corner in his office.

Eric entered the restroom first and quickly checked to make sure no one else was in there. After checking the stalls, it was clear the room was empty. He set his toolbox on the counter and washed his hands in case anyone else walked in, but it was Becker who entered.

"Are we alone?" asked Becker as he looked around.

"We are. Everything all right?"

"Yes, right on schedule. Did you plant the bomb?"

"Yes, it's in the gyro machine like we talked about." He was not going to reveal he left one of the critical power wires disconnected. The bomb would not go off as planned. It was not a lie that he told Becker. He did indeed plant the bomb as agreed, just without its proper connection to the timer which also held the small battery that would start the ignition. He wanted to change the subject before Becker asked too many questions. "I see you made it past the guards without any trouble. When do you plan to hide your briefcase?"

"Soon. Stevens is going to give us a more thorough tour shortly. We'll take our cases and leave one where they keep the assembled sights. He has the duplicate case in his office."

Eric nodded he understood. He may not be able to stop Becker's bomb from going off, but at least his would not be doing any damage today. "Anything else I need to know?"

"I believe so. Jon discovered who our spy is, but you may have trouble believing it."

Eric could instantly feel his heart begin to race. "Who?"

"It's who I thought. June. It seems she's been working with the OSS. She's probably the one who tried to destroy all the timers."

Eric felt panic creeping into his body. If ever he needed to be calm, it was now. "That's bullshit and you know it! She's just a kid."

"Kid or not, Jon and the rest of us are convinced she's the one. It all adds up. It was confirmed by the OSS officer Jon captured after a little . . . shall we say, pressure."

Eric was now not only afraid for her life but was angered that Jon had tortured someone and most likely enjoyed it. In that split second he felt justified in his decision not to arm the bomb he placed in the gyro machine. "I still don't believe it. I hate to ask, but what's he planning to do about it?" He dreaded the answer.

"What do you think he's going to do? He's going to take care of her once and for all," said Becker, completely emotionless. "She won't be causing us any more trouble."

"Why? We're all going to be out of here in a few hours, then there's nothing more she can do. It's pointless to kill her."

Becker waved his hand to dismiss Eric's argument. "Be that as it may, Jon is heading over to the house to clean things up as we speak."

Eric had to act, and act now if he was going to have any hope of saving June's life. "Give me your car keys."

Becker was stunned by Eric's statement. "What?"

"I said give me your keys. Now!"

"What for?" demanded Becker.

"Because I'm not going to let that animal kill her, spy or not. She means nothing to us now."

Becker laughed. "You mean you're going to leave now and try to save her? I always thought you two were a little too cozy. Even if I gave them to you, you're too late. Besides, you wouldn't stand a chance against Jon. He'd be more than happy to kill you too. You're pathetic."

Something came over Eric, an uncontrollable rage that was taking over his body. A rage that had been building for some time now, ready to burst. He grabbed Becker by the neck and slammed his head as hard as he could against the wall, then again slammed it down on the sink with just as much force. There was a sickening thud, and then a crack! It all happened so fast Becker didn't see it coming. He fell to the bathroom floor in a heap, his eyes lifeless. Eric reached down and felt the vein in his neck. No pulse. He had killed him.

Quickly he knelt down and searched Becker's pockets. The car keys were not in the first two he searched, but he did find them in the right, suit jacket pocket. He placed them inside his own pants pocket, then grabbed Becker's body from behind, hooking his arms behind Becker's. Eric had to hurry; if anyone walked in, all was finished. He dragged Becker to the last stall and propped him on the toilet. Blood was now trickling down Becker's nose, dripping onto his white shirt. Eric stood looking at the man he had just killed. This was the man who saved his life on the beach that terrible night he came ashore from the U-boat. Even so, he felt no remorse. Becker was an unfeeling monster who had no respect for human life: the mission was sacred, and anyone who got in the way was expendable. Becker would take no more lives, and neither would Jon if he could make it back to the house in time.

He closed the stall and realized he had to get moving. Jon might already be at the house. If so, June was as good as dead. Eric was going to do everything he could to prevent that from happening. He hastily removed his work overall and threw it in the trash. He paused a second before exiting the restroom, then opened the door and forced himself to walk slowly to the same plant exit he walked out of each day. This wasn't the plan he and June had devised the night before, but he had to move fast to save her.

No one really noticed him, as he was still wearing his employee badge. One female worker finally did notice him walking by. "Hey, Keller. You getting off early today?"

Eric continued to walk past her but decided it best to acknowledge her. "Just heard my cousin had an accident. I'm going to the hospital to see how he's doing. I'll be back later." An obvious lie, but she seemed to believe it.

"Hope it's not serious. Good luck." She went back to work.

He looked back at her as he continued to walk to the exit. "Thanks."

Once outside Eric looked around, searching for the green sedan. After a few moments, he saw it in the guest parking lot. To his surprise the two gate guards were walking around the car, one of them writing down the license plate number. The other, the one he offered the cigarette to earlier, was leaning over and peering into the driver's side window. Eric realized this was not a positive development and that their covers had most likely been exposed. Their plan was going to fail. Perhaps he could still save June.

Quickly Eric ducked down and crept up to another vehicle several spaces from the green sedan, doing his best to avoid being seen. He heard one of the guards speaking to the other.

"We better call this in, I don't like it."

"Me neither," replied the other guard. Both men then began walking back to the guard shack.

As soon as they were out of sight, Eric began to work his way to the sedan in a crouched position, hurrying as much as possible. Since June was in grave danger, there was no time for the extreme caution he would normally exercise. Once he reached the sedan, he knelt beside the driver's door, reached for the keys, and unlocked it. Peering through the sedan windows, he saw the two guards approach the shack and round the corner, just out of sight. He opened the door and got in. He started the car, placed it in gear, then quickly sped it out of its spot. He rounded the sharp corner and was approaching the gate at an increasing speed.

Just ten feet from the gate, the speeding sedan attracted the guards' attention. Eric could see one of the men with a phone to his ear, while the other looked on. The two military guards immediately recognized the sedan. One guard dropped the phone and raced with the other to the door. Eric was traveling so fast that by the time they exited the shack, Eric was already twenty feet past them and beginning his turn onto the road, tires squealing. Astonished, both guards stopped and looked at each other, in complete disbelief at what had just happened.

"That was Keller!"

"I think you're right!" yelled the other guard. "Just what the hell is going on?"

"I don't know, but we need to let plant security know Stevens's guests may not be who they say they are!"

Langer and Stevens were sitting in his office making small talk until Becker returned. Langer glanced at his watch. "I wonder what's keeping Becker?"

Stevens looked toward the office door, then at the clock on the wall. "I'm not sure, but he's been in there for some time now. Do you think there's a problem?"

"I don't know. If he's not back in a few minutes, I'll walk down there and see what's going on."

Stevens nodded. Just then they could hear footfalls running down the corridor, and three armed guards ran past Stevens's office door. Both men looked at each other in fear.

"Trouble," said Langer calmly.

"I think so. What could possibly have happened?"

"I don't know, but my guess is somehow Becker's been discovered. You better get me out of here, and quick!"

"Of course, let me think a second," said Stevens.

Langer was about to grab the briefcase which contained the timer and explosives, but then thought better of it. He rose from the chair and turned toward the office door.

"Hold on," said Stevens flatly, but with authority.

Langer turned and was about to ask why Stevens was delaying his escape when he saw the gun in Stevens's hand, an Army-issue Colt 1911. He was, for the moment, dumbfounded. "What's this?"

"This, Herr Langer, is the end of the line for you and your team."

"What are you talking about? You are supposed to be helping us, not detaining us!"

"First of all, my name is not Stevens. It's Morgan, Lieutenant Morgan. I'm with the OSS. Stevens was a double agent. We've been onto you for some time. We traded places today, as we had a tip you may make your move this morning. Have a seat while we wait for Mr. Becker and Mr. Keller. They'll be along shortly, unless they try to resist."

Langer was in complete shock. He focused on Stevens's pistol and did as he was told. He reluctantly sat back down in the chair. His mind began racing, still in disbelief they had not only been discovered, but now captured. How long had the OSS been aware of their plan? How did they know their timetable had been moved up? How, how, how?

"Just relax, I'm sure your partners are in the process of being detained as we speak. We also have a man on his way to the house you've been living in to pick up Mr. Kahn. We've been watching him for some time now. I'm just going to make a call, so please remain seated."

As Morgan turned to the credenza and picked up the phone, Langer reached inside his pocket and felt the small .32 caliber pistol in his suit pocket. He knew if he was going to act, it had to be now. If Morgan placed the call, there was no possibility of escape. He quickly pulled it out and began to raise the pistol toward Morgan.

Morgan was a man of much experience and expected Langer to attempt such a move; he realized Langer was a trapped animal and would think unreasonably. In an instant Morgan had the drop on him and fired once, hitting Langer in the right shoulder. The sound was deafening and reverberated from the office walls and the corridor outside. The impact forced Langer and the chair backward, both hitting the ground simultaneously. Langer's pistol fell and slid several feet back toward the office entrance.

Morgan quickly got out of his chair, raced around the desk, and looked down at Langer who was searching for his gun. "Give it up, Langer. I could have killed you if I'd wanted to. American prisons aren't that bad. You can live out the war in relative comfort, if you cooperate." He could see from the look in Langer's eyes that he did indeed give up.

There was nothing more Langer could do. He relaxed and decided to wait for medical help. Perhaps Morgan had a point; there were much worse options than waiting out the war in an American prison. "All right," he capitulated.

Morgan smiled. "Smart decision." Morgan walked over and picked up Langer's pistol, pointing his own .45 at Langer the entire time. He walked back over to the credenza and picked up the phone once again. He dialed a few numbers and waited a few seconds. "This is Morgan. I have Langer in custody. Better get a doctor."

✦

Eric pulled into the driveway of the house and stopped just short of the garage. There were two other cars parked there. One of them was Jon's, and he didn't recognize the other. He paused for a moment before he got out of the car, being careful not to slam the driver's door. He quickly trotted over to the side kitchen entrance and peered through the kitchen window. He could see a body lying facedown on the kitchen floor in a large pool of blood.

Eric slowly opened the kitchen door as quietly as possible. He looked around for any sign of movement, knowing at any moment Jon may walk in and happily put a bullet in his head. He walked up to the body and turned it over. He didn't recognize the man. He looked for a gun, but there wasn't one. He stood up and walked toward the swinging door, the door he had walked through so many times over the last few weeks. He had no idea what lay on the other side. He placed his ear to the door and listened. Nothing.

He gently pushed the door open a few inches, just enough to get a look into the dining room. There he saw Gerald lying faceup on the floor next to the table with a large red spot on his chest. He was still moving. Eric quickly ran up to Gerald who was still conscious and lifted his head.

"Where's Jon? Who's that in the kitchen?"

Gerald recognized Eric and with much effort managed to speak in a soft, weak tone. "He's OSS. Jon shot him, then came in and shot me. He thinks I'm dead."

"Why would he shoot you?" Eric was confused.

Gerald began struggling with each word but was compelled to explain before he died. He wanted to protect the young man he had become so fond of during their stay at the house. "I was trying to protect . . . June. I think I knew all along . . . she was helping the Americans . . . but didn't know for sure. She's so young . . . and I knew she would . . . be killed . . . if anyone found out. I couldn't bring myself . . . to betray her. Jon and I . . . were arguing . . ." Gerald was beginning to gasp for air; he only had a minute or so left, and he knew it. "We were arguing . . . about June. I had told her . . . to get out . . . after all of you left . . . this morning. She was . . . about to leave . . . when Jon . . . walked in. He took her . . . upstairs . . . then we heard . . . the car pull in. He came down . . . and shot . . . the OSS agent. Then . . . he came in . . . and shot me. He said that was . . . the plan all along . . . to kill . . . June and me. Couldn't . . . leave any . . . evidence behind."

"Damn!" said Eric. "I should have known."

"Get to June. She's . . . upstairs. There may . . . still be time . . ." With that, Gerald's head sank into Eric's lap, his eyes motionless.

Eric softly placed Gerald's head on the floor and looked toward the stairway. He wondered why Jon hadn't heard the car or their conversation. What was going on? He looked around Gerald's body for perhaps another gun. But again, there wasn't one. He slowly walked to the stairway, looked upward toward the bedrooms, and thought he heard June's muffled cries. As quickly as he could, careful not to make a sound, he crept up the stairs, knowing each second might be June's last. It would be his last, too, if Jon saw him.

The muffled cries were now getting louder and were coming from the end of the hall, specifically, Jon's room. He had no weapon, and Jon had a gun. He crept closer and closer, the cries getting louder and louder. Now Jon's open doorway was just a few feet away. He approached Jon's bedroom door and carefully peeked around the corner.

There was Jon, on top of June. He had ripped her blouse open and was trying to pull up her skirt. June was struggling and putting up the best fight she could. She was gagged with a handkerchief and her hands were tied to the metal bed frame. She was helpless against that animal! Jon was so engrossed in his attack on June he was oblivious to everything else. That's why he hadn't heard the car, or Eric sneaking up behind him.

For the first time Eric heard Jon's voice, and it was the sound of a monster. "It's about time you got what you deserved, bitch!" He kept working to spread June's legs, but she was stronger than he had anticipated and was making it difficult for him. Jon slapped her, and hard.

Eric saw a small lamp on the desk and quickly grabbed it. He calmly walked up behind Jon and, with all his strength, slammed it down on his head. Jon never knew what hit him. He fell to the floor in a heap and lay there motionless. June stopped struggling and looked at Eric with shocked and relieved eyes.

"Hang on, I'm going to get you out of here." Eric untied her hands and then her gag.

Once untied she immediately reached for Eric and held him as tight as she could. She began to cry. "My God, I don't think I've ever been so happy to see you. I thought I was dead."

"I know, me too."

"What are you doing here? Why aren't you at the plant?"

"Long story, but everything fell apart. Are you all right?"

"I think so, but another minute and—"

"Don't think about it, you're OK now."

"What about Gerald?"

Eric shook his head. "He's dead. Jon shot him. Also shot an OSS agent in the kitchen. He's been very busy."

"Oh, no. Not Gerald."

"I'm sorry. He was trying to save your life."

"What about the others? Becker and Langer?"

"I don't know, but I'm sure they're either dead or captured." He would not tell her he was the one who killed Becker. But to Eric's mind, it was either Becker or June, and it was not going to be Becker's life he would help to save. "Listen, we don't have time to talk now, we've got to get out of here. There are sure to be more OSS agents here any time, so we have to hurry."

June's eyes bulged with fright. "Look out!" she screamed. Eric felt a huge blow on the back of his head and went tumbling to the floor. He looked up and saw Jon standing over him. Eric was dazed and the pain was intense. The look on Jon's face was one of complete rage, yet somehow he was controlling it, for the moment.

"I'm going to enjoy killing you, Keller," said Jon with a sinister smile creeping upward from the corners of his mouth. "You've been nothing but a pain in the ass since we saved your miserable life on the beach. We should have let you die right there. Perhaps then we could have avoided all the problems."

June got up from the bed and wrapped her arms around Jon, doing her best to restrain him. She was no match for his strength and rage. He quickly shook her free and threw her to the floor with so much force it completely disoriented her. She missed the corner of the bed frame by inches as she fell. Any closer and her head would have hit it, and June would have died instantly.

Jon turned his attention back to Eric, who was still woozy from the blow. Still standing over him, Jon reached for the pistol in his pocket, but it wasn't there. Eric started to sit up, but Jon kicked him in the face, forcing Eric back to the floor. Blood began running from Eric's nose and mouth. He was on the verge of unconsciousness. If he blacked out now, he realized both he and June were dead. And even worse for June; he knew Jon would then have his way with her before killing her.

Giving up on his pistol, Jon straddled Eric and wrapped his hands around his neck, squeezing tighter and tighter. Eric tried to pry off his strong hands, and then began beating Jon's arms. But it was no use. Eric had endured two powerful blows and was greatly weakened. He could see that Jon was enjoying his triumph over both of them. Jon was going to win the battle and was taking great pleasure in it. To have come so far—to escape from the plant before getting caught, and then nearly rescuing June—only now to die at the hands of a remorseless killer, was more than Eric could bear. He could not let Jon win, but he was feeling weaker and weaker as Jon's grip continued to tighten.

Eric knew he could not overcome Jon, not now. Not in his current condition. He looked to the floor where June had been lying. He wanted to mouth the words "I'm sorry," but she wasn't there. Where had she gone? Just then a shot rang out, shaking the entire room. Instantly Jon's grip relaxed, and even let go. The expression on his face changed from one of sweet revenge to one of shock and disbelief. Another shot rang out, and Jon fell over beside Eric on the floor. As he fell, Eric saw June standing over them. She was shaking and holding a pistol with both hands.

Eric and June stared at Jon's body on the floor, his eyes wide open, staring into space. It was clear he was dead. Eric looked up at June and smiled.

"Thanks," he said in a hoarse whisper.

June dropped the pistol and fell to the floor on top of Eric, kissing his face over and over. "I don't know what I would have done if he hadn't dropped his gun."

Eric's strength was coming back, now that he could breathe again. "I'm just glad you found it." He sat up, regaining his composure. He and June went over and sat on the edge of the bed. Eric looked at this wonderful young woman and admired her courage. He gently reached over and began to rebutton her blouse. June finished the job for him. Both of their hands were still shaking.

Eric looked down at Jon's body where two, clear red stains on his back were beginning to spread. "I never liked him. He was everything that's wrong with my country. I think it was him and Becker that made me decide not to arm the bomb."

That got June's attention. "You didn't arm the bomb?"

"No, I couldn't. After I placed it in the machine, I began thinking of you and how you loved your life and the Americans here. I think you convinced me we were wrong. Germany was wrong."

None of that was important to June right now. Only Eric was on her mind. She reached over and hugged him. "I'm so happy you're alive! I thought that was it for both of us."

"Me too."

"I can't begin to describe how sad I was when you walked out the door this morning. It was bad enough you were leaving for the last time, but I thought you might be killed at the plant. What made you come back?"

"I ran into Becker. He said Jon made you, and he was on his way over here to kill you. I just couldn't let that happen."

June bowed her head, again looking at Jon's body. "He's the cruelest person I've ever met. I think he enjoyed killing and hurting people."

"Well, he'll never do any of that again." Then he turned and looked June in the eye. He gently, but firmly, grabbed her wrists. "We have to get out of here, and quick! There are going to be all kinds of OSS people here at any moment. Once they see the mess downstairs it's curtains for me, and maybe not so good for you either."

"Me?"

"I'm afraid so. Becker told me he and his contacts found out you were helping the OSS. There are a lot of German agents over here. Once they find out you're alive and where you are, your life is in danger. They will look for you and—"

"And what?"

"They will kill you. You are a traitor to them now, and I know firsthand how they deal with traitors."

"They would do that? I don't believe it."

"Trust me, they will. And they won't think twice about it." He looked down at Jon's body. June's eyes followed Eric's. "There are more of him around. You don't want them finding you."

"Oh my God! What about my parents?"

"I don't know. If they're as loyal to Germany as you say they are, they may be left alone. Just the same, I would disappear for a while if I were them. At least until the war's over."

"What about you?" asked June.

"I don't have a choice. I'll still head to Canada and hide out there for a while. Gerald showed me where they have money hidden here in the house. There's enough to help me stay hidden for a long time."

"Let me come with you."

Eric wanted desperately to never leave her side again. He had saved her life, and she had saved his as well. "I thought about that. But I don't think it's a good idea right now. It will be much safer if we travel alone at first. If I'm caught, and you're with me—"

"What?"

"The OSS will believe you're a double agent working for Germany. Then it's bad news for you. You may spend the rest of your life in prison."

"No, please! I know we can make it together."

Eric's face softened. "Do you trust me?"

"Of course."

"Then do as I ask. At least for now." He paused. Tears were welling up in June's eyes, revealing she had acquiesced to Eric's request. "Do you have money?" he asked.

"A little, not much."

"I'm going to give you some from Gerald's box. I want you to get a car. Then get far away from here. Maybe California or someplace south, like Florida. Change your name and lay low. The war is not going to last much longer. Hitler and his grand plans are already lost. He just doesn't know it yet. When the war is over and things settle down, I'll find you."

"How will you do that?"

"Don't worry, I'll find you. I'm an intelligence officer, remember?"

June nodded. It was clear she didn't like this plan. She wanted to leave together, but she recognized Eric had made up his mind and was right in his thinking. "OK, but I still think we can do it together."

"I know you do, but this is the best way."

Tears were now running down June's face. She reached over and they hugged each other as though they would never see each other again. As difficult as it was, Eric took June's arms and pulled them from around his shoulders. "We must get moving, they could be here any minute."

Eric and June hurriedly went to Gerald's room, where they quickly found the box of cash hidden in a false drawer in the desk. June looked at the stacks of American cash, then looked at Eric. She couldn't believe how much money was there, and that it had been under her nose the entire time.

Eric quickly gave June nearly half the money. She resisted taking so much, but his only response was, "Take it right now, money equals safety." June took the four stacks of bills, and then both of them ran down the stairs into the dining room. June paused when she saw Gerald's body. She was about to lean down to say something, but Eric grabbed her arm.

"No time, June, we have to get going." He pulled her hand and led her through the swinging door into the kitchen. He turned before she could see the dead OSS agent on the floor and the extremely large pool of blood. He had been shot twice. Once in the chest, then once more in the face. It was completely disfigured, and Eric knew if June saw the body, she might faint.

He stopped her. "Close your eyes and hang on tight to my hand. Don't look. Promise?"

"Yes." June closed her eyes and followed him as close as she could.

Eric slowly walked around the body, leading June so she wouldn't step into the blood and possibly slip. He looked out the kitchen window and saw that nothing had changed from the time he arrived.

He opened the door and told June she could open her eyes but she shouldn't look back. He looked into the OSS sedan and saw the keys still in the ignition.

"OK, the keys are in it. I want you to take this car and drive at least four hours before you stop. If you need petrol, do it quickly and talk with no one. Get out of Indiana. Find a small motel and clean up. Tomorrow I want you to take some of the cash and buy a different car. Leave this one in a busy parking lot somewhere. Got it?"

June nodded.

Eric continued. "Get a map and decide where to go. I would go south, toward Florida. California has too many military personnel out there. Think about a name change. Get a job as a waitress or something that doesn't draw attention. Don't make any friends at first, wait until things die down. This is sure to be in the papers, but people will soon forget and move on to something else. Just use common sense and that beautiful head of yours."

June smiled. "And what about you?"

"I'm taking Gerald's car. I'll switch it out tomorrow and head north to Canada. I still have some friends up there from when I studied over here. They'll help me." Eric paused, looking at the road out front, knowing they both needed to get going. "It may be a year or two before we can contact each other. They'll be looking for us, you can count on that. The OSS for me, and German intelligence for you."

"I still don't know how you'll find me."

"When you change your name, pick something that I'll recognize. I'll figure it out." He was throwing a lot at her right now, so he decided to stop. There was so much more to tell her, but it would only be lost now in the confusion of the moment. June held his hands and looked into those eyes she had fallen in love with.

"This is really it, isn't it?"

He provided the warm, reassuring smile she needed right then. "Yes, but only for a while. Now, kiss me and then be off before both of us get caught right here in the driveway."

June stepped closer, tilted her head upward, and they kissed each other long and passionately. She broke it off and stepped back. "OK, this is never going to be easy." She turned and walked to the car with the stacks of money in her purse. Eric watched her get into the car and back up slowly, stopping at the driveway entrance. She stuck her head out the window.

"Kahn!" she yelled.

"What?"

"Kahn! That's going to be my new last name. In honor of Gerald for trying to save me!"

Eric nodded he understood, then watched the black car pull onto the road and disappear down the street. June was heading south. Then a few moments later he got into the dark-green sedan and tossed the sack with the rest of the cash on the backseat. He started the engine and backed out to the end of the driveway. He paused and took one last, long look at the house. So much had occurred there in just a few short weeks. Much of it unpleasant, but also the best memories he had ever had. Memories of June. He knew he would see her again.

He checked once more for oncoming traffic. There was none. He backed out and turned the opposite direction of June. He was heading north, toward Canada. As he was pulling away, he couldn't help but watch the beautiful home they had all stayed in slowly disappear in his rearview mirror.

CHAPTER 10

ENDINGS

PRESENT DAY

David Keller placed a sheet of his grandfather's papers facedown on the kitchen table, laying it carefully on top of the stack of other sheets, now nearly two inches thick. He sat back in the chair and stared ahead, deep in thought. Never in his wildest imagination could he have guessed his grandfather, Eric, was a German intelligence officer during World War II. Yes, his father had mentioned from time to time how Grandpa had fought in the war, but he refused to provide any details. Even as a small boy, David could recall Grandpa talking a lot about Germany. He seemed to know so much about life there in the old days, yet he never explained how he knew. He always had a sparkle in his eye when referring to what he called "the Fatherland" of his youth.

If his story was to be believed, it was the story of stories. At least for the Keller family. David wanted to call his father and tell him what Grandpa had left him. He wanted to ask his father how much he knew about Grandpa's story, if he knew anything at all. But that was impossible, as both his mother and father had died in a boating accident twenty years earlier. It was then Grandpa Eric had taken such an interest in David, overseeing his education and eventual enlistment in the army. Of course it was in military intelligence. He always implored David, above all else, to be honorable, steadfast, and to always consider another's viewpoint. After all, they may be right. It was all making sense now.

Why, David asked himself, didn't Grandpa share his story while he was still alive, when he could still answer the scores of questions David presently had? What was he afraid of? He must have been afraid of the truth while he was still living. The man he had ignored for several years and was ashamed of visiting was at this moment a person he wished he could sit and talk to—for hours. He longed for more information, he yearned for more details. And, most of all, what had happened to June?

The morning was now nearly over, and David needed to get his work done. But this was more important, more compelling, than anything he had ever experienced. He glanced down and saw only a handful of papers left to read in Grandpa's handwriting. He picked up the first sheet and began to finish reading them.

Leaving that day from the house was the most difficult thing I've ever done. I wanted so badly to go with June to wherever we could be together, wherever that might have been. But I knew that was impossible, at least then. The OSS had proven their skills and tenacity at finding people, and they would surely look for me. And if they found me, they would find June as well. I could not take that chance. I dearly loved June, and I would do anything to protect her. True, I had saved her life. But she had saved mine, in more ways than I could count.

I had become a new person. A better man. She opened my eyes to a new way of life. A life of love, caring, and doing what's right in spite of one's allegiances. Our last day standing in the driveway, I was confident we would be together again soon. That was not to be.

Yes, I did make it to Canada, crossing into Ontario near Windsor. It was after midnight when I crossed. Nearly every moment, I desperately wanted to know where June was and what she was doing. I could not get her out of my mind. If it were not for my good and loyal friends, I surely would have gone mad. They saved me.

My friends did all they could to help me stay hidden throughout the war, sometimes at great risk to themselves. The war went on much longer than I ever could have imagined. As much as I tried to restrain myself, I did make several attempts to locate June using the last name Kahn. I searched mainly in Florida, where I believed she would hide. But I always ran into dead ends. I desperately wanted to leave Canada before the war was over and begin searching for her, but my friends convinced me it was both foolhardy and dangerous to do so. I reluctantly heeded their advice and remained in Canada until 1947. Only then did it seem reasonably safe to venture back into the United States and begin my search.

In spite of my friends' protests, I kept the name Keller. I knew it was a risk to do so, but I wanted to make it easier for June should she be looking for me. Keller was a common name, so I believed there wasn't much to fear. I went to Florida and spent more than six months looking for a young woman using the name Kahn. A week before I planned to move on, I learned such a young woman, who gave violin lessons, lived outside a small town by the name of Naples. Driving there, I found where she lived, but the landlady told me she had moved, and she didn't know where. She thought perhaps New Orleans, or maybe Birmingham. I knew it had to be her, and my hopes were raised. Traveling to those cities I again was unsuccessful in finding her, and I was beginning to lose hope.

I continued to work, doing odd jobs and traveling the country until 1951, when I realized the search was going nowhere. I was at a dead end and needed to get on with my life. I didn't even know if she was alive. What if she was indeed discovered by some German loyalists and killed? I would never know.

At that time I decided it was safe to return to Indiana. Maybe, by some miracle, she had also moved back to her home state. Maybe, by some miracle, she was living there and someday I would see her walking down the street and we would be reunited at last. I could still hope. Even so, as much as I hated to admit it, my memories of her were beginning to fade. And if mine were fading of her, then I knew hers were of me too.

Once in Indiana, I took a job in sales at a pharmaceutical company and did quite well. During a sales call one day, a customer was telling me he was once a guard for German prisoners at Camp Atterbury here in Indiana. I asked him if he ever had a prisoner by the name of Langer. This was a huge risk, of course, but I was curious about what had happened to him. He did indeed know a young soldier by the name of Langer. He was killed a few months after arriving during an escape attempt in early 1944. It was big news at the camp, and he never forgot it. It then hit me I was the only survivor from the mission. Kurt, Lars, Becker, Gerald, Jon, and finally Langer. Gerald's death was the only one I truly regretted. How I was the only one to survive I do not know, but I was obviously happy to be alive and living in Indiana, June's home area.

I met another woman in 1955 and, after a long courtship, we got married. June had been my first love, and always would be. It was hard to let her go. But I needed to move on, to settle down and start a family. We had two children, as you know; your father and Aunt Alice. Even though your Grandma Ruth was a wonderful, loving woman and gave me much happiness, I still saved a special spot in my heart for June. Even though I thought of her often, I finally accepted the fact that it was meant to be.

In 1961 your grandmother and I attended a benefit concert in Indianapolis. There was a full orchestra playing, and who did I see playing in the second chair but June. My heart raced! Even after almost two decades of separation, I knew at once it was her. She looked so happy! And she was doing what she had always wanted to do; play violin in a large metropolitan orchestra. I waited until after the concert in hopes she would see me and perhaps chat for a few minutes. I wanted her to know I was doing well, and I needed to know she was doing well too.

When she came out of the dressing room, I saw a handsome young man with a boy walk up to greet her. The man gave her a hug and kiss. I could tell he adored her. Instinctively I knew he was her husband. When the young boy became restless, I heard the man call him Eric. My heart nearly stopped! It was a moment later when June looked up and our eyes met. She instantly knew it was me. That beautiful warm smile I remembered so well greeted me, just as it had many years ago each day in the kitchen of that house we shared. She whispered something to her husband, and he and the boy headed for the exit.

June walked up to me with tears in her eyes and we hugged, just as we had in the driveway years earlier. She was so relieved I was alive and doing well. She told me after the war her parents convinced her I had been captured by German spies, sent back to Germany, and executed. No doubt a ploy by her parents to dissuade her from looking for me. She continued to look for years in spite of their claims, but finally gave up.

She met a man while in Florida, fell in love, and then married him after finally believing I was indeed gone forever. Her last name changed after getting married, making it nearly impossible for me to find her. By then it was too late. I asked about her boy, and she was so proud of him! And yes, she named him for me. It was one memory she would never let go of.

June had a real family, just like me. And most important, she was happy. That was what I really wanted for her all along, and she was just as happy for me as I was for her. We talked for half an hour, when her son returned and reminded her they were waiting for her. Our time was up. We entertained the idea of staying in touch, but we thought better of it for the sake of our families and because of the potential consequences of seeing each other once again. The exact words were not spoken, but we still loved and cared for each other. Very much.

After I returned home that night with Ruth, I was conflicted. I looked at this wonderful woman I had made a life with and knew I was truly blessed. I suspected she knew my heart was never totally hers. Even so, she loved me and devoted her life to our family, and for that I was grateful. To rekindle what June and I once had would only hurt those we loved. That we could not do. So, we continued to live our separate lives. Sometimes fate deals cards other than what we hope for, yet we still end up with a good hand, which both of us had.

Not often, but a few times, I saw her at a distance in a store or on the street. For some unexplainable reason, our eyes would always meet. We'd exchange a smile and wave, knowing our lives had somehow become permanently intertwined with a love and affection that could not be broken by time or circumstances.

About ten years ago I received a letter from June. She confessed she had been carrying a secret for many years, one that involved me. One she could not bear to keep any longer. Her son, Eric, was indeed my son too. We had conceived a child that one night we shared together. I think that night at the concert I suspected it, but I didn't have the courage to ask. June stated her husband had taken them in and provided love and support when they were most in need. Her husband was a good father and husband, and I should be happy our son had the good fortune to be loved by many. She was right, of course. Her son did not know about me, and she preferred it that way for the time being. Perhaps, when the time was right, she would tell him our story. And then he could make his own judgments about us.

After your grandma died, I was quite lonely and considered contacting June once again. I could have used her friendship. But she had since moved out of state, and I didn't know where she was.

Now, as I struggle with this terrible illness, I must relate this story to you before I pass on. With God as my witness, all I have said here is true. And, as you now know, you have another uncle. Eric, June's son. I hope, by the grace of God, you will have the opportunity to know him someday. One of my regrets is that I did not have the pleasure of knowing him as a son. But I cannot turn back the clock, and I have led a full life, so regrets are vain and wasteful thoughts.

Let me close by saying how proud I've always been of you. I know we parted on less than cordial terms. I take responsibility for this and pray you will forgive me, an old and foolish man. Perhaps I should have shared my story with you long ago, but I was not yet ready. I love you and hope you will not forget me and my story.

Love,

Eric

David set down the last page, totally amazed with the story he had just read over the last few hours. He couldn't wait for Emily to read it! He was sure she would feel the same way. Just when you think you know someone, you find out that you really know very little.

✦

Over the next two days, David worked with a local funeral home in making final arrangements for Grandpa Eric. He wasn't sure whether to have Grandpa cremated or interred. It was only after examining the box more closely that David found yet another small piece of paper in Grandpa's handwriting requesting a cremation. He asked that his ashes be disbursed in the Atlantic off the New Jersey shore. His reason, he wrote, was that this was where he first came ashore in this country and where he began a new and exciting life. It seemed only right his remains rested there.

The next day in the paper, David read the announcement of Eric Keller's death and of his memorial service to be held at McComb Funeral Home, just two blocks from the Regency Senior Care where Eric had spent the last years of his life. David assumed few would attend; mainly some friends and perhaps some staff who had come to know him.

David spoke with Logan from the law firm that had held Eric's box and asked for the name of the pastor at the church down the street from Regency, the one that had inherited all the money from the widow. Would they be willing to do the service? Logan made the arrangements and said he would also attend.

The next day the service was held at two o'clock. David wasn't surprised when only a dozen or so attended. Even Emily was too sick to attend, just two days after her latest chemo treatment. The pastor did a terrific job with the little information he had. Most of the attendees were from Regency. Their van had brought them over. Most were in wheelchairs or used walkers. David believed he and Logan were the youngest people there.

Following the short service, every able-bodied person walked up to David and conveyed how much they would miss Eric, and how much his grandfather had talked about him. It was clear Eric did in fact think the world of David, which made him feel even worse about ignoring the man he really never knew. Even Logan came up and said one day he would like to have a drink and know the story of the box.

Most everyone had made their way to the exit when one last elderly woman in a wheelchair started making her way to the front. She was pushed by a smartly dressed man, probably her son, he assumed. As she approached, something caught his attention. It was her eyes. There was something about them. Then he noticed the man carefully pushing her wheelchair. He looked somewhat familiar, yet David could not place his face or name. Slowly they made their way up front. David waited until she was directly in front of him, her blue eyes sparkling.

"I don't know if your grandfather ever told you about me. I'm June, and this is my son, Eric."

THE END

AUTHOR CONTACT

If you would like to contact Jeff Funk, find out more information, or purchase books, please contact:

Jeff Funk
JeffFunkNA@icloud.com

www.ingramcontent.com/pod-product-compliance
Lightning Source LLC
Chambersburg PA
CBHW021216250626
47155CB00008B/2829